Sex Ring in a Small Town

Coming soon,

The Old Airforce

Ravenhawk™

Books

Sex Ring In A Small Town
JOHN PELHAM
Ravenhawk™ Books

This is a work of fiction. All characters and events portrayed in this novel are either fictitious or are used fictitiously. Any similarities to persons living or dead is purely coincidental and should not be inferred.

Sex Ring In A small Town
Copyright © 2005 by "John Pelham," d.b.a.
All Rights Reserved

All rights reserved, including the right to reproduce this book, or portions thereof, in any form.

A Ravenhawk™ Book

Cover design by Brandy Parker
Original art "Passion at Midnight" by John Pelham
Library of Congress Cataloguing-in-Publication Data
Pelham, John -
Sex Ring In A Small Town/John Pelham- 1st ed.   p. cm

"A Ravenhawk™ Book"
ISBN 1-893660-00-1
I. Title
2004091344   LCCN
Printed in the United States of America

Dedicated in fond memory of

Mamie Stover

John Pelham

PROLOGUE

Small towns have an undeserved reputation for being virtuous. By undeserved I mean yokels are as libidinous as the worst Hollywood can boast ~ otherwise modern movies wouldn't play worth a damn at the local Bijou at umpteen bucks a pop. Nonetheless, the virtuous small-town veneer stands up because rustics must learn how to be sneaky. By the time a kid condemned to growing up in a small town is four or five it plays through that everyone around is potentially a vice detective. And let's not forget the Heartland's devotion to those precious family values ~ their appearances, at least, which are guarded like gold. That's mostly because the church still has a big voice in things. So small town people have to worry a lot about what "other people" will think of them.

Sex Ring in a Small Town

There is as much dyspepsia from the nagging fear of being found out, or even suspected of something, as from the local diets of meat, potatoes and gravy three times a day. That leaves no choice but to "sneak" in order to sample forbidden delights. And who can resist them? So much for maintaining appearances. In any case sneaky sampling of forbidden delights in the suffocating small town environment is what this book is about.

Finally, bear in mind that this story is set sometime back, circa, 1980, and contains references to big names of the time, the characters as well speak in the era's jargon and slang.

John Pelham

CHAPTER ONE

I guess I had a pretty typical marriage. Sex wasn't dull because we were dumb, but because we were bored with each other, I suppose. Nonetheless, I wasn't thinking about "sneaking." I tried it once and it was more trouble than it was worth. But my wife heard the Pied Piper and jumped the fence, tossing her ass out the window and trying to fuck the whole world. We were headed for a divorce when she totaled herself and our Caddy in a head-on collision with an ore truck.

Shortly after the funeral I stumbled into a unique, new business to supplement my income. It hinged on something I'd learned years before, from a nightclub magician, of all people - hypnosis. It's simple as hell. All the hocus pocus attached to it avoids the obvious:

that the hypnotic state is a natural condition.

That brings to mind Mandrake the Magician an old comic strip character, who was always "gesturing hypnotically" to achieve some magic illusion. It hardly requires magic to tap a natural function.

I applied hypnotism a couple of times to help people quit smoking, or for innocent parlor entertainment like showing that everyone has a built-in clock and, under hypnosis, can keep time to the second. In the army, sitting around the barracks bored out of our gourds, I had used hypnotism for entertainment, even taking some of my buddies home on furloughs entirely in their minds. They could describe to us what they were doing at home, participating in whatever was going on, so I have no doubt that it was realistic as hell.

One day a man in my company, whom I hardly knew, watched one of my performances then approached me privately and said, "I'll give you twenty bucks to take me on one of those hypnotism trips home."

I told him, "Hell, I don't charge for that sort of thing."

He said, "You might want to for this one."

I suspected he might be up to something crooked. But, like everyone in the Army I could use twenty bucks, especially back then when it was a lot of dough. "What's the deal?" I asked.

"I want you to take me home to see my girl."

"I can do that. It won't cost you a cent. Why should I charge for that?"

"I want to make love to her. Can you make me think I am?"

I laughed. "How the hell do I know?"

"Will you try it?"

Twenty bucks talked. I was broke as usual.

I didn't have any more scruples about something like that than the average man, and in fact was curious as hell about the outcome as soon as I started to think about it seriously. He wanted to do it somewhere where no one would know, so he drove us into town in his old car and rented a motel room.

The Army thought nothing about two GIs renting a motel room together in those days. Today some asshole might call the Army C.I.D. so they could slip down with cameras and see what two GIs were doing to each other. Back then they figured it was just two guys out on the town, saving dough by sharing room rent. Get this picture. Here is this guy stripped off on a bed, with me hypnotizing him and curious to know what was going to happen. Without going into a lot of details it came off like clockwork.

His dong got hard, he started thrusting his hips like he was screwing, got down to the short strokes, breathing hard, and creamed all over himself. In the Army, where everyone was horny all the time, that could have led to a lucrative business.

He wanted me to fix him up on a regular basis and his buddies too, but he shipped out before he could pressure me into it. So I didn't start a psychic whorehouse.

But the sneaky little thought must have stayed in the back of my mind. For years I really didn't think much about hypnotism. It was after I retired from the Army that it entered the picture again. My neighborhood banker, a hot-looking lady who lived across the road, recalled that I'd casually told her I once had cured someone of smoking through hypnotism. She sent me a customer.

A word about my neighborhood banker. Her name was Dorothy McCann. She was one of those mountain flowers, plucked by a clod ~ as in Breakfast at Tiffany's ~ but you'd better believe it happened only with her connivance because she recognized the clod as her vehicle for escaping Appalachia. That sad geography may not thrive economically, but I can vouch for the fact that it nurtured at least one first class brain.

Dorothy had even taken voice lessons and got rid of her pone, pellagra and prejudice twang. I'm sure if she hadn't she wouldn't have risen in the world to be a bank manager.

Of course one can't discount that old military promotion system for the distaff side known as "fucking up." Dorothy was sure constructed to do that if she wanted to.

She'd been sixteen when her fat-faced husband-to-be came home to Sow Hollow, or wherever, as a military police lieutenant, and she grabbed his coattails and flitted away with him. The dumb shit probably thought he swept her off her feet.

Dorothy suggested the idea to me of a stop-smoking clinic, using hypnotism. And, as I said, sent me my first victim (whoops! client) shortly after my wife died. I really didn't suspect Dorothy of ulterior motives. I should have ~ or at least interior motives. For example, even before my wife died, Dorothy had suggested we jog together, " . . . because a lady shouldn't be out on the road alone." Knowing she was married to a hulk of an ex-M.P., I didn't want to invite complications, such as a set of loose front teeth. Nonetheless, when she made her business suggestion, I only thought Dorothy was trying to help me supplement my income. Maybe the banker angle blinded me to the fact that she was also human.

To avoid anyone suspecting she had me in her sights, she even delayed tripping across the road, like a sympathetic neighborhood good wife, with hot buns and sympathy for the bereaved.

Since her husband was by then chief of security for the dominant local business, branch of a big international mining enterprise, she had reason to be circumspect. At that time I was forty-four, retired early from the Army as a bird colonel working on contract for the government and not particularly liking it. The worst part was driving thirty-five miles to work and having to get up too damn early to do it. I lived in a bedroom community (prophetic, as you'll discover).

I moved there because I found a nice big place ~ the kind I wanted to grow old gracefully in ~ a lot cheaper than I could get one where I worked. The point is I was looking for another retirement, or at least something to do closer to home.

I'd thought of renting out the semi-detached wing of my place to a professional man, maybe a doctor. I didn't know I was going to be the doctor. A trifle closer to witch doctor than M.D. My first "victim-whoops-client" showed up chaperoned by her husband, who came to the door alone, as is the Hispanic custom (since husbands make the best duennas of all).

He took his hat off, so I knew he wasn't a drug dealer who'd got the wrong house. Oh yes, down there close to the border we had those ~ in fact I lived in one of the dope capitals of the world, but they don't bother anyone who doesn't bother them.

I wondered who the hell this was at the door early on a Saturday morning when I wanted to sleep in. It was a man I'd never seen before.

I woke up fast, trying to keep my Rottweiler, Curtains, from taking out his asshole. After we settled that, the man said, "I heard from Dorothy," motioning across the street with his thumb, "that you can make my wife stop smoking."

It was tough not to say, "Aw, shit!"

But I got a glimpse of his little dove out in the car and decided I'd like to get a look at the whole woman, especially since my morning piss hard-on had just gone down and I still had that horny tingle down there. I said, "Let me lock the dog out back, brush my teeth and comb my hair. Bring your wife in and have a seat anywhere."

I waved my arm around the living room, which by the way was about as big as a tennis court; they built those old Spanish-style brick piles big before World War II. As I said, Dorothy McCann had planted the idea that really took hold while I brushed and combed that morning. Maybe there were a lot of people who wanted to quit smoking and needed help to do it.

Maybe I could use the big, empty wing of the house as Dr. Pelham's Stop Smoking Clinic and make enough dough to quit work. Hell, I wouldn't even need a license. Besides it would be looked on as virtuous, and therefore precious, in a small town. (Ah, Big Apple, you may have Lincoln Center, but we have virtue.)
This young lady who wanted to stop smoking was sure as hell worth looking at.

One of those Latin lovelies who hadn't got fat yet. She was at that stage of full bloom that usually lasts about two years, then fades. By thirty that type is usually fat. However, in some rare cases that glowing beauty lasts a lifetime, since it is as much character as flesh.

I wondered if she would be one of them. She was a living example of the kind that would raise a hard-on on a dead man. It was a good thing my bathrobe was a big loose one. Her name was Carmen. Imagine. Carmen. For Chrissake! I thought, *Carmen? Is the Almighty doing a number on me, staging an opera in my living room on Saturday morning with a cigarette girl?*

When her husband introduced us, she took my hand with a warm little patty and looked directly into my eyes. She had a pair of luminous dark peepers you could drown in. I almost creamed my pajamas. The husband was still doing all the talking. He said again, "Dorothy told me you hypnotize people and can make them stop smoking." This guy's name had to be Pedro, and it was ~ Pedro Gonzalez.

I thought it was damned unusual for a pair of Hispanics not to have heard from the priest that Svengali had been a very bad man and that any form of hypnotism not exported from Rome was a no-no, but I thought, *What the hell, why not be a fuckin' philanthropist?* (Boy was that prophetic.) I heard myself saying, "It's easy to help someone quit smoking. I've done it hundreds of times to guys in the Army."

Two times, to be exact, but if my clients had looked like Carmen there might have been hundreds of them. In fact the only reason I didn't fluff the two off was that I liked being around Carmen. I do my best work with at least half a hard-on.

I found myself blandly saying to Pedro, "You will have to be here anytime I hypnotize your wife. It may take two or three times, but I feel a sacred obligation about hypnotism, especially with women. There must always be a chaperon, or even several of them." Then I got a true inspiration and softly added, "When God has given one a gift, they must treat it in a sacred manner." (It was almost a direct quote from the title of a book I'd just read about Native Americans, called In a Sacred Manner We Live. The dying lamb looks both of them gave me when I said that reminded me of one of El Greco's luminous-eyed, astigmatic holy paintings.)

I was actually beginning to feel even more elevated, especially when I noticed how Carmen's tits tried to escape from her blouse. I said, "Why don't we all go into my study and start?" I was still wearing my bathrobe; not as good as white doctor's overalls, but what the hell, I was new at the game. I led them into my den.

Actually it was a semi-detached wing with four big rooms. One had my books and a big desk and leather executive chair with a matching leather guest couch and chair. I'm not going to go into the details of hypnotism. You can read them in any book on the subject. There are lots of techniques; they all work on someone willing who simply follows your instructions. Carmen did.

She dropped off like a rare jewel. And so did her dumbshit husband, can you believe it? He was out cold, gone into a trance in his chair, getting a good rest through the whole thing. What a fuckin' duenna ~ I really should have put him out cold and done my own idea of the treatment that Carmen more likely needed.

Instead, I simply impressed her with the fact that she wanted to quit smoking, and therefore would do it. Just like that. I also left her with post hypnotic suggestions that would simplify putting her into a hypnotic state again. I told her over and over (and there was nothing sinister about doing so just then) that whenever I looked her in the eyes and counted to three, she would be back where she was. It's a simple way to make it easier to hypnotize a subject the next time.

Moreover, I cautioned her that she would not consciously remember any part of the whole business. A hypnotist doesn't want people getting self-conscious or embarrassed after the fact. Then I awakened her, and her dunce husband, sure that he too would be a simple subject the next time if I wanted to work on him, and that he'd consciously remember nothing.

"What happened?" he asked, looking groggy and giving his wife a quick, guilty look, or maybe he was smarter than he looked and was checking to see if her clothes were rumpled.

"It worked like a charm," I said, avoiding any mention of his going out like a light. I had a notion he'd just as soon have forgotten that part of it, if he even knew what happened. I added, "You'll have to bring her back a couple of more times just to be sure it takes, but a subject with good Catholic character like her will quit smoking since she wants to anyhow."

Then I remembered the con used by an Encyclopedia salesman on a cow-like waitress I once knew and added, "Besides you're obviously both extremely intelligent people or I wouldn't be doing this for you. I wouldn't for just everyone."

They were at least intelligent enough to pick up on that and not insult me by offering to pay me for my philanthropy. Maybe I should have said, "I'll send you the bill," but I was *intelligent* enough to realize that might queer my chance to do some more mental masturbation on Carmen at close range. They both thanked me profusely and I again took that little warm patty in my hand, feeling a sensation a lot lower down than my palm.

I would have liked to return Pedro to a deep sleep and thrown Carmen into bed right then. I was having my coffee at last, and smoking a cigar, when Dorothy came across the street with hot buns and sympathy for the first time since my "late" had got "lamented."

Curtains was on the front porch again, but he knew and liked Dorothy and didn't see any reason to warn me that she was coming. I couldn't imagine what she was doing making a call on me, especially that early. I didn't suspect that her husband's absence from town had something to do with her timing.

Sex Ring in a Small Town

CHAPTER TWO

Money is not the root of all evil, a fact which George Bernard Shaw, or someone, observed, adding: "lack of money is the root of all evil." It sounds like GBS. Very likely I wouldn't have got involved in anything that followed except for my relative lack of money. My father left me only enough money to get into shape to need more. When I had elected to stay in the Army and told him to shove the family business, he disinherited me for all practical purposes. When he croaked, the family was probably worth fifty million on the low side. The business was milk processing. I haven't got anything against it, or milk, except that I'd have had to live in Wisconsin to take over the business. So, I got three hundred grand when the old boy died, just enough to buy more house than I could afford unless I worked to augment my "overly generous" military retirement.

The quote is from the Grace Commission that Reagan appointed. I had a notion to write Grace and ask him if he ever heard of anyone killed in a riot trying to be first into a military recruiting office. Anyhow an "overly-generous" house was where I was living, on the edge of a small town, also on the edge of a high cliff from which there was a superb view of a wide valley with mountains on the far side.

The swimming pool was on the "superb view" side behind a privacy wall. I had twenty acres and the only house on that side of the curving road, which wound around a hill above me.

Hot Buns and Dick Tracy had the house across the road. There were only two other houses for half a mile. We were practically in the country, yet had the blessings of city water, trash pickup, road maintenance, mail delivery, ambulance service and all those goodies.

A word about my background is probably in order here. I did pretty well in the Army due to General Harboldson, or actually due to his wife, in the first place. I was lifeguard at an officers' club pool when I was still an enlisted man ~ an off-duty job to bring in a little extra dough. Mrs. General observed that I was an Olympic class swimmer and diver. I was summoned to the presence of her serene highness.

A little digression is in order about military highnesses. Here's how that works: at that time her husband was only a two star or serene highness; later he was a four star and Mrs. General became a Royal Highness.

Anyhow, she wanted me to teach their daughter to swim and dive like I could. She was sure that any general's daughter could get the hang in five minutes a day or so of what a mere enlisted swine could do after only fifteen years of hard practice. I thought, "Why the hell not?"

After I saw their daughter, a luscious, nubile fifteen, I really thought, *Why the hell not?* I suppose I wondered how long I was apt to be in the pen at Leavenworth if I did what I had in mind to supplement little Agnes Harboldson's swimming and diving lessons. At that age, who gives a shit? At least little Aggie's private lessons didn't get her pregnant ~ even then I had sense enough and self control enough to pull out my tally-whacker and shoot my wad on her belly button every time instead of in her. I'd have used a condom, but I never could keep up a hard-on while putting on a condom. To be fair to the girl, I always thought it required pulling out and coming on her tummy, whether it's as much fun or not, and in this case, of course, it was a matter of keeping my head on. Generals can be real bastards where their daughters are concerned. (And at all other times too, come to think of it.) Anyhow, in addition to Aggie, I finally entered the consciousness of her old man, who took a liking to me. "You ought to be an officer," he told me one day. He wasn't exactly a complete patrician, but whatever he was, he was pragmatic enough to know that even officers who hadn't been anointed by West Point, had it a lot better than enlisted swine.

To make a short tale of it, I went to O.C.S., then flying school, and a few years later I was Harboldson's pilot and aide, riding his coattails, which was how I eventually retired as a Colonel rather than a Sergeant.

Besides I could play bridge like a pro. You can't imagine what that will do for a military career of even someone who came up the "enlisted swine" route. For the first year after I retired I played bridge on the Love Boat circuit with Mrs. Harboldson along, helping her get her life master. By then the General had retired, too, and went with us for a long rest, but he wasn't even the short rest type.

Sex Ring in a Small Town

He almost went out of his mind. It's a wonder he didn't organize a mutiny, commandeer the ship, and head for some Banana Republic to liberate it from communism or something.

Actually he was waiting out passage of the statutory year following his retirement, after which he'd be legally allowed to steal from the government through sweetheart contracts with the other old boys.

My late wife did better than anyone on Love-Boats. At that restless age, as they say, she laid every ship's officer on at least four cruise ships. The only man I'm sure she didn't lay was me ~ her whole act turned my stomach. I never climbed in that saddle again. She turned me off women entirely, which may be at the root of much that happened that I'm telling about here. Anyhow, as soon as the law allowed, General Harboldson started a consulting firm to do business with the Dept. of Defense. (You may have heard how *old boy* connections can rake in big bucks.) So I ended up working for him, and the government, driving thirty-five miles a day each way to a job I really didn't care for ~ but there was that big house with the view and swimming pool. Pity my old man was such a shit; he could have left me a million and I'd have made out, even sleeping till noon. You may not believe this, and I don't give a damn whether you do or not, but, due to psychological castration, the morning Dorothy finally came across the street with hot buns and sympathy I hadn't had a piece of ass for at least five years. You also may want to know, if you believe that, what I did to keep from exploding. A little trick I picked up in Japan at the famous hotsy baths: Jergens lotion and mother five fingers augmented by Centerfolds and a big dose of fantasizing. It actually can be liberating, as Thomas Wolfe observed, and if a certain class of women get much more precious, Jergens and centerfolds may replace them.

There's an old song that goes: "I'd rather have a paper doll to call my own, than have a fickle-minded real live girl."

A "paper dolly to call my own" sure as hell replaced my wife. I can remember her gleefully "buying" the lib program and snidely saying, "The pill liberated millions of women." (I applaud what that means: no more "double standard.") But pursuing her new freedom with total lack of tact and discretion liberated her from my concerns. She didn't have the foggiest notion of the meaning of "what you don't know won't hurt you," and, as a consequence, did a real number on me. The term for it is psychological castration; it only gets in its deadly effect, or at least did in my case, where real live girls enter the picture. I couldn't get a hard on with one because I had to really respect one to do that, and I couldn't. Or maybe I was afraid to give one the power over me she'd have if I respected her. Yet, a man in my shape still can't avoid the physical urge. So he gets his outlet (all alone) because he's scared to death of flesh and blood women. Pity!

I read an article by some liberated sexologist "tut-tutting" over her discovery that many men, "who could make a lot of women happy," were relieving themselves in private instead. (She didn't mention, if she knew, that they'd turned off the whole thing as a pain in the ass not worth the trouble.) She was dead right as far as she went. If she really knew why men turned off, she soft-pedaled it. The reason, of course, is Women! They don't raise 'em right in the U.S. Never did. I'm not criticizing, but rather sympathizing. The root reason is actually hypocritical men. It's not a case of women not wanting to be natural; it's a case of "can't" in our society. Boy, was I about to learn that in spades during the next couple of months ~ and about a lot of the dumbshit men behind it.

I was surprised to find Dorothy at the door when I answered the bell. Even more surprised to see her in tight white shorts and some kind of black T-shirt affair that made it pretty obvious she wasn't wearing a brassier and didn't need one.

I wondered what the hell she wanted. What a simple shit I was then, forty-four and naive as a virgin at a High School prom. That was the first time I'd seen all of her legs, well tanned and something to write home about. Of course, she wasn't literally bringing me hot buns, or if she was, they weren't the kind carried in a basket with a napkin over them.

"Out of cigarettes?" I asked. Sometimes she used to come over and borrow a pack from my late wife.

"No. I wish I were. I'm trying to quit."

A real opening in view of the new business I didn't yet know for sure I was in. She did though. Why didn't I say, "I'll help," then put her into a hypnotic trance and do something unspeakable to her?

Quien sabe?

Probably because women scared the shit out of me, especially good-looking ones. Of course there may have been a vision of that big ex-M.P. husband of hers in the back of my pea brain. More likely I was too busy looking at her. I wonder if my jaw dropped. I did fumble my cigar and have to pick it up off the tile floor.

"You can say 'shit!' if you want to," she said, smiling like a Crest ad.

It wasn't exactly what I expected her to say, but it broke the ice nicely. I wondered why I'd never really looked at her before, then I remembered my wife's cobra face if I looked at another women, even someone's grandmother. Dorothy was beautiful.

I stood there with my mouth open too long and she had to ask, "Can I come in?"

I got off my first even moderately bright line. "Why the hell not?"

She waltzed in and looked around as though she'd never been in the place.

"It's immaculate," she said. "You're going to make someone a great wife."

"I've been," I said, "wife, husband, whatever I was. They can shove marriages."

That must have got her attention. She looked as though she'd like to get close enough to smell my breath to tell if I'd taken up morning drinking. I got off another great line. "How about some coffee?"

"You've got a customer."

"What are the chances that your keeper will show up and challenge me to a duel if you stay over here long enough for coffee?"

"Very dim. He's out of town . . . thank goodness."

I wondered what the hell that meant. Still frightfully dumb. Significantly, it was the first time he'd been out of town since I'd become a widower. "Fix your own brew," I said. "I'm not good at mixing it like anyone wants it."

We went out to the kitchen together and she sized up my coffee setup and re-lit the teakettle. "I like instant," she said. "It's the only way I can make a cup the same twice."

She leaned back on the sink counter while the water and I heated, and eyed me amiably. "You don't exactly look like a mourning widower."

"I'm not. I'd be a liar if I said I was. That sort of thing is a shock, but I'll let you in on a secret if you promise not to bruit it around town."

"Let me guess. You like it this way."

"I was thinking about a divorce anyhow."

"I'll let you in on a secret too, if you don't tell," she said.

"Shoot. I'm compared to the Sphinx on occasion."

"I'm thinking about a divorce, too."

She was watching me closely for reaction.

I let that sink in for awhile. "I haven't heard any screams over at your place, so I guess the big gorilla doesn't beat you. Why do you want out?"

She thought about that for awhile before she answered, as though she wasn't too sure herself. "I was young and dumb when I got married. Sixteen. We have no kids to prevent me escaping Dullsville. I'm not built right for fetching a pair of slippers and a pipe to a clod that's flopped in front of the TV swilling beer. And I'm still dumb!" She looked right at me when she added, "He's the only man I ever knew," and something unmistakable happened to her eyes when she said it ~ and that something ran straight down me . . . at least half way anyhow.

Even Dumb John Pelham began to get the picture. I wondered if my morning was about to pick up right smart. "How about having our coffee out on the patio?" I suggested, for no particular reason except that's always the way it's done in movies. I added, "The patio is screened," thinking of flies bothering us, especially her in shorts.

She mistook my thoughts and gave me a look. "Sounds great," she said and led the way.

I didn't miss the view while she went ahead. She had what I've always thought of as a *classic* ass, one that juts right out and has just enough padding, complemented by ample hips and a narrow waist. Her butt wiggled like Marilyn Monroe's; she was probably doing it on purpose. I started to get a hard on again and wanted to; the hell with embarrassment. Even unused erections are one of life's great pleasures.

Besides I didn't give a damn what she thought in case she noticed before we sat down. She wasn't slow. She noticed all right. The next thing I knew she'd set her cup down and was standing in front of me. She took my cup and set it down too, then came very close and looked up at me. It was a ways up, since I'm six four and she was about five six.

Her blue eyes had turned almost black. I'd read about that somewhere. A sign of passion. I didn't do a goddam thing. I was scared to death. Scared that if I did what I suspected she wanted I'd get my face slapped. So many of them revert to prom queens after they sucker you in. Besides, there was Dr. Ruth's good advice. If this was leading to the casting couch, AIDS can be forever; there was that clod husband of hers to think about ~ maybe she never had anyone else, but what about him, his frequent travels? Was he the saintly type? If he was a monk it was only because women had good judgement; and good eye-sight.

"I hate to seem like a dumb shit," I practically stammered, seeming like a dumb shit, "but you're going to have to call the signals."

She laughed, "I thought I was."

I felt better. This was not your usual woman. I told her, "I've had my face slapped by forty year old matrons just for what they thought I was thinking."

"The world is full of assholes. I'm not going to slap your face for anything you say, think, do or don't do. I'm at least as dumb at this as you seem to feel you are. But I'm willing to learn." She averted her eyes and looked down, but didn't move. "I just have a feeling there's more to life than I've been getting out of it."

She sounded like a little girl that missed out on Christmas. This was neat. I was dealing with a mature human being; and, in my limited experience, an unusual woman. A dead honest one. She wanted something and wasn't ashamed of it. She thought I might be able to give it to her. She was dead right up to a point. But a lot of what I could give her depended on her. I had a notion she'd accept that too.

I pulled her to me but kissed only her neck. I was afraid to kiss her on the mouth. Hadn't I read that AIDS is transmittable by saliva? I thought, *This is bullshit. AIDS has killed recreational sex deader than a doornail.* She seemed to like what I was doing well enough by itself, at least for starters. In fact she was squeezing me hard enough to break ribs on a less durable soul and had started to breathe rapidly and hard.

My guardian angel who all those years I flew airplanes had obligingly repealed the law of gravity for me, stepped in at that point and took over my role. It was a good thing. I was still scared spitless. I (or one of us ~ my angel or me) took her by her shoulders and pushed her away far enough to look into her eyes.

"Look," my guardian angel (G.A.) said for me, "there're smart ways to go where we're headed and dumb ones. We're already hot and horny but we haven't made love. We've got to cool down a little before we do anything else."

She seemed to come back from a long ways off. "Cool down?" she said, not seeming to understand."

"Yeah, cool down. We can do a hell of a lot of love-making provided we do it smart," the angel went on. "Do you read Dr. Ruth?"

That seemed to penetrate.

"Never miss her, why?"

"Well, I believe you when you say you've never messed around, but how about your roving boy?"

Several thoughts registered on her face, none of them dumb, and none disapproving. After awhile she said slowly and from a long ways inside herself, "I know what you mean. I don't know how many he's played around with ~ there's one regular one; that's one of the reasons I'm going to throw him out."

By this time her breathing had returned to normal and my hard on was folding up nicely. I thought, *What price survival?* Also, *Oh shit!*

"So where do we go from here?" she asked, sitting down rather resignedly in one of my patio chairs.

"Right where we were going, but I'm not sure we should even kiss until we know it's safe. Do you remember Dr. Ruth saying whether

AIDS is transmittable by saliva, I can't remember."

For just a moment she looked panicky. "If that sonofabitch has given me AIDS playing around, I'll get a .38 caliber divorce!"

The glitter in her eyes gave me a clue why she was a good banker. The little girl that had been there a moment before had evaporated. She looked off across the valley and gritted her teeth noticeably, took out a cigarette and impatiently lit it, inhaling deeply.

She looked at the cigarette and said, "I wish I could quit these goddam things. They're a crutch. So where do you think we should go from here? And how? You know a lot more about this than I do, I think."

Guardian angel stepped in again. "There's a lot we can do without even kissing and end up satisfied. If you're serious about this we're both going to have to stay away from anyone else for six months, and even be careful what we do together, then take an AIDS test. After that . . . "

She looked expectant. "And after that?"

"Let's get to before that first," my G.A. said. "Come into my parlor."

I led her into the hot tub room. She didn't hesitate even slightly. She stepped out of her shorts. She wore nothing under them. She then whipped off her T-shirt. I wasn't slow in following her lead. I didn't miss the fact that she was a real blond.

"Show me," she said.

This time when I held her there was nothing to prevent feeling all of her. I nuzzled her face all over, kissing her neck and hairline, caressing her hair, kissing the hairline on her forehead then her closed eyelids softly while my erection throbbed against her like mad.

There is absolutely no mental state in life to match the exhilaration of a "first" passion with a superb partner. I slipped some Jergens (my old friend) onto my finger and gently rubbed her lips with it.

She opened her eyes briefly then worked her lips eagerly against my finger as it simulated a kiss.

"Not as good as kissing," G.A., or at least one of us, said, "but it'll have to do for now."

"Mmmmmmmm," she said. I led the way into my deep hotsy tub. It was happily just the right depth, the water level a little below her nipples so I could kiss them, gently and long, without being in danger of drowning. I gave them a Jergens treatment too, with both hands, gently massaging, and watched her face captured by spasms of naked passion, her eyes still tightly shut.

I wondered what she was thinking, but not for long. She was making little delighted humming noises and straddled my leg with a scissors grip that would have done credit to a wrestler. I worked my hand between her and my leg, which wasn't easy till she sensed what I wanted and relaxed. I soon found what I was looking for.

"What are you doing to me?" she gasped.

A funny idea entered my mind. Maybe she really didn't know. At her age she should have. Besides her clitoris stood up like a marble. "Don't you know?"

She opened her eyes briefly and gasped, "No!" Without the faintest hint of guile in her eyes.

"Hasn't the gorilla ever done this to you?"

"No."

"And you've never done it to yourself."

She looked startled. "No. Stop talking! Please!"

I'd met women who'd never learned to masturbate, but they were rare. I didn't doubt that she was one of them. I thought, *Jesus Christ, how sheltered can you get?*

Of course she could have been putting on a great act. Later I found out she wasn't. This creature, although she was made for absolute pleasure, had been going around for thirty-five years, sex starved.

Of course I'd been going around in the same shape for five and knew better, but at least I had Jergens. "Let's go in on the bed," I suggested. No argument there.

I managed one of my better performances if I do say so myself, kissing her nipples and massaging her clitoris with a lotioned finger and she had the goddamndest orgasm I've ever been spectator to.

She cried out, "What's happening to me? What's happening to me? Oh my God!"

Toward the end I almost came just watching her. She raised her back into a huge arch and kept thrusting her hips at an invisible lover, then collapsed into my arms. When her spasmodic breathing had subsided a little, she whispered, "I never knew. I just never knew. That's the orgasm I've been reading about, isn't it? I just simply never knew. My God, what I've been missing. You darling. You dear, darling man." Then another thought grabbed her. "That sonofabitch. All these years! I never learned a thing!"

"He never did that to you?"

"He hasn't even kissed me for years. He wakes me up in the middle of the night by pinching my nipples, then has me get up on my knees and he forces it in like a damn bull from behind, takes a few strokes and collapses. I guess I should be glad he doesn't take long. I always know my torture is coming for sure the day he gets his Playboy in the mail; I hate to see Playboy come in the house."

I didn't, but then I had a different outlook on Playboy. I thought, *Well, Heffner, I suspect I won't be needing your centerfolds as often from now on.*

"What are we going to do about you?" she asked. This was not your typical woman who forgets all about a man as soon as she's satisfied, then cries *rabbit* if she gets the same treatment."

"Do you know how to get a man off using your hand?"

"I never got a chance."
"You didn't do that to him?"
"I tried once. He thought it was kinky."
"I sure as hell won't. Here, put some Jergens on me and your hand and do what comes naturally."

It's the formerly dumb ones that are the best at doing what comes naturally. They put their hearts into it. She brought me off fast; I was thrusting as wildly as she had, and gasping like a dying fish, so entranced by it all that I couldn't believe it. Of course I'd had quite a warming up exercise. I thought as I was jetting off, "Ah, Dorothy, if you weren't my Heaven-sent neighbor, I'd have been doing that myself with my paper dollies anyhow about now."

I am a horny bastard. Occasionally, during an exceptionally horny cycle, I've jerked off two or three times a day. On the other hand, I once tried to quit, or at least lay off for a long while; just to see how long I could last. I found myself getting erections in Safeway checkout lines, driving past the High School when the girls were out at gym, and sometimes while just sitting around. One day I stumbled across some old friends. A centerfold collection I kept in a file folder. I opened it up. The end was in sight. I whipped into the bathroom, got out the Jergens and quickly shot off so hard the first round flew clear over the washbowl and splattered on the mirror.

I brought Dorothy off twice more ala finger after that first classic, then we dipped in the swimming pool au natural and I did it once more in the pool before she headed home, not showing the faintest evidence of being exhausted; quite the opposite. She turned as she went out my door and said, "That dumb bastard is never going to touch me again, I promise you. Mark the calendar. Six months and I get AIDS tested."

God bless you, Dr. Ruth. She didn't once suggest that I needed to take an AIDS test as well, although I was sure I didn't. I hadn't screwed since way before AIDS arrived on the scene. I didn't tell her how long I'd been without, although she probably would have believed me.

I watched that *classic* ass undulate back across the road and thought, *Dorothy, I love you, baby. Sort of.*

I wondered if I'd be able to get a hard-on with her for the real thing when it finally came down to it and I felt a moment of panic. *How the hell will I explain that to her if it happens?* I asked myself.

Then I was consoled by the thought that at least she'd know I could get one. "G.A.," I said to my guardian angel, "Are you listening? When the time comes, if I flunk the course, you explain it."

Sex Ring in a Small Town

CHAPTER THREE

I had some time off coming and decided to call Gen. Harboldson and get a week off. The sonofabitch doesn't know what time off is and gave me a hard time, but finally agreed. I had a notion to say, "Look, Norbert," (ain't that a darb of a name for a fuckin' general?) "how would you like to take your job and stick it?"

I almost said it. At the end of that week off I was going to tell the bastard exactly that, but I didn't know that then. Actually I like the old fart. We need his kind; the only distinct class that expects water to run uphill and, by Christ, gets it to do it about two out of three, through childlike faith.

I took a swim after Hot Buns left, not much of a swim admittedly, since I didn't have all that much strength. Swimming always got

Curtains' attention and he came out from under his Loquat tree and joined me. Curtains weighs in at about one-fifty. He averts the bother of traveling salesmen and Jehovah's Witnesses at the front door. They may ignore my "no soliciting" sign, but Curtains looks a lot like he might solicit a big chunk off their asses . . . he would too.

Back inside I turned on Mozart's Salzburg Symphonies while I got dressed. Curtains had already read the signs of going out for a late Saturday morning breakfast and came right behind me, not about to let me out of sight.

After I finished breakfast he knew I always brought him out a regular order of ham and eggs with hash browns on a Styrofoam plate. (None of your chintzy scraps for the kid.) Then we usually went downtown, him reluctantly on his leash where he had to behave, rather than rid the world of other male dogs, which he considered his assigned mission in life. Boy, is he good at it.

I hit the sack for a siesta right after we got home. Didn't stir till almost sundown, then rolled out and took another swim. It was getting a trifle late in the year for that, but it was nice as long as I stayed under water.

I was just wondering when I'd see Hot Buns next when I heard a yodel over the wall, "Hey, lover, it is I!" That got Curtains attention and he went over there to see for sure that he didn't have to kill anyone, then wagged his almost nonexistent tail. "I'll get the gate," I yelled. I don't leave the latchstring out, believe me. Too many drifters come through there and have light fingers ~ not that they'd come in with Curtains on the job, but there's no sense in setting up a homicide.

She had a portable 'beeper' telephone with her. "In case Oscar calls," she said. "He's apt to get out the National Guard if I don't answer the phone when he calls for his daily report."

"Oh yeah?"

"No shit . . . what's to drink?"
"What do you drink?"
"Scotch and Soda."
"A heavenly body after my own heart." (G.A. handed out that line too.)
"I'll fix . . . point me at it. I'm wonderfully useful."
"I noticed that earlier."
"You're pretty useful yourself."
"My Boy scout training. Cheerful, Kind, Reverent, Helpful, Chicken, Horny ~ all of those."
"If I understand all I've read, pretty well hung too."
"Anything under eight inches doesn't make a record in Kinsey."
"You measured it?"
"Why not? Every day, in case it's growing. At my age, good news is important."
"Oscar has a little nubbin."
"Fuzz usually do. It's a qualification for the job ~ not much on either end."
"No shit?"
"No shit."
"You haven't pointed me at the fixin's."
"I got a whole bar over on the porch where we were this morning, refrigerator, sink, booze . . ."
"And I take it you want a Scotch and Soda too?"
"Right."
I watched her going away and I'll be goddamed if I wasn't getting another hard-on. That's the way honeymoons are. A man should have one every month or so. Maybe women should too, but I never met one with sense enough to realize it. I'm talking about those utopian Zipless Fucks which, aside from not meeting all technical requirements, was just about what Dorothy and I fell into that morning.

She looked just as good coming (no pun intended) as going. I thought, *This woman either has the world's biggest set of little tits or littlest set of big tits.* In either case they came as close to perfect as any I'd seen up till then.

She set our drinks down on the poolside table, one of those big mothers with an umbrella; this one was set in cement so it couldn't blow away.

"You don't have any cuts around your mouth or inside, do you?" she asked. That took me by surprise.

"No. Why?"

"We can kiss then. I checked on AIDS transmission. I have an almost overpowering urge to kiss you."

We did a real number on each other for about a minute. Here again, like all the under-experienced ones I've known she was aces at her work. She grasped me where it did the most good and got in a little preliminary work. I had a hard-on a cat couldn't scratch by the time we broke the clinch.

"I have an overpowering urge to fuck you," G. A. said. "But I ain't gonna."

She looked genuinely sad. "Pity I may be carrying the plague."

"How about me?"

"Could you be?"

"I ain't had it in anything but my hand for over five years."

"You poor thing. That bad?"

"That bad. I didn't think it showed."

"I used to wonder why you hung in there every time I looked at her, especially those cobra eyes. But who am I to wonder?"

"Habit in my case, I guess. Besides we had some good years early on. Maybe I thought I owed her, considering the crummy places we had to live in. She never complained once. Then, one day, bang! Just like that."

"Did you ever love her?"

"Whatever that means, I guess I did . . . once, at first. Or maybe I just had the hots."

"You can't tell the difference?"

"Can you?"

"I never knew what the hots were till this morning."

"And about love?"

"I think I know what love is."

She didn't say she'd found that out just that morning. She didn't have to. A real blow-torch-look went with the word love. I've been around a few women who really liked something I did to them ~ can read the look, but I never got one that matched that one. I was getting a dangerous feeling myself, sort of like I might be falling into something more than the hots. I thought, *Imagine that big jerk Oscar jumping this magnificent woman dog fashion and not having the foggiest notion what he could do with her if he had any smarts.*

We sat together and watched the sun go down, she occasionally taking my hand in hers. I had an evening cigar, happy as I'd been in years. I'd sat in that same spot the night before, with Curtains licking my hand occasionally, but the future had looked pretty empty, much as I liked being free again. Free isn't enough. You've got to be free to do something and know what. I was beginning to get a notion what it could be. I'm not cut out to be a bachelor; few men are. Unfortunately, most of us aren't cut out to be husbands either. I had an idea I could do better at it with a second chance.

Dorothy searched my refrigerator and pantry and manufactured a helluva meal of steak, fries, broccoli, which she was surprised to find in my crisper since "men never like what's good for them" and a big salad. The rest of the evening went even better. She slept with her beeper phone on the table next to her side of the bed.

I have observed before, not in print, that there's no better way to sleep than snuggled up to a lovely woman's back, with your arm around her, an ample tit in your hand and a throbbing hard-on up against a 'classic' ass. We half-awakened once and played with each other, this time able to kiss, especially sweet when you're coming. It's my view that nothing beats what you might call a "sexation" as the best way for a man and woman to get well acquainted.

John Pelham

CHAPTER FOUR

Even the smartest women can be damn fools when passion creeps in (or storms in thrashing and flailing). Dorothy made a real great observation while she was being domestic the next morning, making ham and eggs. "I wonder if that buffoon had some of his snoops watching me while he was gone? I wouldn't put it past him."

"What buffoon?" I asked, knowing all too well which one, and lamely hoping somehow to make my sinking feeling go away by putting off the grim confirmation another second or two.

"Oscar."

"Beautiful. Just beautiful. This is a hell of a time to think of that. Has he ever done it before?"

"I'm not sure. I wouldn't put it past him."

What a great way to spoil breakfast. "Shit!" I said. "What the hell are you going to tell the bastard if he thunders in and demands to know what you were doing over here all night; tell him you were afraid to stay in that big house all alone? I don't think he'd buy that."

She gave me a disgusted look. What the hell, I already told her I was chicken, in addition to being helpful.

"No, she said, "I'm not. I'm going to tell him the same thing I was going to tell him anyhow."

"Which is?"

"To get the hell out and stay out. That we're over."

"Suppose he decides to kill you? Kill me?"

"He's not the type. Inside he's yellow."

"How can you be sure?"

"I just know. Meanwhile, let's not let it spoil breakfast."

I wasn't very convinced. I thought, *Why don't I just fuck her if I'm going to die anyhow? At least that'll be once.* Did you ever notice that it takes about a day for the fuckin' snake to slither into the act just when you think you've discovered a new Garden of Eden?

After breakfast she said, "I'd better stick close to home today, much as I hate to be away from you for even a minute now that I've found you. The bastard may come roaring up without warning if one of his gumshoes has been spying on us."

Maybe it was something in the ham . . . . "Fuck him. I have some other plans for you." She eyed me closely, waiting.

I said, "Better yet, let's just fuck. If I'm fated to die anyhow I want to go even happier than I am."

That gave her something to think about. I watched the wheels turning. "One of us has to keep our head screwed on straight so let's not rush into anything. I'm not going to be the one to kill you."

"What a way to go. Besides you don't know what you're missing.

"I know what I'm missing. I say, let's do it, and smarts be damned!"

"And I say, let's not!"

I had to laugh at how serious she looked when she said it.

I suggested, "How about next best thing before you go?"

"You're on. Whatever it is."

I was *on* too, very shortly. I showed her something else not apt to be deadly and almost as good as the real thing. Did you ever try a shot of lotion between a woman's thighs to slide a nice big erection up and down in? (I don't mean you, ladies.) If you haven't, my fellow men, I can recommend the technique without reservation. Useful while your gal has the curse, for instance. It gets contact with enough of the lady even under those circumstances to bring her off too. I believe this is what they refer to as clinical details. Great! We need more of them to cure America's chronic duncehood at sex.

As for the novelty of it, Roman and Greek historical writing is full of references to the frictional qualities of a young male slave's thighs for the use of young men till they're old enough for wives; they slipped up a trifle here, in my opinion, but maybe all the young female slaves were being used by older men.

We were on the phone with each other every half hour or so all day, like a couple of High School kids. On about our third call I said, "If old Oscar calls he'll be lucky to get through."

"Fuck him! Besides he always calls on our unlisted number, which come to think of it, I'd better give to you."

I wrote it down backwards in the front of my phone book, just in case, and put a New York area code in front of it. Christ but I felt good, even if maiming or death were impending.

I thought, *When you're not in love, you're not alive.* And I confessed to myself that I was indeed in love, not just afflicted with the hots. What a lovely feeling, what a wonderful woman.

I keep Curtains in the house at night. On the front porch he might go through the screen and kill somebody. His growl woke me up even before the imperative pounding on the front screen door. That really set him off barking. I told him to be still, went to the window overlooking the door and flipped on the front light from the switch I'd had installed there. It was Oscar. And he looked agitated. I thought, *shit! I wonder what he did to her?* That gave me guts to answer the door. Curtains beside me helped; also the fact that I didn't see any gun about him and had my old GI forty-five charged and ready in the deep pocket of my bathrobe.

I did preserve enough caution not to open the screen door right away. "What can I do for you?" I managed to ask, without too big a quaver in my voice."

"I need help," he said. "My wife just went crazy, I think."

At least that sounded like she was still alive. "What happened? What makes you think that?"

"She took a shot at me. Didn't you hear it?"

I almost laughed from relief. I managed to summon my best histrionic ability and said, "I hope you grabbed the gun. She might be after you."

He looked apprehensively behind him. Across the street I could see their front yard light on and his car still parked in the circle drive. I opened the screen and let him in. Curtains, the epitome of discrimination, started for him. "Get down!" I yelled sharply. He really didn't want to, but he's trained out the ears and did what I told him, still growling. Oscar was so agitated he hardly noticed.

"I need to use your phone to call the police," he said.

I couldn't let that happen even if I had to shoot him. "Get a grip on yourself first. Don't do anything you might want to undo in a little while. Let me give you a stiff snort of something and then tell me what happened. If she comes after you I won't let her in."

He looked relieved. Also grateful as hell.

"Have a chair," I suggested. "What do you drink?" I knew the sonofabitch was a beer drinker, but that wasn't worth a shit in an emergency.

"Anything strong." He was breathing hard yet, and had started to sweat. I remembered what Dorothy had said about being yellow. It was sticking out all over him. I fixed him a water glass of brandy. He downed about half of it, and I'd bet he didn't even know what he was drinking. This sonofabitch didn't know which end was up. He'd had a very hard time and showed it.

"You got any cigarettes?" he asked, looking around.

I got him a pack of Camels and he lit one, his hand shaking.

"Thanks," he said, "I needed that drink, too. Christ!" He gave me a grateful look, like I was the Good Samaritan who'd just cold cocked the mugger who had a knife to his throat. He went through his cigarette in about five big drags and lit another one off of it.

I was curious to get the details and thought I might, since he was beginning to see me as the "good cop" after the bad one had just worked him over. I decided to take the offensive. "Tell me what happened and then we can decide what to do." I put that "we" in there to try to get my foot in the door and take command of this situation.

He didn't seem to notice, in fact appeared grateful. "I got home and tried to get in the front door with my key. It didn't work, so I rang the bell. How the hell could she have had the locks changed on the week end?"

A damn good question. Not only that, but I knew it had to have been done on Sunday. I shrugged. "Search me. My first wife did the same thing."

I hadn't had a first wife, but this was my second ploy to get into the *good cop* role. "She did? What for?"

"Said she was tired of me and wanted a divorce. What did yours say?" He looked dumfounded.

"The same damn thing. Said it with the door barely cracked open with the night latch on."

"Ditto. So what did you do?"

"I kicked the door in."

"I didn't. I hauled ass. I taught my first wife to shoot. She was a crack shot."

He almost groaned. "I did the same thing. So is mine."

"So she didn't really want to kill you, just scare you."

He thought about that. "I never saw a look like that in her eyes. She'd have killed me with the next shot. I know it." He sighed. "What a hell of a mess."

"That's exactly what I thought. Let me tell you, when they get like that it's time to get out, make the best settlement you can and start over."

He was silent awhile, then finished the brandy in a gulp and lit another cigarette. He already had one going in the ashtray, noticed it, then stubbed them both out, looking disgusted. "Filthy habit."

A great idea grabbed me then. "It is," I said. "I quit years ago. I'm starting a clinic to help people quit. I can make you quit before morning and make you feel a hell of a lot better at the same time. A good night's sleep and you'll see this thing in a different light."

He looked interested. It wasn't easy to do with a face like his, which was jowly and pig-like, but his shifty eyes had a gleam of hope in them. If only he trusted me. I'd talked to him once or twice before and he'd treated me like a captain normally treats a colonel, even though he'd been out of the army for years. What an asshole. But that was another plus in grabbing his confidence sufficiently to hypnotize him.

"How the hell are you going to get me to quit smoking before morning?"

I didn't tell him right out, but said instead, "I did it to hundreds of people in the Army. Now I'm going to start a clinic and charge for it ~ work right out of the house here. I've already got some local customers. I've got a Masters Degree in psychology and used hypnotism clinically at the University."

What a crock of shit. I did have a Masters in psychology though; I got it in the Army because they thought everyone ought to have some kind of degree, the higher the better. If they knew what the University was teaching about institutions like the Department of Defense, they'd have keeled over kicking and twitching. Advanced degree, my ass; what they needed for the most part was a bunch of rabid morons with muscles, like Oscar, especially muscles between the ears. (Note to the Dept. of Defense: consider what would happen if service people really got educated. Note to taxpayer: it would save money. DOD has served in place of the WPA long enough and has yet to build a park.)

Poor old Oscar. He fell into my net like a ripe plum. I had him in a deep hypnotic sleep in a back bedroom, and knew he was thinking subconsciously, due to post hypnotic suggestion, that I was his best friend. I knew from past experience that he wouldn't wake up till 8:30 A.M. to the second, unless, as I'd instructed him, I or some life-threatening disaster awakened him. It was a good thing I got him put away before the phone rang.

"Hello, did I wake you up?" Dorothy's voice said.

"With the shot or with the phone?"

"You heard the shot?"

"No, but Oscar sure as hell did. As far as he's concerned it was the shot heard 'round the world'."

"He's over there? Is he where he can hear you?"

"He couldn't hear a twenty megaton explosion right now."

"Did you hit him with something? If I'd known he was headed over there, I'd have come after him with the gun."

"Good thing you didn't."

"What happened?"

I told her. She gasped, "I don't believe it. Or, come to think of it, I do believe it. What luck. What are you planning to do with him?"

"I haven't decided. What would you like me to do with him?"

"Put him on a slow boat to Singapore. Induce suicidal tendencies in him. Whatever you want. I leave it to your good judgement. What are you going to do now?"

"Do you have any good Scotch?"

"Why?"

"I thought I'd invite myself over for a drink."

"Are you sure it's safe?"

"One thing I can tell you for sure from past experience; Oscar is going to sleep until precisely eight thirty to the second unless I, or something like the house burning down, wakes him up." There was a long silence. I could hear her breathing.

Finally she said, a trifle breathlessly, "All right. Come on over."

"I thought you'd never ask." I turned the porch light off and crossed the road under a full moon. It was just turning decidedly cool at night as it does in late September in that country. She met me at the door wearing absolutely nothing but a look of obvious anticipation and still dangling the pistol from her right hand ~ a case of great confidence in either me, or the gun, whichever applied.

You want a story about savoir faire? You want to guess what I blew my brains out doing twice in the next three hours?

Stark *nekked*, she kissed me good night outside her front door while the moon still rode high and bright and I returned to my silent abode.

Curtains met me at the door, looking hopeful, as though I might let him in the back bedroom where he knew there was a stranger sleeping that he didn't like. Sleeping very soundly.

CHAPTER FIVE

Oscar hadn't come to yet and wasn't scheduled to for another hour and a half or so when I got my first customer Monday in my new trade as *witch doctor*. That first customer Monday was the same as my last one Sunday - my only customer to date ~ Carmen. I was startled to see her. I hadn't told her to come back alone. Obviously Curtains liked her since he didn't try to get through the screen door and alter her appearance.

It looked like I was destined to greet her mostly in my pajamas. I'd rather have done it out of my pajamas. I thought, *I love my neighbor but, oh you kid!* She looked even more adorable than the day before, wearing a skirt and high heels this time and an equally inadequate blouse.

(She must have known she was wearing a two-size-too-small garment. Would a good Catholic girl do this? You bet!) But I didn't think she was thinking about tossing her assets around just then; I read fear in her eyes. "Please let me in?" she said in a little, breathless voice. "I have to talk to you."

"What's after you?" I asked her, but she acted like she didn't hear me. Naturally I wondered what had her in an uproar, wondering if Pedro was hot on her trail, but I let her in anyhow.

Curtains sniffed her, wagging his excuse for a tail, but didn't try to sniff where dogs usually do. (I hate crotch dogs, which most are. Curtains was my style dog. Patrician.)

"C'm' on in and have a seat," I invited.

"I can't stay long. Pedro would kill me if he found out I was here and what for."

I was all ears. But, recalling suspicious Latin male minds and proclivities, I thought, *How about me?* "What the hell might Pedro do to old Ish if he finds out you're here and what for?" I asked. "What are you here for, by the way? Didn't the smoking treatment work?"

She looked confused by that question. "What smoking thing?" she asked, sounding vague. This kid was really shook. "Oh?" she said. "Smoking. Yes. It worked. I haven't smoked since I left here. But that isn't what I came for. You must help me!"

I thought, *The hell you say?* Thinking more about helping both of us, especially me, I asked, "Where is Pedro?"

"He's at work. He works at Holt."

Holt is a small border town thirty miles from us (interestingly known to locals as "Tail Holt," by the way). I felt a lot better knowing he was at least that far away.

Then she added, "Unless he followed me."

I felt a lot worse ~ even though Curtains wasn't apt to let him in; at least not in the same condition he arrived.

Later I learned that Pedro was locally known as Cuchillo Pete, since he'd done time for a knifing. Boy was I rapidly getting into a hell of a fix and that was just the warm-up period. Happily I hadn't yet heard that fascinating snippet about Pete or I might have started throwing sox and underwear into a bag for an eternal vacation somewhere. "Does Pedro follow you much?" I asked.

"Sometimes, when he's suspicious."

I thought, *When he's suspicious? With a wart hog face like Pedro's, if I had lucked into marrying a dish like this, I'd be suspicious all the time. Also keep her away from optometrists.*

The phone rang and I scooped it up and cautiously said, "Hello." I wasn't really anxious to talk to anyone on the phone just then. A familiar, neighborly voice said, "If I recognize the car over there, you must have some interesting company. Is he with her?"

Christ, what neighborhood bankers know about customers. "No. I wish he were."

"You're sure of that?"

"I have mixed emotions."

That netted a short laugh and a sarcastic, "I'll bet."

"Relax. I can't even spit." Another laugh, then a silence.

I could hear her thinking. I asked, "What's your schedule for today?"

"I'm going to take the day off. Get rid of Oscar and I'll fix us breakfast."

"Cool. That's the second thing I'll do."

"And the first?"

"Clear out the whole place," I said, hoping Carmen didn't clue in whom I was talking to.

"Good luck on both counts. Should I come over with my six-shooter and lurk in a closet?"

"Suit yourself. I'd probably feel better if you did."

Sex Ring in a Small Town

Boy would I have missed out on an experience and a half. "I have complete trust in you, darlin'. Let me know when the coast is clear. I can hardly wait for a full report."

I was praying I'd survive long enough to make some kind of a report, even half a one. Carmen's eyes had been on me steadily.

As soon as I hung up she said, "Please help me!"

"If I can. What's the trouble?"

"I love Pedro."

Boy, that was trouble. I wondered again if she'd ever had an eye exam. "So?"

She blushed, obviously uncertain how to unburden something.

"Women like him too much. Women are crazy. Even my abuela."

I thought, *Women are really crazy.*

For those who don't speak Spanish, an abuela is a grandmother. We obviously are all descended from abuelas. "I suppose Pedro likes women too. Is that part of the trouble?"

She nodded, close to tears.

I melted and ended up with a great, suicidal idea. I said, "Follow me back into my office where we won't be interrupted if anyone comes."

"If Pedro comes and you do not answer the door," she said, "he will kick it down."

This kid had a pretty mouth, but it sure could make dumb noises. I thought, *Fuck Pedro!* That was the first outcropping of my new professional attitude, the trait anyone in what was becoming my new business needs most . . . balls.

I stopped by and shoved my forty-five into my bathrobe pocket again. If the bastard got by Curtains, I was ready to give high odds he wasn't bullet proof. On the way back to my study, which I'd just re-dubbed an "office," since that's what doctors call their lairs, I did some nimble skull work. It was obvious this doll wasn't ready, or able, to level with me.

So I'd whip her back into a hypnotic state and get right at what was biting her.

She slipped back into a deep trance at once ~ and never mind how I do it. Let's just say my prior post hypnotic suggestions worked like a charm. What an opportunity, if only:

(1) Oscar wasn't crapped out in the back bedroom,

(2) his consort might not get second thoughts and trot across the street with her .38, or;

(3) Cuchillo Pete might not be lurking in the oleanders;

(4) if I hadn't been dehydrated in a remarkably delightful cause. (All of which is to say, I guess, *if the dog hadn't stopped to take a shit, we'd have all had rabbit*). Oh yes, I forgot to mention,

(5) If only I wasn't a fuckin' Boy Scout at heart. Just like old Clark Kent. I hope everyone is impressed with my remarkable talent for getting my ass on the firing line with no prior practice. Just then I'd have liked to be like Clark Kent in more ways than one. For starters, bulletproof. (If the name doesn't jangle you, he's Superman. Did you ever wonder why the bastard never fucked Lois Lane? I always did.)

Back to my act. I said to my lovely victim - ah - whoops - client. "Now, you are absolutely alone. You are talking to a friendly voice that will always be ready to listen to your problems. You can see no one and nothing; you are floating in a pleasant place and hear nothing but the sound of my voice, your inner friend. You can be absolutely honest and open with me since no one will ever know what you say except you yourself.

"Now say whatever is on your mind and remember you are talking to a friendly confidant that always has been inside you, like God, who listens but never reveals your confidences." Hold your socks, fellow Americans. I should have been, but wasn't wearing any. This is what came out in an absolutely bitchy, nasty voice.

"That son of a bitch, Pedro, is fucking Angelita!"

"Who is Angelita?"
"My sister. I could kill them both."
"I wouldn't do that. There are better ways." I was numbly casting around for one.
"Are you sure?"
"I came home from shopping one night and peeked in the bedroom window."
"And?"
"They were doing it! His ass was humping up and down like a dog. She was moaning and squealing, the slut, and gasping, 'Oh Madonna! Oh Madonna!' over and over. I wanted to die. I wanted to kill them both. I should have."
"Why didn't you?"
"I love them both. Besides it would be a sin. Angelita is my sister. Also, I knew she couldn't help it. And I'm scared to death of Pedro. He has an insane temper . . . what a lover he is though. I really love him so."
"Did you ever have anyone else?"
"No."
"How do you know he's a great lover then?" No answer to that one.
"Did you ever want another lover?"
"Sometimes."
"What do you mean by that?"
"Handsome movie actors."
A great light went on in my mighty think-tank about how to make her happier ~ and independent of Pedro. I remembered how I'd been a sort of madam for that other long-ago imaginary piece of ass I'd arranged for a horny buddy by hypnotism. I knew what I was going to do with this innocent lamb, and my asshole puckered at the idea. "Would you like to get your pick of handsome movie actors right now ~ without anyone ever knowing?"

A long pause.

"And get even with Pedro and Angelita?" It's the best way."

Not so long a pause, then she hissed, "Yes!"

One of the four rooms in my study wing had a king size guest bed in it. Later all of them would, but that's getting ahead of my story. I led her in there and convinced her she was absolutely alone, then told her to take her clothes off. What a killer body. My dong came twanging up like a startled cobra, and it normally doesn't jump up like that.

I told her to pick a movie star and gave her a blow by blow set of instruction about what was happening. I got a real shock right off. The first thing I told her after having her imagine she was being kissed a little bit was that he was starting to play with her clitoris. Nothing happened. She just lay there.

"What's the matter?" I asked, as the disembodied voice that was conducting the ceremonies.

"What's my clitoris?" she wanted to know.

Jesus Christ! Two innocents in two days! It was almost too much for me to believe. I carefully locked the door and, with an almost clear conscience (after all I was doing this professionally wasn't I?) played with her myself. Talk about Oh, Madonnas! Then I threw in a nice, slow, imaginary fuck so she'd know what real fucking was all about. It was pretty obvious she'd never had anything but a rabbit climb on her. Many more Oh, Madonnas! She must have come a half dozen times. So much for great lovers. Later, as her friendly, disembodied voice, I was telling her over and over what a jerk Pedro really was and also suggesting that if Angelita was a smoker, she bring her around ~ even bring Angelita as her chaperon, if her sister didn't want a treatment.

By then my hard-on had gone down and Carmen had her clothes back on. My last instructions to her were, "You will consciously remember nothing. What happened to you was a beautiful dream of how it really can be and you won't forget that.

You'll want to come back here to do it again and again." And, of course, my reminder to come back for further treatment included bringing her sister ~ but not Pedro. It was almost time to work on Oscar's case again by the time I packed Carmen out the door and put Curtains in the back yard to avert a dismal fate for Oscar.

He staggered out right on time. "Coffee?" I asked, not surprised that he appeared a little disoriented.

"Did all that really happen last night?" he asked, looking around, knowing it must have since he was in my place.

"I'm afraid so. Your wife decided to off' you."

"Yeah! The bitch! I never did anything to her." If he'd added, "that counts," he'd have been closer to the truth.

I gave him my most *sincere* sympathetic look. "Like I told you, they get that way. Better stay away from them when they do or the coroner might be working on you."

He still looked stunned. "Yeah," he said, the word sounding like it came from the bottom of a barrel. Then, "I guess I'll have that coffee." After awhile he said, "Your first wife pulled the same shit on you, huh?"

"Sure as hell did. Actually it turned out to be the nicest thing she ever did for me. I had a broad I liked better hid out."

His mouth opened like he was about to say something, then closed, then opened. He finally said, "Me too. Do you suppose Dorothy knows?"

"They have radar about those things."

A look of dawning comprehension got the best of his face. "You suppose that's why she took a shot at me?"

"Maybe. She probably did it just at that time because you were trying to kick the door in, I'd guess."

"Yeah, that was pretty damn dumb wasn't it?"

"Under the circumstances. Been even dumber if you hadn't

hauled ass."

"Funny thing," he said, "I was wondering how to shit-can Dorothy when she turned the tables. That really pisses me off. I wanted to do it first." He let out a short laugh.

Dumb, but honest, you almost had to like him for the remark.

"When you find out they don't want you it can cut your balls off for awhile. You even feel like you might want them back. But you get over it."

"Did you?"

"I didn't have to, but I felt just a little bit like you do for a short time. Forget it. It goes away pretty quick."

He was obviously thinking that over. "I sure don't want her back. Shit, she might off' me."

"Yeah. She might. A thought like that's enough to chill your ass."

"You can say that again . . . I wonder how the hell I can get my stuff out of there?"

"I might be able to do it. You want me to try?" Ah, how noble can a neighbor get? Especially when his fondest dream looks like it's paying off. Goodbye, Oscar!

"Yeah. I'd sure appreciate that. Would you?"

"Sure. You got anywhere to stay for awhile where I can drop you off right now? In fact I may be able to get your car for you. What's your phone number over there? I can call up and see what I can do."

"What the hell would you say?"

"That you're over here and told me you had a little falling out and you want to know if you can get your car. Hell, just tell it straight."

"Try it."

I did. I made it sound like I'd almost never talked to her ~ told her who I was ~ the whole bit. What a smooth shit I was getting to be. Oscar almost licked my hand ~ the poor simp didn't suspect a thing. I had him on the road inside of ten minutes with my promise to phone when I got his clothes out for him.

I phoned Dorothy and told her he was gone and repeated my opener of a few minutes before, "Good morning, I'm your neighbor from across the street . We met once when you were over seeing my wife."

She interrupted, "I remember. You must think I have a short memory like you, since you seem to have forgot that it wasn't too long ago that I jacked you off the last time."

"Oh, yes. It's all coming back to me. How would you like to come over and hear what happened?"

"I'm on my way." When she was inside she said, "I'm all ears."

I nibbled one of them before I told her a convincing bunch of shit about Carmen's earlier visit and then the straight story about poor Oscar. By then she was putting together breakfast, looking enchantingly domestic in another pair of very brief shorts. I'd have bet a bunch there was nothing but Dorothy under them. And let's not forget a tight T-shirt. I was getting my second hard-on of the morning, this time with better prospects of doing something about it fairly soon.

God how you can manufacture the old juice when there's a good reason for it. Enhancing my 'budding-shitass' personality, while I watched Dorothy, I wondered if Carmen's sister, Angelita, had a body like her sister's. I'd forgotten to ask Carmen if Angelita was married. Ah well, time would tell. Was I shocked over my callous lack of concern to stay absolutely true to my new love? Not really. I had already wondered how soon it would be before she too pulled a shitty on me and invited me to slope. You lose some naive niceness when you've been shit on once too often. It plants the nasty suspicion in you that it'll only be a matter of time till it happens again. Life can never be such a happy affair afterward. The whole business encourages a "take what you can get while the getting is good" attitude. As the French say, "A fair exchange is no robbery."

CHAPTER SIX

My second legitimate customer in my new capacity as witch doctor was Dorothy. She lit up an after-breakfast cigarette, took a deep drag on it, then looked at it disgustedly and stubbed it out. "I want to quit these damn things once and for all before they kill me. You said it's working on Carmen, so how about hypnotizing me?"

"Why not? I'll give it a try. Some people aren't good subjects."
"And you think I'll be one of them?"
"Sometimes very bright people are."
"Thank you. Do you really think I'm bright?'"
"Damn straight. Beautiful too."
"Thank you again."
"Shall we go into my lair?"

Sex Ring in a Small Town

I let her precede me, anticipating the view. Jesus, the erections that I was to have walking down that corridor during the next couple of months. Of course, at heart, I'm just an impressionable boy. Also an *ass* man. Shapely asses turn me on quicker than anything, though I also have an appreciation of tits and legs. But mostly, come to think of it, I'm a mind man. That's what I'd be working on in Dorothy's case, but I suspected what I wanted from her mind was already mine, at least for the time being.

She was in love for the first time, as only a strong woman who knows she's finally found what she wants can be in love. Despite my roving eyeballs and normal, nasty male mind, I recognized my own symptoms pretty clearly. This was the woman of my dreams ~ even if I couldn't fuck her yet. What the hell, courtships used to last years. Those days must have been the golden age of masturbation. Nonetheless, although fists are adjustable, the real thing indisputably has them beat all to hell. (So much for you, Heffner, and the crowd that Norman Mailer dubbed, "those fist-fuckers over at Playboy").

I used a hypnotism technique on Dorothy that's almost sure-fire for overcoming cautious minds, and it worked the first time. Then I convinced her she really wanted to quit smoking, and gave her the usual instructions to assure that it would be easy to return her to the hypnotic state again to reinforce her desire to quit smoking. I was already developing a standard approach to the legit part of my business without knowing it yet. It's best, in my opinion, to make sure that your subjects can't consciously remember anything unless you want them to.

So when I woke Dorothy up she asked, "What happened? Did it work?"

"Like an exercise video; you're actually a good subject."

"I don't remember a thing. Did you pry out my darkest secrets?" She gave me a look, perhaps half-serious.

I wondered what dark secrets she might have and made a note about that for future reference. "Nary a one. Do you have some?"

"Doesn't everyone? And to change the subject abruptly, I think we can put your talents to an excellent business purpose if people don't remember anymore than I do about it."

"Which is?"

"I'll tell you later."

"Uh. Uh."

She eyed me suspiciously. (Was this an early warning sign I missed? Was the snake in the wings ready to crawl into the garden? Guess.)

I eyed her right back. Finally she said, "Do you like money? Need some more? A lot more!"

"I wouldn't if my old man hadn't been a shit."

Her eyebrows raised. Bankers always like financial statements, even informal ones ~ perhaps that kind most. I answered the obvious question. "The old boy died from falling off his wallet. Worth at least fifty mil. My mother was dead ~ my brothers split it, me left out in the cold."

"How come?"

"I was a bad boy and stayed in the Army; or, worse yet, out of the family business. I got only enough to buy this place ~ not enough to live the life of Riley though. So I have to work."

She looked around my digs. "Could be shabbier. This ain't too bad to come home to, podner."

"Gets better all the time." I leered at her to emphasize my point. What an accent piece she was.

She said, "So the answer to my question then, was "yeah, you could use some more money. I'll tell you how after I check around. I don't want to raise any false hopes. OK?"

"O.K. So let's take a morning dip."

Sex Ring in a Small Town

We three, she, I and Curtains had a little nude swim together. If he saw anything unusual about that, he didn't mention it, after all that's the way he always swam. Curtains is a jewel. He wasn't too crazy about my shutting the bedroom door in his face a little later, but he even took that philosophically. He was beginning to like Dorothy real well. Many men have probably never experienced the pleasure of simply holding a naked woman close and kissing her a lot for a long, long while. Most men are rabbits anyhow, but even some who are a trifle above mistaking foreplay for a quantity X that's located roughly between three play and five play, have confessed to me they'd never done it. In fact, can't. Of course, it's a hell of a lot easier when you're pretty drained already and can't do much else. But do try it boys. I suppose many of the new rabbit generation of females might belly-ache about it and demand a quick, automatic hard on whipped in them as the just due of their beautiful silky bods, but that's their tough shit. Anyhow, Dorothy and I had an early siesta, all wrapped up in one another's arms. I wonder if you could call that some sort of sexual act? Who cares? It's great just to be close as you can get to someone you love.

John Pelham

CHAPTER SEVEN

That was Monday. Not a bad day. I got four more customers. News travels fast in a small town. Surprising how many people would like to kick the cigarette habit if it doesn't take discipline to do it. Over two bucks a pack ought to help. Imagine a twenty-five year old couple that kicked the habit of smoking only a pack-a-day apiece, at that price, and put the dough into savings. At a lousy 6% compounded they have over $114,000.00 stashed in the bank at age 65 instead of possible cancerous lesions stashed in their lungs.

The long-range possibilities, however, were far from the minds of most of my customers. They just wanted to kick the habit. They'd probably blow the savings on something else. So shortsightedness could deny them $253.07 a month when they reached age sixtyfive

Sex Ring in a Small Town

A nice Social Security supplement for someone with not much else. In time I'd toss in that kind of information with witch doctoring. The thing that prompted that angle was people like Al Gomez and his wife, nice but not too sophisticated old folks.

Al was my handyman when I needed one. He was a type everyone has seen in Westerns when we still called them Mexicans. He was the peasant who got the shaft from corrupt revolutionary soldiers and humbly slunk away from his half acre of corn, shoulders slumped, while some drunken general humped his beautiful, virgin daughter in his rude cottage. Later, of course, he joined Villa or Zapata and took the occasion to gut shoot the general and remove his head with a machete. The cowardly general would always plead on his knees for his life and the beheading always occurred off screen. Would Al Gomez do something like that? Never underestimate righteous wrath; or a nice guy. At least I always gave Al fair pay and got fair work ~ usually about a day and a half of anyone else's work for a day's pay, because that's the way Al was built.

Curtains liked him too ~ a big plus. Of course if Curtains hadn't liked him I'd have got damn little work from him unless I shut up the dog. Al did mostly landscaping, but also carpentry, plumbing, electrical work, painting, car washing and anything you can think of. Why would an old guy in his seventies work his ass off? For one thing he didn't know anything else; would have died of boredom sitting in front of a TV. And did you ever try supporting a sickly wife on $320.00 a month Social Security? They couldn't even afford a corn shuck cigarette habit, yet they both lived on them. It was a damn good thing pinto beans were cheap. (I heard, too, that there were many strange disappearances of dogs over around the Gomez place. One can't help but wonder what Dog Tacos taste like.)

Al's Mrs. had never been in my house, although she'd probably heard about it and was itching to look it over. In their eyes I was a *rico*.

Al left his wife in the car and came to the door, taking his hat off as I came out. Curtains was glad to see him and got a pet as soon as Al came in. Al looked like he was thinking his wife wouldn't be welcome. Besides, maybe what he wanted would cost too much. I had a hard time convincing him to bring in the missus. They were both good subjects. I gave them their treatment and tried to make it a treat. He wasn't having any and reached for a thin, worn billfold.

"No way," I said. "You can do some work for me. A couple of hours will cover it."

"One day," he said, and wouldn't have it any other way. He was careful always to pay his way, full measure. "If we can quit smoking it will be worth a lot. More than a day's work, even."

I paid him $5.00 an hour even then, when a lot of people tried to pay $10.00 a day, and for wetbacks merely a promise of ten a day. Then they made a call to the Border Patrol about the time payday came around. Lots of people did that. Lots of people are dirty low-life shits too.

Mrs. Gomez hadn't said a word, only crossing herself before we started, but as they left she gave me a gap-toothed grin and took my hand, giving it a little squeeze. "You are a good man," she said. It was an opinion I'm sure will carry weight with St. Peter when the time comes.

Anyhow, Al and his wife started me thinking about what to charge for witch doctoring. Regular doctors charged a heap for whatever results turned out. I decided on $100.00 for a successful cure, regardless of whether it took one visit or ten, and nothing if it didn't take. If I could just get ten victims a month at that rate, I could quit working for old Norbert over at the fort and squeak by ~ with twenty customers I'd be in tall clover.

Al hadn't been gone ten minutes when the phone jangled. "Look out the window quick," Hot Bun's voice said. "I want you to get a look at the bastard just leaving."

Back on the phone I said, "I didn't know you knew Dirty Harry."

"I didn't till about ten minutes ago. He's one of my pig husband's gumshoes."

"He looks the part. What'd he want?"

"In exchange for eternally sealed lips . . . guess what?"

"I shudder to think."

"My jewel beyond price."

"No shit? Sealed lips about what?"

"You can guess. The bright-eyed sonofabitch has been snooping around the past few days. He thought we were beating quite a trail between our two houses. That could be big trouble. He didn't report to Oscar yet, thank God. In fact he asked me where Oscar was. Obviously he wasn't snooping when I took a shot at fatso."

"What did you do to get rid of him?"

"You gave me the idea. I told him I'd caught something fatal from my beloved and was planning to kill him."

"How'd he take that?"

"I hoped he'd break some furniture heading for the front door on the off chance I might be desperate enough to off' him too."

"And . . ."

"No such luck. This one is tough. He just grinned and said, 'I guess this is going to be a money instead of an ass case.' So I gave him all the money I had in the house to give us some time to think this out. The bastard said, 'A neat down payment; I'll be in touch.' I really did have a notion to do the .38 number on him. Anyhow, unless you can give Oscar amnesia, we've got a real problem."

My mind was already whirring on that one.

"Are you still there?" she asked.

"Yeah."

"Any good ideas?"
"I just thought of a killer."
"What?"
"What you don't know won't hurt me. What's the gumshoe's name?"
"You won't believe this."
"Try me."
"Sheridan Millikan, so help me. He even gave me his card."
"No shit, what does he list as his occupation, blackmail?"
"It ought to read sonofabitch," she said. "Do you want his address?"
"Why not?"
 "Are you going over and off' him?"
"Hardly anything that crude."
"Do you suppose we should stop seeing each other for awhile?"
"No. Fuck Sheridan! My oracle tells me his omens are evil."
"You should do that speech to the opening bars of Don Giovanni. I suppose you're still not going to tell me your game plan."
"That's a roger. I ain't. See you later."
"All right, lover. In thee I trust." She hung up softly.
A line that rhymed with her last words ran through my mind:
"And shoot if I must!" What a babe. Whoops! Pardon me N.O.W. Also, "Up-yerz!"

As I said, I got three more customers on Monday. The first two were ordinary couples. Funny thing, I was to find that people come to witch doctors in pairs the first time, then a hell of a lot of them come separately later. It was to be a pattern. And the solo visit was almost never for what they'd both come about. I noticed I was already becoming more deft at my business. People sense confidence in a hypnotist, or as they are now fashionably called, a hypnologist ~ sexy eh? It's probably like a horse or dog reacting to a vet, or a skilled trainer, anyone who understands them. If the person loves animals, so much the better. I loved at least two of my animals already ~ Hot Buns and Carmen, and was prepared to extend my warm nature like a blanket over other worthy objects.

My last customer was a threesome. I got a phone call from Pedro Gonzalez about 6 P.M., just as I was expecting Hot Buns over for a swim. I headed her off with a call right after Pedro hung up. "I've got three late customers, and in this case you'd better be scarce. Gonzalez, his wife and her sister."

"Did you ever see her sister?"

"Huh uh. Anything like Carmen?"

"Even better. I'd better hurry over and minister to you after those two leave."

"Be my guest. I'll give you a jingle the minute they're gone."

"Don't bother. I'll be snooping around the front drapes."

"Shame on you. You sound like my mother-in-law. I used to call her Nanny Nosy."

"Actually I'm gonna take a soak in the Jacuzzi. So call when the coast is clear. Bye."

I thought, *Well. Well. And a Well. And a few other things*. This was almost too good to be true. Someone up there liked me. Or as my old man used to say after he'd screwed someone out of a million or two, "I'd rather be lucky than have a license to steal." Very modest in his case to give luck its due.

In the prescribed Latin manner, Pedro came to the door alone. Recalling his debut earlier, I had Curtains in the back yard to avert a castration, not that I wouldn't have liked to see him get one.

"Like I said," he said, "my sister-in-law wants to quit smoking too."

"Bring her in."

"How about my wife? She's out there too."

"Her too. We can reinforce her urge to stay quit with cigarettes."

"How about me?"

"You too. All for one price."

I settled the four of us in my lair. Dorothy sure as hell had Angelita's description right. She was sensational. Carmen plus. No one could fault Pedro for ministering to a yen on Angelita's part. And come to think of it ~ none of them knew I was in on their secret.

Looking at the two ladies, I thought, *"Cripes, how these kind can look like the Virgin Mary and carry on like Elizabeth Taylor.* Angelita met my eyes directly, just as her sister had, but the look was demure, and totally inscrutable. I was tempted to say, "Oh, Madonna!" to see if it got a reaction. Only the reaction might have been Cuchillo Pete's after he thought it over.

Everybody went into a trance like champs. Very good. According to plan. I gave Angelita the standard stop smoking hocus. Then I reinforced an instruction in Carmen and Angelita that they would go wait in the living room and be unable to hear what I was saying to Pedro, or anyone else until I called them back in. I watched two world class asses undulate to the door and out. What to say to Pedro? Plenty. All, of course, in the cause of right and justice. I concluded the session with all three together, assuring that Angelita knew she should come back (with a little private whispered suggestion in her ear that she do that alone) then saw them all to the car, sure that none of them had a conscious recollection of anything that had happened. (But, oh those subconscious recollections!)

I was feeling quite elevated when I called Dorothy. I said, "The coast is clear unless Sheridan is on the job with a sleepless eye."

"As you so aptly put it, fuck Sheridan! . . . Do you need urgent help? A ministering hand? Hot lips? A yielding bod, thrusting and writhing?"

"Actually, I'm feeling virtuous as hell. But come on over."

"Bullshit!"

I forbore to mention that a fellow feels most virtuous when drained, just like ladies get especially virtuous around homely men who don't have money. Life was picking up right smart. I had steaks thawed and the salad made, plenty of Scotch, and Curtains, outside the back door, was going, "Woof!" (Read as: "Hey you! Fathead! You in the house!") "Woof! Woof! Let me in. I know steak scraps need to be devoured."

CHAPTER EIGHT

It may occur to someone that I was in deep trouble. It did to me. Disturbing? Not really. What should have been disturbing was that I liked it. Faust's conversations with Mephistopheles were probably no more literal than mine. Old Nick does deliver. The number one item on my shopping list for delivery was probably on her way over. Every time I thought of being near her, something happened to my breathing and pulse rate ~ a constriction grabbed my chest, I could feel my heart bumping, even feel my pulse throbbing in my neck and head.

Christ, I thought, *I'm in love like a dumshit High School freshman.* Cool, yeah?

At forty-four a lot of men are so bored (or terrified) with life they

Sex Ring in a Small Town

can't even manage a morning "piss hard-on." So, you may ask, should I have taken a bow? Hardly. It was my new lover who'd kick-started me. Of course she had me in her sights for her own purposes, as I already more than half suspected. Yeah, I can see now ~ in case it ever happens to me again ~ that you've got to circle around life and kick it in the ass when things don't suit you. It's that or the rocking chair, and "then comes night," the fuckin' yawning abyss. Piss on that!

That night things went just great. Dorothy didn't even keep her beeper phone next to the bed. Unfortunately, something kept disturbing Curtains. About 2 A.M. I let him out into the back yard and stood out there listening, with my old GI cannon charged for bear. But nothing was stirring.

Curtains eventually lost interest. Whatever it was had gone away. Sheridan Millikan? A coyote? Maybe a porcupine rattling around. And what would I have done with the charged cannon? Well, I hate to brag . . . the hell I do . . . anyhow, in Nam I got shot down and walked out of the stinking jungle. Whenever Charlie or his first cousin, got in the way of my prospects for a future cold beer, I blew the sonofabitch away with a private little Uzi insurance policy. Know what an Uzi is? A sub-machine gun that zaps slugs out so fast it whines. I shot everything that moved, even a goat. (I don't think I killed it; I hope not.) I was a one-man Mai Lai massacre. Was I ashamed of myself? Only for being so scared sometimes that I almost shit down my leg. John Wayne never got scared. Was I scared to go out there in the back yard? Strange to say, not really. After you're blooded and survive you get a "tough-for-the-other-guy" philosophy. You've got to believe they haven't made the weapon that will get you. Macho? Sure, but not the hot air variety. If old Sheridan Millikan had been out there I might have blown him away. And about the dead meat? Slipped him into a couple of those plastic bags that an old comedian used to advertise on TV. Or trussed him up in one of those smooth blue plastic tarps and hustled him to some abandoned mine shaft or prospect hole. There were plenty of them around there, and I knew where a lot of them were from hiking the hills with Curtains. However I had made some other arrangements for Sheridan, provided they worked out quickly enough. Blackmail is a chancy thing for both parties. For example, if Sheridan took Hot Buns' money and squealed, just because his kind are congenital shits. Oscar would be just the pig-headed HillBilly fucker who would decide to stay around forever to even a score. Well, the Mexicans have a handy medicine that takes care of that, called *Los Muertos No Hablan.* The dead do not speak.

TUESDAY, 9 A.M. The damn phone rang. I jumped. Don't ask me why. It was apt to be Hot Buns telling me she got to work and making "kiss-kiss" noises on the phone from the privacy of her office.

"Hello," a sweet lady-voice warbled. "You don't know me yet. I'm Pat Sunderland." Pause. "I'm president of the Civic Uplift League."

I'd heard of both. Sunderland spelled money. Big money. Uplift meant bullshit regardless of its dimensions. I thought, *Holy shit. Fancy that. And, so what?*

"We've heard about the good work you're doing."

I thought, *"I'll bet a million you haven't heard the half of it, sweetheart.* But what I said was "Oh, good."

"Yes," she said a trifle breathlessly, "and we wondered if you'd do us a big favor."

I liked her voice. Somehow it sounded like it was coming out of a bouncy matron, thirtyish, probably voluptuous, probably just getting a little restless in double harness. I'd seen a lot of the type among officers' wives. If you looked at them with daddy around it was the cold, cold shoulder, but if he was sent overseas without them . . . Awesome!

I could have said a lot of things to this one, based on such an assumption. A few days before I'd have been anxious to meet her. Just now I was cautious. "What kind of favor?"

"A lot of us want to quit smoking. We understand you can help us do it."

Superman just thought he traveled fast. News in a small town has him in the bush leagues. I heard either John Pelham, or his guardian angel, saying in his new suave, professional voice, "Why yes, I undoubtedly can help you ladies." I didn't exactly add, *but it'll cost you.* What I said was, "You understand no one can guarantee results in this business, but if the therapy . . ." (get that therapy shit?) . . . isn't effective there'll be no charge."

"That sounds more than fair. How do we arrange appointments?" She didn't even ask me about the tab.

I said, "Appointments can be fitted to your schedules. How many of you will there be ~ and do any of you work?"

"I work, but just for something to do as a community service. Some of the others contribute their time to various things."

Our town has a lot of money. I interpreted her smooth rejoinder as, *Great heavens! A job? Us? How demeaning!* "Would you want to coordinate appointments for the group, or, if it would work out better, each lady can call and set up their time. I'm very flexible." And, I could have added, quite truthfully, even limber in my current condition. "Actually we were hoping to come as a group." She giggled, a nice, girlish touch. "It could be so much fun." She was practically warbling again.

She sounded as though she'd have thought Betty Friedan was an asshole for assuming women with *time* on their hands had a problem. She'd probably never heard of Betty Friedan. Femi-nazism wasn't big right around there, except for a few malodorous, hippie broads with unwashed hair that looked like frayed rope, who had enough leg and armpit hair to stuff a respectable pillow.

I was beginning to get a mental picture of the Uplift crowd as Blondie Bumpstead and her overfed bridge club. I could see me serving tea and watercress sandwiches to a campfire circle in my tennis-court living room and, later, theatrically making a few Svengali hand passes like Mandrake the magician, to put them all in a trance at once. Pelham gestured hypnotically . . . and all that shit. Don't laugh. Was I ever in for a surprise.

"We were going to have our weekly get together at eleven today, then go to the country club for lunch. I have time to call all the girls and we could meet at your place. It would be lovely if you joined us for lunch afterward."

That invitation sounded a lot like General Emeritus Norbert Harboldson in his best democratic style, prefacing an order to fly to Mars with: "You wouldn't mind if I asked you to . . ." Translated, it meant, "You play ball with me or I'll shove this bat up your ass!" I heard myself saying, "That's agreeable with me. I'm just getting the business off the ground, but I'm sure we can manage."

"I understand. I can come out a little early and help." She laughed. "You don't have a receptionist yet, do you?"

I thought, *It sounds like I do now.* If I'd known her as well as I was going to, I might have said a lot more. Such as, "Why don't you come right over. I'm sure we could manage to occupy our time till eleven somehow."

Such as skinny-dipping in my hot tub, or even my swimming pool. Instead, the best I could manage was, "That's very thoughtful of you. Come whenever you want. Do you know where I am?"

"Oh, yes. Everyone knows your place."

No shit! Think that over. I was. Did other restless matrons besides my Hot Buns make a practice of reading obituaries to see who was newly eligible? Were speculative eyes appraising my bulging biceps in Safeway, and I innocently unaware? Maybe. I am built like Mr. America and stay in damn good shape too.

Ask me: did I rush around after her call like a housewife, plumping pillows on the couch, quickly vacuum, dust, worry about the bathrooms and the kitchen drain board, hastily make my bed? Fuck no. I had coffee and a cigar on the back porch.

But I was back where I could see out the front picture window when Pat Sunderland unloaded from a BMW sedan in my circle drive. Unloaded was the right word too. Pat, as the saying goes, was amply stacked, with everything. She looked like Suzanne Sommers before some idiot talked her into a nose job. (Did you ever see the Playboy shots of Sommers? I Like them.) In so many words, the ingredients for a nice, wholesome, American romance, more or less.

Like Sommers, Pat looked as though she knew it. Moreover, when I came to unhook the porch screen door, she dazzled me with a smile that an orthodontist might kill to use for his ad. She appeared to be a genuine honey-blond and had hazel eyes, a deep tan and wore a powder blue suit that would have looked cheap and flashy on 999 women out of a thousand, but just the opposite on her. Of course, she'd have made a potato sack look sensational. The blue simply complemented her tan.

Since Curtains almost never objected to women, except religious freaks who must give off a hypocrite musk, he was right with me to greet Pat. She put out a beautifully manicured hand for me, and said, "I'm Pat Sunderland, as you probably suspect."

All I could manage was a weak, "Hi. Come in."

Then she made the move on Curtains that would have put Cuchillo Pete into intensive care. She darted down and cuddled his ugly mug right up to her cheek and warbled, "Oh, you sweet, big thing. Aren't you adorable?"

Curtains almost fainted, then made a lightning recovery and grinned, starting his stub tail oscillating at the same time. And, I might add, the softheaded idiot licked her ear. He's no ear licker. Nor hand licker either, except mine. It was the first time I'd ever seen him lick an ear. Traitor!

"You've made a conquest," my guardian angel said.

"Sometimes I do," she said, and looked directly into my eyes, down my gullet and out my urethra, in one dazzling flash.

Holy shit, feller Americans. Hot Buns on Saturday. Vulva Woman (i.e. Navaho deity) on Tuesday. I was really flying. Pat affected me a lot different than Hot Buns. I simply knew her husband wouldn't be a dumb shit that played around and risked AIDS, for example. I knew she'd never played around, and maybe never would, despite her knowing look. If she'd said, "Let's fuck," I'd have slipped old Roscoe in her in Olympic class time. I'd probably also have shot my wad trying to get it in ~ or maybe managed a whole, long, deep stroke and apologized later, without even blushing. And somehow I knew she'd understand and forgive that.

Boy can I fantasize. And "let's fuck" is exactly what she said, two steps inside the front door. I'M KIDDING! Maybe Mickey Spillane can get by with that kind of improbable horseshit, but it simply never happens. I never met a woman like that, and if there is one, she'd be mighty risky.

What Pat actually said was, "What a nice place." Later I'd discover it looked like a ghetto packing crate compared to hers. Later yet I'd discover that she was married to Croesus. Also Methuselah in the same package. He hadn't risked AIDS, that's for sure. He hadn't got laid since about the time Pearl Harbor was bombed, which was to say about twenty years before she was born. This was a bought woman and a goddam careful one, or I missed my guess. She had "right school" and breeding stamped on her. A thoroughbred, a patrician . . . and a volcano of unpredictable proclivities.

She gave me another smile that would have jumped the Sphinx

across the Nile, and said, "A few of the girls may be a little late. Is that all right?"

"Certainly." I wished by then they'd all be about two days late. As it was, she was earlier than I'd expected. "How about some coffee out on the back patio?"

"Wonderful. I can smoke my very last cigarette ever. I tried to quit before and always gave in and started again over a cup of coffee. They just seem to go together."

"Let's hope it's your last one." I was leading the way to the kitchen, only because I couldn't figure out how to gracefully get her ahead of me. And with another sensational blond in tow.

"Oh, I just know you can stop my smoking. I hope I don't start eating to compensate and blow up like a basketball. I couldn't bear to be fat."

"We can treat that tendency too. Hypnotism works on a lot of things." A masterpiece of understatement.

Out back over our coffee, she looked around and said, "You have a lot of acreage. Her little place, just over the mountain I later discovered, was larger ~ six hundred sections more or less. In case you're a trifle vague on what a section is, it's six hundred and forty acres, a square mile. In others words, her little place (actually Methuselah's) had 384,000 acres. And in case you're vague on acres, what difference does it make? We're talking about something ten miles wide and sixty miles long, or twenty miles wide and thirty long, cut it how you will. You can't throw a rock out of it from the middle at any rate.

This woman was filthy rich, as the vulgar saying goes. Super goddam rich. And super goddam beautiful. As I said, Mephistopheles delivers.

I might end up in her expensive drawers if I played my cards right. But let me add that I think the world's screwed up about Old Nick.

The devil is so clever that he has people thinking he's God. Got that? Jehovah is actually the devil. Proof. Any son of a bitch that thinks suffering is gratifying, and fun is sinful, is fucked up. Impossibly fucked up. And go take a gander and see what they do in churches. They glare at each other's clothes and hats; gossip about one another, try to fire the minister if he doesn't cowtow and instead goes after sin hammer and tongs (which, inevitably, reflects on the congregation).

If I were going to join a church it would be Catholic, where the management excommunicates you if you fuck with them. After all, aren't they God's minion's ~ or, as I said, somebody's? Anyhow, the point is that I was doing just fine with Old Nick in my corner. I had an awakening about the local Uplift girls vs. Blondie's bridge club when they showed up. Not a one was overstuffed, had blue hair, or wore tennis shoes. They were an eye-full as far as grooming went and I'd bet not a one was pushing forty yet. Pat was probably the only one with really big money, but the rest were all "comfortable," if you know what I mean. Not apt to suffer even if another Great Depression came along. Old mining money, old cattle money, old money-money, even the heir of some old grey beard who'd invented some kind of metal fastener, a rivet or washer or something. Day and night, all over the world, every second, a dozen little doo-dads were stamped out at a mill apiece royalty. That means his granddaughter was raking in $378,432.00 a year, before taxes, over seven thousand dollars a week ~ a lot better than even the top bracket of Social Security.

Not as good as I'd have done if the old bastard hadn't cut me off, but pretty damned good. What a load to have an old man who's a reprehensible shit. You may think I spend a lot of time thinking about money. You're right.

Almost as much time as I spend thinking about fucking. I'm almost as bad as a woman. And, speaking of such, there wasn't a single valiant uplifter in that crowd that I'd have tossed out of bed; not all beautiful, but not ugly either. And rich, let's not forget rich.

Briefly my session went about the way I conjectured it would earlier, except for the watercress sandwiches. Tea I had. And chocolate chip cookies. The ladies took over there, suspecting I'd probably maim myself in a kitchen. Little did they know. Shit, I still have my GI can opener on my key ring and am pure lightning with K-rations and a Sterno one-burner stove.

I had them all sit as a group. All were eyeing one another (and me) cautiously.

"Clasp your hands together in front of you," I told them, which they all did dutifully, fingers interlaced, except one dark haired, dark eyed, diminutive little beauty named Stacey, who simply held one hand with another, as though she wasn't really listening, and might not really be with us.

I walked over and stood in front of her, pointed and said, "I should have said with your fingers intertwined."

She smiled uncertainly at me. "I'm sorry."

"No need to be."

Here, I thought, *is a woman with some kind of problem.* I didn't know how bad it was yet, or how little she was aware of it. She was twenty-nine, going on thirty, and technically still a virgin. Her husband had a Madonna complex. He'd jumped her once, got her pregnant and never slept with her again. (Of course I didn't know that then.)

"Now ladies, keep your fingers interlaced and rotate your arms up over your heads." (This, by the way, is an admirable position for tit watching.) They did as I told them. "Now shut your eyes and relax."

(This is an even more admirable position for tit watching. You won't be caught at it, in case you're the sneaky type. I'm not.)

They all shut their eyes, whether they relaxed or not. Time would tell. "Now, try to blank your minds. Imagine a big black void in front of your eyes and try not to think of anything distracting. Listen to nothing but the sound of my voice. Relax. Try to listen to nothing but the sound of my voice. You must have confidence in me." I said all this in a low, caressing monotone. That's part of the technique. I repeated the same instructions several times.

Then I said, "I want you all to concentrate on this. You can't take your hands apart. Don't try it yet, but concentrate on the thought *you can't take your hands apart.* Think about that and listen only to the sound of my voice and do just as I say. You will have extreme difficulty disengaging your hands even if I tell you to try it. Now try it. You can't take your hands apart! No matter how hard you try you can't take your hands apart."

As I anticipated from past experience, most of them were very suggestible and really couldn't get their hands apart. They were half hypnotized already and didn't know it. This exercise separates the good subjects from the more difficult ones. Since their eyes were still closed, none of them knew which were which.

"Without opening your eyes, put your hands back in your laps. Be sure to keep your eyes shut. Now all of you unclasp your hands. Open your eyes."

The ones who were the best subjects looked a trifle groggy, as is usually the case. I carefully noted who they were. I had expected Pat to be one of the tougher subjects, but she hadn't been. I looked them all over like a good speaker, swinging my eyes over every one of them in turn.

"I know you wanted to do this as a group. In fact if any of you come to me individually, I will always insist a third party be present." (Such as Old Nick, who is omnipresent just like Jehovah ~ and maybe more so. Number two tries harder.)

Did I see some disappointed looks quickly covered up at the notion of being with me only with a chaperon?

Sex Ring in a Small Town

I told the group, "I'm going to hypnotize Pat first, so you can all watch and see what happens." It worked like a charm. Women are always far more serious about such business than men. There was no snickering. When I finished and Pat was herself again, she consulted her watch.

She exclaimed, "We're going to be late for the Country Club if we don't hurry! Can we do some more this afternoon?"

"Certainly," I said. "I'm at your service. This is my business." (Well - sort of).

Pat insisted on whipping me out to the Country Club in her BMW. Whipping explains exactly the way she drove too. This lady was a pistol. On the other hand she'd kissed Curtains goodbye on his cold, wet nose before we left.

She drove admirably, with almost total concentration, like a race car driver. It takes an airplane driver to appreciate coordination. Few women really have it. They tend to be mechanical, rather than animal.

"I'm glad I met you," she said, eyes straight ahead on the road.

I glanced her direction and took in a wonderful profile, but just then she was poker-faced. Undoubtedly on purpose. I wondered where the hell that remark was intended to lead us.

"Do you ride horses?" she asked.

"I don't fall off, if that's what you mean."

"Good," she said. "I have eighty of them."

CHAPTER NINE

WEDNESDAY MORNING, 10:00 A.M.

Remember Norbert? Gen. Harboldson? My patron? He was trying to cut a deal. I had him on the horn submitting my resignation. I was out from under his thumb at last ~ or at least I thought so. After all, I'd drummed up over two grand in my new business the first couple of days. If that wasn't a fair market survey, I was planning to marry Dorothy anyhow.

I hadn't made a market survey of what she was planning, but had a good idea. (I didn't know the half of it.)

"You can't resign!" Norby growled.

I thought, *Why the fuck not?* He might have read my mind.

"We need you down here, especially now!"

True. I was the brains of the stinkin' place, if it had any. The "especially now" referred to the first real work we'd had in the two years I'd been there.

"Are you trying to hold me up for a raise?" Followed by a short, unhumorous laugh. (They always think you're still wearing a uniform ~ a lot of them still are, in their heads, like Oscar.) "I was just going to make you project manager on this Safety Shield thing we just got the contract on."

No doubt. I'll bet. I could see me doing all the work for the ass kissing bastards Harboldson had pulled in from his misty past, as far back as the fabled plains of West Point.

I thought, *If you think I'm going to spend the rest of my life trying to pump studies through a bunch of illiterate, retired Brigadier Generals - half of them nicknamed either Buck or Old Steady, guess again, Norby.* They'd expected me to salute them, bring their coffee, stand at attention, and refrain from farting while they held the papers I wrote for them upside down and tried to read the title, like a bunch of monkeys trying to screw a football through the inflation hole.

"Well, speak up!" Norby barked.

"I did speak up. I quit."

Instead of having apoplexy he got reasonable, after a fashion ~ a most dangerous situation with generals. He said, "Bullshit! You're up to your ass in bills. I'll give you two grand a month more than you're getting."

Too late. I got a sharply etched picture of that 70-mile round trip, shoving off while the east was just getting light and my body was begging for just one more hour of sleep. Worse yet to go listen to the stale jokes of a bunch of superannuated coffee coolers. Some of the bastards were so dumb that even the rest of them noticed it.

I said, "Look, general. Don't think I don't appreciate everything you've done for me . . ."

"What the hell do you expect me to think? We really need you and you're trying to desert."

How military. How goddam preciously military. Desert, my ass.

"Are you planning to have me shot?" I was ready to tell him the hell off. He probably suspected it.

He laughed and said, "I'd like to. And don't get smart with me."

I had a notion to say, "Nobody smart would have spent twenty years in the Army."

Has anyone happened to notice that most generals are real assholes? I can't have been the only one. On the other hand, the twits they like to keep around to *yes* them have to have their wives tie their shoes and send them off to work in the morning, so maybe not too many have noticed. In fact the ideal career officer is a gorilla who can't tell the difference between right and wrong ~ next best is one who doesn't give a shit even if they can tell the difference.

"General, you may have noticed I don't wear those green overalls anymore. I'm a civilian."

"You always were."

"I come from a long line of them."

He was obviously desperate or he would have blown his stack. Instead he stayed reasonably cool. He knew that without me he might have to do some work himself.

He cooed, "Look, you're tired. I can tell the signs. Like combat fatigue." (*Asshole* fatigue would have come closer.) "Take a couple of weeks off. A month if you think you need it. Grab a space-available flight somewhere. Get laid by some of that tight pussy in Taiwan. Get skunk drunk a few times. You've been working hard and just had a shock losing your wife."

I can't imagine how he knew I was working hard since he was never around, and didn't think he'd noticed I was a widower now. Anyhow, the notion occurred to me, *Why not cream this sonofabitch for a final month's pay. There was always the chance too, that my new racket would bomb. Why not take out a little free insurance and accept a gratuity for being so benevolent?*

I said, "At the new rate of pay?"

He said, "What, at what new rate of pay?"

"A month off at the new rate of pay." I almost added, *asshole.* I did add, "You just gave me a two grand a month raise, remember?"

"You bastard. All right, at the new rate of pay."

"And a whole month off?"

"Long silence. "You're really pushing it, aren't you?"

Shit. He acted like it was his money. Come to think of it, that was almost true, since he was out of the Army. Usually they never discover they aren't still on active duty, where, if they blow it, it's back to the drawing board and stick the "ignorant taxpayer" with the bill. In this case, he'd figured out he was sticking himself with the bill. Give Norby high marks for a general.

I hung up the phone, and it rang before I let go of it. "You don't know me," a voice said. "I work for Oscar, your neighbor across the street."

I knew him all right. Dirty Harry. I hung up. As I expected, the phone rang again in about the time it takes to redial a number.

"Look, Sheridan," I said, "your omens are evil."

"So the bitch told you?"

"What did you expect her to do ~ this isn't TV or a grade B movie where all the actors have to act stupid to keep the plot moving? What the hell do you want from me, as if I didn't know?"

"About a grand would do for starters."

I thought about that. "O.K. if I deliver in person?"

"Maybe. Where?"

"You know where all those old abandoned mine shafts are up on Ocotillo Hill?"

"Very funny. If something happens to me certain people will have all the scoop to put you and that blond bitch on the hot seat."

I doubted that and decided to give him a jolt. "Speaking of that blond bitch, have you ever jerked off thinking about getting some of that?" Of course he had.

"What are you, a pervert?"

Great. I'd bet he'd done it thinking of tearing off a little with her within the past twenty-four hours. I'd done it often enough and I'm a clean-cut, perfectly normal American boy, even if I'm not a blackmailer. I didn't answer his question.

"Well?" he said. "What's the word on the dough-re-mi?"

"How do you want me to get it to you ~ and don't say in small, unmarked bills or I'll die laughing and you won't get anything."

"You got that much around there? I'll drop out and pick it up."

I was thinking fast. I wanted some time to work on his case.

"I don't keep that kind of scratch around. How about tomorrow? I'll meet you at the VFW bar at noon, we can have a drink and I'll pass you an envelope."

"Why the VFW bar?"

"It's light and full of people. I don't want you getting suspicious and fading for your hardware like Mike Hammer."

He actually laughed. "O.K. I'll be there."

I thought, *Good. Your omens are getting more wicked yet.*

Shortly after that a car pulled into my circle drive carrying an interesting cargo. Stacey Greer, hot, cute, wiggly, bright-eyed, and, alas, a technical virgin. Curtains announced her, though with only a small woof that denoted no homicidal intentions. The big oaf liked women, just like someone else right around here.

"Hi," she said, still outside, "I've lost Beano again."

"And who, pray tell, is Beano?"

"My dog. The maid or gardener always forget and lets her get away. Last time I found her in your yard."

"Good thing it's a her, or you'd have found her body in my yard. Curtains is death on boy dogs. C'mon in. No sense in yakking through the screen. How about some coffee?" (A sneaky way to keep her around awhile ~ she was a class act to look at too, in a different way than Hot Buns or Pat Sunderland, but still nice.)

She came in willingly enough. If I had a little more suspicious mind, I'd have wondered if Beano was actually lost.

I indicated the way to the kitchen. "Lead the way, and I shall precede," I said.

She turned and blessed my punkin head with a radiant smile that would have ripened a retarded tomato crop. "Oh, I love it, you're a Mrs. Malaprop fan, too. You read Sheridan?"

I said, "I'm guilty, I guess. I read a lot of things."

By then she was ahead, going down the hall. Something about our little town must drive matrons into wearing tight shorts. Something about tight shorts drives me to a hard-on. I could feel the boy starting up and had a sense of deja vu. Would she notice? And what if she did?

She'd been in the kitchen with the ladies and remembered where the makings were. I'd been in the kitchen with three ladies ~ her, Pat and Dorothy, and I knew where the *makings* were too. In those tight shorts.By now my pants were standing out fair to middlin'. If she noticed, she pretended not to.

"How about out on the patio?" We sipped our brew out there with my *rail* a lot less noticeable sitting down.

"What does Beano look like?"

"She's Heinz Fifty-Seven. I think Scotty, crossed with something a little longer in the legs. She's mostly black. Scotty ears. But she's a real watch dog." She laughed. "The bishop came up one day and I told him to stay in the car till I got Beano on her leash. He must have felt a strong spirit protecting him and got out anyway."

"What happened?"

She guffawed. "You can guess. It was like the Hound of the Baskervilles. He made it almost twice around his car before she caught him. We bought him a new pair of pants."

I could hardly forbear asking if he ripped them, or shit them, or both. I said, "I wonder if he reported it to the pope?"

"Oh, he's not a Catholic bishop. My husband is a Mormon."

"And you're not?"

"Huh uh. I'm not a much of anything."

"Doesn't your husband get on you about that?"

She looked as though she were debating whether to say more and obviously decided to trust me. "I support him. Mormons like money."

"Don't we all? Does he make you tithe ten percent?"

"Fat chance."

She was the heir I mentioned earlier who got another coin dropped in her sack every time a lock washer or something was punched out. It didn't sound like she was too enamored with her consort. I'm the kind that makes a note of that sort of thing. Maybe she'd be a grass widow someday. If all my contingency options folded, this was not something I'd throw out of bed. Au contraire. Besides, she read Sheridan. Simply reading would have been an improvement on most of the Army officers' wives I'd known, for example, though a good many of them filled out tight shorts rather well, not to mention blouses. Sad to say, it is, as yet, an imperfect world.

Suddenly Stacey pointed and said, "There she is, up there!"

"There who is?"

"Beano."

She had better eyes than I. "Where?"

"Up there nosing around in the Yucca. We'd better get her before she noses into a snake."

She headed out the back gate, Curtains and I "followed." It was a hefty jog, despite my daily run, I had trouble keeping up. This broad was spring steel.

Beano saw us coming and headed over the hill, Stacey in hot pursuit. She finally collared her fair and square and pulled a leather thong out of her pocket.

"Gotcha, you little blucka-bluck."

I could imagine what a blucka-bluck was. She finished the job hardly breathing fast. "That's my place down there," she said, pointing. "There's a path down from here. C'mon down. You might as well see where I live. Besides, if you ever catch Beano down at your place you can bring her down and lock her in if no one is home. I'll show you how."

Obviously "no" wasn't going to do as an answer. I noticed she said "my" place rather than "our." Also that there was a bird's eye view of my "secluded" back yard. I wondered how much skinny-dipping she'd watched me and Dorothy doing. Or me all alone, more to the point.

John Pelham

CHAPTER TEN

Somehow I felt pretty light-hearted about my impending tryst with Dirty Harry at the VFW. As though I had a premonition that his omens really were evil, that something permanent might happen to him. The feeling got such a strong hold on me that I almost didn't drop by the bank and pick up a grand in cash, except that I needed some "fresh" around anyhow. I didn't bother to put it in an envelope though.

The VFW is located in an enclave called Freeport, which is midway between the two sections of town, the canyon district and the flats. The area was half boarded up because of a local depression that set in when the mines cut back work a few years before. The VFW used to be a J.C. Penney store.

I found a spot to park the Caddy up the street a half block. I was just getting out when a gaggle of police cars, followed by an ambulance, screeched to a Hollywood halt in front of the VFW building. The street was suddenly full of fuzz, running for the front door of the VFW, drawing pistols like the Lone Ranger. Curious people came to the doors of the few operating businesses still left in that neighborhood and gawked up the street. None of them had the nerve to go up to the excitement. I waited a couple of minutes, then started up that way and got a couple of "are-you-out-of-your-mind?" looks. People get killed for real around our neck of the woods ~ dope and illegal immigration contribute to a sort of fatal climate more than occasionally.

There was no point in trying to get into the VFW. A cop was guarding the door like Cerberus (except for being shy a couple of heads ~ maybe all three, come to think of it) I had a pretty good idea what had happened, and didn't bother to ask the watchdog at the door. By the time I got up there, they already were carrying someone out on a stretcher. I was feeling charitable enough by then to wonder what kind of flowers I should send to Dirty Harry's funeral. However, I wasn't feeling charitable after they carried the body past me. It wasn't Dirty. It was Cuchillo Pete, white-faced, eyes closed tightly, gritting his teeth in pain, even though he'd probably been pumped full of painkiller. Obviously he'd had a serious accident. If I'd got there a little sooner I'd have heard the shot; sooner yet, I'd have seen it happen to him because I'd have been inside, but as it was I had a pretty good idea what had taken place.

Back at the Caddy I peeled a cigar, got it going and sat there thinking out a good next move. The one that looked best was to whip a few things in a traveling bag and slope for parts unknown, with Curtains of course; then wire back to have a "For Sale" sign put in my front yard.

Then it occurred to me that a guilty conscience might be about to make me do something stupid. I thought, *nobody really knows a goddam thing ~ not even Cuchillo Pete, for all practical purposes.* Dirty Harry was just the rotten sort of bastard to smell a rat though. The question was how to get him off the scent. The best way was to find out what really happened, then play innocent as hell, and arrange to deliver the thousand later. I was sure I couldn't call him up for a few hours yet; not while the cops questioned him, assuming what I thought happened actually had. The best way to find out quick occurred to me and I dug out for home in the Caddy, after edging past an arm-waving traffic cop who was, by then, about as necessary there as a soup kitchen.

Once home I hotfooted in the house and got Dorothy on the phone. I had to assure the girl who answered that it was important, since her boss was with a customer.

"Hello," a very different Dorothy-voice said, all business. "This is Dorothy." (How fuckin' crisply-democratic can you get?)

I quickly said, "I was just down in Freeport and got tangled up in a mess of squad cars and ambulances. Has anyone come in there yet and said what was going on?"

"Just now," she said . . . , "I'll have to look it up and I'll get right back to you after I finish with this customer."

What the hell did that mean? I fidgeted away a couple of minutes, carrying my telephone with me. Curtains kept a cautious eye on me, sensing my mood. Five minutes went by, and I flopped in my recliner and tried to read an article in *Newsweek*. The words made no sense, as I read and reread them. It was a good ten minutes before the phone rang and by then I was getting snappish.

"Yeah," I growled at the phone.

A sweet-voiced thing at the water company told me I'd forgot to sign the check when I'd sent in my bill.

"I'll send you another check," I snapped, and then cut her off.

The poor girl must have thought, "I hope I never meet *him.*"

I hope she doesn't.

When the phone rang again, right after I hung up, I was a little nicer. Dorothy said, "I just called and got a busy signal."

"The goddam water company called. Doesn't some idiot always tie up your line when you're expecting an important call? So what happened? I'm all ears." I'd like to have added that she took her sweet time getting back to me.

She must have sensed what I was thinking and apologized. "I had to get the customer at my desk taken care of. He told me what happened at the VFW, but I had to get him out of there before I could talk to you."

"Why?"

"Because I want to know what you knew about it before it happened."

"What does that mean?"

"Well, something happened to one of your customers."

"Customer?"

"Pedro Gonzalez."

"What happened to him? I saw him being carried out on a stretcher, but had no idea why."

"Oh?"

"He tried to knife a man named Sheridan Millikan and Millikan beat him to it and shot him. I thought you might have an inkling something was due to happen like that."

"Did it ever occur to you that a bunch of shits like bankers have all the company phones tapped, or at least monitor them occasionally?" I added, "Anyhow, how would I know about something like that?"

"You said something about evil omens. I thought you might be psychic."

"Well, Pete's omens were, that's for sure. What did he and Millikan say to each other, if anything?"

"Pedro said something about Millikan paying too much attention to his wife, according to people standing near them, then pulled a knife. Millikan pulled a pistol and shot him."

"I don't blame him. Did he say anything?"

"Maybe he said, 'take dat!' Do you suppose?"

"You've been seeing too many gangster movies. And how come you're talking so freely? I thought you thought my phone might be tapped"

"Not really. Banks are too cheap to pay for that sort of thing."

"Thanks. You're reflecting on my life work. I'll see you tonight, or this evening, or both."

"Okay, baby . . . later."

What a pretty kettle of fish, to coin a frightfully original phrase. If Dirty Harry didn't suspect me, or her, or both of us, of trying to have him *off'd,* he was smarter than I figured he was. And what do I mean by that? I mean, would we pay a five-thumbed moron like Cuchillo Pete to take him out in broad daylight at the Corner of Main and Broadway when we live where we could buy a professional job out of Mexico at bargain basement rates? (Note to the effete East: conditions like that make for real polite people, as a rule, just like carrying guns does; in fact, may lower the homicide rate in both cases, reducing it to only those who deserve it.)

In any case, with respect to the immediate case, it was no joke. Dirty, unless I missed my guess, could play rough. It wasn't only a question now of whether he'd blow the whistle on us to Dorothy's dimwit husband, Oscar. That would be bad enough. But he might try a little hard ball playing of his own. Like tit for tat. One small comfort was that he wasn't apt to tell the cops he suspected a pair he was blackmailing had hired a hit on him. Only we hadn't. Not technically. She had had nothing to do with it. I'd got her into a hell of a mess, along with me. I decided I'd better get the nut cutting over with. As soon as Dirty Harry reasonably could be expected to be home I phoned him. He was in. I hoped my voice didn't sound too shaky.

"I tried to deliver the dough but there was a swarm of cops down there. What the hell happened?"

"You must be the only one in town that doesn't know."

"I came home and took a siesta awhile. I figured I could get in touch with you later and find out what happened."

"I shot a greaser."

"You what?"

"Shot a goddam greaser. He pulled a knife on me."

"The hell you say? Was he drunk?" There was a long pause. Was I overacting?

Finally he half-snorted and said, "The bastard said, 'this'll teach you not to play around with my wife.'"

"Were you?"

He really laughed this time. "Only in my dreams."

Christ did I feel relieved. I was home free, assuming he hadn't been snooping around when Cuchillo and the girls were at my place. If he knew that and put two and two together ~ a lot of people already knew I was hypnotizing people, playing Svengali . . .

If he knew the first damn thing about hypnotism, and the potential of post hypnotic suggestion, a nasty, suspicious mind like his would put two and two together in short order. I said, "Mexican men are jealous as hell. Maybe he saw you looking at his wife in a way he didn't like."

"Maybe. Everybody did." (Tell me about it, Harry.)

"Are the police planning to charge you?"

He snorted. "Are you kidding? This is still a company town. They're more apt to give me a medal."

"Is he dead?"

"Not the last I heard. He's the one'll do time, with a record like his."

He told me about Pete's record, which was the first I knew about that. I thought, *Holy crap! And I was in a fuckin' room with him, ogling his two private pieces.* I innocently skirted around asking Harry who the Mexican was, changing the subject. "Well, I'll have to get the grand to you some other way."

"Suppose I drop over to your place?"

I almost blurted, "Don't do that!" I didn't want to be anywhere near him if I could help it. Unfortunately, I wasn't apt to be able to help it sooner or later. I decided to take the bull by the horns. "In the A.M.," I said. "The bastard I work for is throwing a shindig and I have to trot over and dance attendance on a bunch of Army lame brains." A crisp, quick lie. I sure as hell didn't want him dropping in on me about the time Dorothy got home from work, and was apt to come tripping over.

He guffawed. "Army lame brains! That about covers it! Officers, no doubt."

"You got it."

"Somebody told me you was a colonel . . . "

"I'm afraid so."

"You got more brains than the average colonel."

What the hell did that mean?

"What time should I drop over in the A.M.?"

"Make it tenish."

"O.K." he said, and hung up.

This was a dangerous sonofabitch that I'd have to be damned careful with, especially now. My best bet to get out of this whole mess was to convince Oscar he'd be better off on that slow boat to Singapore that Dorothy had mentioned. Was that just a couple of days before? Christ. It seemed like a month.

I was suddenly dog-tired and sleepy. A siesta would fill the bill.

I locked up and hit the sack. Did you ever notice how you sleep to avoid facing what you don't want to think about? There was plenty

I didn't want to think about. And plenty more that I did.

I didn't want to think about having a warped Viet Nam conscience that would set up a hit without the slightest compunction, except about getting caught. I dropped off thinking, instead, about how it had felt to give the fully disrobed Mrs. Cuchillo Pete a finger job and got a rail-on recalling her bod in full Technicolor. Also recalling the breathless, "Oh Madonna!" cries. She'd be free now to come and go as she pleased. She'd also be horny pretty soon. I made a note to counsel her wisely about that.

John Pelham

CHAPTER ELEVEN

I wonder what quaint notion prompted me to assume that Dorothy may not have been aware of the visit to my place by the Civic Uplift girls? Maybe because she didn't ask me about it the evening after they were there. Such being the case, mentioning it must have slipped my mind. Do I expect anyone to believe that? At any rate, she probably wasn't aware of Stacey Greer's romp with me into the hills after her mongrel, Beano (who'd bit the bishop).

The matter of getting past an eventual discussion of that with Hot Buns paled alongside a meeting with Dirty Harry. I'd put that off a day to buy time to work out some strategy. Pity some strategy didn't occur to me in the meantime. I didn't really sleep well that night.

There was a strong possibility that the son of a bitch had a suspicion I'd set him up for a coffin. In that case, judging from his looks and action, he wasn't above coming over with intent to kill, in the gritty language of the courts. Somehow the notion that Mrs. Pelham's little boy, John, was destined to check out as a "murder one" victim didn't appeal to me worth a shit.

Obviously I'd have Curtains present for our meeting. My old .45 would be a little obtrusive. Besides, unless I held it in my hand, pointed at him, it would also be too slow, with someone who'd beat Cuchillo Pete's knife with absolutely no warning. The best thing to do would be have a witness there ~ or several witnesses, better yet. But who? I really didn't have a close friend in town. Who the hell wants a bunch of *sanitation engineers*, and garbage carriers for enlightened conversation, even if they are aldermen and the mayor. They're almost as bad as old maid schoolteachers (or "young maid" schoolteachers).

Then a stroke of genius rescued me from my concern. Over my morning cigar and coffee it occurred to me that I had some business to conduct with Dirty Harry's boss, Oscar. Why not kill two birds with one stone? I reached for the phone to get Oscar on the horn, just as it beeped an incoming call.

"Hello, lover," Dorothy's voice caressed me. "What're you doing?"

We'd decided discretion demanded we spend our nights apart till her divorce was final. "Thinking," I told her.

"About what?" A hopeful tone there.

"About that too."

"I'm coming over. I don't have to go to work for at least an hour."

Could it be possible that the lady had the hots? Could it be possible that anyone as well-drained as I, could feel the first stirring of another hard-on? I thought, *At least I won't die horny.*

Five minutes later we were having a preliminary dip in my hot tub. Twenty minutes later I was blowing my brains out the head of my dick. Just as though I hadn"t last done it at ten P.M. the night before.

Naturally, the night before we'd managed to work into our busy schedule a talk about Dirty Harry's impending visit. Over coffee, after our morning calisthenics, we continued it.

About that she asked, "Have you decided anything?"

I couldn't help but observe that she looked absolutely adorable with a "recently-played-with" look. Regarding her question, I said, "Yeah! Why don't we jump in the Caddy and send back for our things?" I divined from her expression that she was half-afraid I might be serious. I should have been.

She actually asked me, "Are you serious?"

"Would you do it, if I were?"

She thought about that. "I might. It depends."

"On what?"

"Whether you really want to run." The word *run* said a lot the way it came out, like, *O.K., if you want to be a chicken-shit, yellow-belly I'll always have to be ashamed of.* It was the indomitable Southern female spirit that had killed off half a generation of Confederate chivalry about a half century before their time, keeping a war going two years after the chivalry had brains enough to recognize a "Lost Cause." Also the spirit that kept the Hatfields and McCoys going, down in her home digs, the generation after the shooting Civil War was over. (The War itself, as is obvious to "any blue-bellied Damnyankee" who goes down to Dixie, is still going on in millions of pinheads.)

In direct reply to Dorothy's question, I said, "I'm not leaving a mess like this unsettled."

"Should I lurk in a closet with my hardware ready?" she asked.

I seriously turned that over in my mind. "Maybe you should." But I decided the situation wasn't that crucial yet.

I said, "Curtains and I can probably handle him. You call about 10:15, and if I don't answer the phone, or if I pick it up and say 'Pelham here,' send the Marines quick."

* * *

Dirty got there right on time. The first thing that went wrong with the deal was that he eyed Curtains knowingly. The dog didn't bark at him or show signs of hostility, which should have clued me that he sensed something very unusual. He was thinking and just sat and eyed Dirty through the screen with an unwinking stare.

Harry said, "First of all, the dog goes in the back yard or I don't come in, and all bets are off."

I thought that over a few seconds while Dirty stared at me. If I knew what he knew, and why, I'd have let Curtains out and jerked the neat little .32 PPK out of my vest pocket while Dirty was busy, and blown him away on the spot. It was going to be my last chance. "Okay." I finally said and led the very reluctant Curtains to the back door. He started barking wildly out there as soon as I left him. What is it about supposedly sane people that they can't read and heed warning signs that plainly say: "Facrisakes, smarten up! Your ass is getting in a real mess!" I could have hit the back trail over to Stacey Greer's and called in the Marines. But what the fuck would I tell them? The truth? Fat chance. My alternatives were, face Dirty down or blow town (or one worse than either).

I went back and let him in. The first thing I did was pass over the envelope with the grand in it. He opened it and counted out the ten big ones inside and grinned, eyeing me with the strangest pair of yellow-green gunfighter eyes I could recall seeing. They sent a real chill up my spine.

For lack of something better to break the tension, I asked, "How about some coffee? I can lace it with something."

He continued to stare at me. This was a real nasty specimen.

"Are you trying to butter up the bully?" he sneered.

Smart and nasty ~ that's exactly what I was trying to do, come to think of it. I recalled trying the same thing in school with a bully that scared the shit out of me. It didn't work then, and I knew it wasn't going to work now. Only a fight had chilled the bastard in the fifth grade, and things hadn't changed all that much. (If Lyndon Johnson had only known that, we'd have got out of Nam with our reputation intact.)

Dirty took out a cigarette. I watched his hands carefully as he did it, expecting a pistol to come out instead ~ God knows why. How could he really know anything?

"How long do you plan to keep up the blood sucking?" I asked him. "The lady is getting a divorce. I'm thinking of leaving town."

He lit up and flopped into one of my overstuffed chairs, blew smoke out his nose, carefully dropped the match into an ashtray and looked at me with those terrible eyes. They had a slightly dark ring around the irises, like cartoon eyes. He didn't say a word, blew another big puff of smoke toward the ceiling and looked at it.

"I hear you can make people quit smoking with hypnotism."

Oh! Oh! I thought. *This guy has the inside dope he needs to put two and two together. Or is the bastard just interested in getting off the weed?*

What I said was, "Yeah, I can do that." It was like we were talking in a dream though. An awful suspicion ran from my toenails up and made the hair stand up and tingle on the top of my head. Something was telling me ~ too late ~ that I was minutes, maybe seconds, away from being seriously dead. I was praying the telephone would ring.

I looked at my watch. It was only three minutes since that bastard had got there. Christ! Did time ever go so slow? Then I remembered lying face down in the brush in the jungle with Charlie sneaking all around me, fully aware I was there somewhere, listening, practically sniffing, darting those muddy brown eyes around. My Uzi was under me where I dropped on it as I dived out of sight. I wondered then if it was full of dirt and might not work in case I had to roll over and shoot it out with a half dozen VC. My bowels felt like they were going to let go. And right now the same bowels felt the same way, reminding me. I wished I had that old Uzi pointed at Dirty. Maybe, too, I was having the worst case of nerves and guilty conscience any chicken in town had had that morning. The thought ran through my mind that surely no one else in town could be in that sort of suspense just then.

"How about hypnotising me then?" Harry finally said.

My hopes took a great leap. I tried to keep my voice steady as I said, "Okay. We can do it right here or go back into my study."

"Why not back where you do it to the others?"

Did I hear that right? It was then I was certain that this one was wise to my whole game, somehow ~ that he knew too much.

He gave a nasty laugh that confirmed it. "You son of a bitch . . . you don't think I'd really let you hypnotize me and maybe send me down to the girl's gym or uptown, to expose myself and get carted away to the "crazyhouse" do you? He beat me to the draw by a mile and I let my hand fall away from my vest pocket (and probably let my mouth fall open). He'd got a nickel-plated detective special out like lightning, jerking it from one of those upside down shoulder rigs.

I stared at it like they tell you rabbits stare at a rattlesnake.

"Now," he said in a poisonous voice, "just use two fingers and fish out that dude and drop it on the rug real careful."

I did what he told me, wondering if I could grab it for business at some point on the way down. No way. He had the .38 cocked and ready, and his eyes on me every second.

"Now back away," he said, and when I did, reached down and scooped up the PPK, but kept his eyes on me constantly. "Now we're going back to your office," motioning that way with his gun barrel. He'd obviously been in there before, no trick for an experienced Security man (such as any FBI agent).

I weighed the possibility of dodging down the hall to my bedroom, slamming and locking the door, and getting to my .45, and decided my chances were nada. Anyone that quick was also a dead shot. In this sort of situation you play for time, hoping some break will show up before the dirty, dirty end is unavoidable.

In my study, he said, "Turn around and don't make any dumb moves."

He slipped a pair of nippers on me with their chain laced through my belt in back. It makes it hard to unzip your fly, or do much of anything else either, which is the idea.

"Now sit in that chair." He indicated the big one I used for customers to be comfortable in. Just a few days before, Carmen's little, warm pussy had throbbed right where I was sitting. What a useless fucking speculation, but nonetheless the thought passed through my mind. Pussy doesn't mean a thing anymore when your ass is on the line. I felt like puking. My dong was puckered up to a hole in my belly, and my asshole was cutting rivets. The old heads who wrote the bible knew about that and mentioned, "girding your loins" so you wouldn't shit your pants. I girded mine, though I'll be damned if I know how.

Harry said, "I'm gonna show you something." He climbed on my desk, pushed up one of the soundproofing panels and took out a little black box, then jumped down. "Know what this is?" he asked, shoving it under my nose.

I knew it had to be a recorder for bugging the place, but I didn't say a thing. I was about reconciled to where I was headed, and had started to get a "fuck-you" attitude. The only way he could have got that damned thing in there was when I was out somewhere with Curtains along. This man was a real snake. Obviously he'd been watching my place with binoculars for at least a couple of days before he put the thing in, to know enough to get in undetected.

He said, "With one of these, if you push a remote radio control, it plays back to you up to a mile away." He shook it under my nose again. "If I'd played it back sooner, I'd have known you set me up, you son of a bitch! I'd have waited till you and your greaser hit man were both in the VFW before I showed up, and I'd have got you with a stray shot after I settled that dumb fuck's case."

Only the laundry people now know if I kept my loins girded after that little shot. The phone finally rang. I almost fainted from relief.

"Answer it, I'll hold it up for you and no dumb breaks ~ get rid of whoever it is."

He held the phone to my left ear from behind me, his .38 to the right. "Pelham here," I then heard a click on the other end. "Whoever it was hung up. Must have been a wrong number."

"What was that 'Pelham here' shit?" he asked. Did this smart bastard think that might be a code? I was beginning to suspect he wanted to keep me alive awhile yet and didn't want to upset the apple cart.

"It's Army," I said. "We always answer the phone like that." If I'd known Dorothy had seen too many detective movies and was trying to handle this herself, I'd have died of a heart attack.

Dirty sneered, "Why didn't you answer the phone and say, Colonel Pelham?"

"I'm trying to live it down." It was the right thing to say to a guy like him who'd probably been a corporal in the M.P.'s for a hitch and taken an infinite amount of shit from colonels, to say nothing of second johns. (Listen up Army recruiting, if you wonder why things aren't rosy for reenlistments . . .) I divined that he really wasn't going to blow my head off just yet. No doubt later.

He took a nylon cord out of his pocket. "Move your ass over here," he ordered, and trussed me into a straight chair. (Did I hear the thunder of cavalry hoofs approaching? Nary a thing yet.) He did a thorough job of it and taped my mouth to boot. I'd have been lucky to be able to burp. If I puked, and I still felt like it, I'd drown in my own ick. What a lousy fuckin' way that would be to go.

"I'll be back." Make yourself comfortable."

He was gone a couple of minutes, during which I prayed for the arrival of the troops around the flank, but no luck. I wondered what the hell he was doing. I'd have been mightily relieved to know he was putting his pickup truck in my garage out of sight. He was probably going to hang around and off me after dark, then dispose of my bod in some abandoned mine shaft. He knew Hot Buns would come over after work and this was his chance to get us both clean. He obviously would have to get her sometime before she could blow the whistle after I disappeared.

When he got back he poked his face in front of mine, and said, "Hello, Colonel, sir. Did you make yourself comfortable?" He let out a really nasty laugh probably the only one he had in his inventory.

I wondered what the hell kind of experiences had made him such a winner, then wondered why I was wondering. He was probably raised by wolves. He hopped up on my desk again and brought down another treasure. He waved it at me just as he had the bug.

"Know what this is? It's a $25,000.00 item I borrowed from the company. A wide angle camera that shoots through a needle-size hole. They use it to snoop on their faithful servants. Even the top exec's, sometimes, when the rest of the good old boys get suspicious that someone is a bigger shit than them. Just like the Army C.I.D."

He snorted at some recollection, then said, "I put one in a general's can once and we played back a shot of him jerking off with the Playboy Centerfold just like a dogface." Harry yakked again over remembering that.

I noticed he didn't say like *us* dog faces ~ he was pure mudsill and thought jacking off was demeaning, even though he probably did it more than the average.

His back was to the door when it slammed open and Curtains hit him dead center and knocked him sprawling. Dirty rolled and went for his .38. I got a terrible picture of Curtains drilled between the eyes. Only the huge dog was quicker than Cuchillo Pete had been, quicker than Dirty, and trained by experts for just what he did. Dirty got the .38 out and had his arm mangled a microsecond afterward by jaws that had tons of pressure in them. The pistol dropped. Dirty made some sort of sound, not a scream, not a groan, a gusty sigh like a sacked quarterback. I could just reach the gun with my toe, and kicked it away. I really didn't need to.

Did you ever see a one hundred fifty-pound killing engine pull out a jugular vein and Adams Apple, along with half a neck in one monstrous twist? I just did. I loved it. Dirty died hard but quick.

Dorothy burst through the door just a trifle late for the real show, her .38 ready. She had the Hatfield - McCoy look on her face. If Curtains hadn't got the job done first, and Dirty had shot her, I'd bet she'd have lived long enough on sheer grit to 'off the bastard. In fact I thought she might be going to put a couple of big lead pills in his head anyhow, for good measure. I let out a muffled protest, warning her not to with a violent shake of my head.

It took awhile to get me untied and uncuffed, especially since she had to get the keys out of Dirty's pocket without getting bloody in the bargain, but first she unzipped my lips. I fed her the details of what had been going on while she got me loose.

She said, "I let myself in the back way. I could hear Curtains raving out there and figured he'd lead me to you. I hoped the son of a bitch didn't look out the window at the wrong time, if he was still here. I didn't know but what you might be dead, since no car was out front."

"His pickup is in the garage. He expected to get us both when you came over after work, I'd guess. He was a cold one."

"What should we do with his body?"

What we figured out to do with him was a masterpiece. Of course we could have used his own pickup and simply hauled him out at night. We could have called the cops and had a lot of unnecessary red tape, and possible complications we didn't need. And if we hauled him out ourselves, there's always the technicality of bloodstains to get rid of. They never come out beyond chemical detection. And Dirty mentioned someone would be looking into the matter if something happened to him.

So I opened my safe and left the door ajar, then spread the thousand dollars around between it and the mortal remains of Harry, as though Curtains had caught him just as he got the loot out.

Before Dorothy and I went to lunch (lunch? Why not?) I disposed of the adhesive tape in the trash and burned the tapes from the recorders, then stashed both machines in my patio refrigerator. I'm the thrifty type where big-ticket items are concerned. On the way into town I tossed the nippers, wiped clean, into the ditch. Were we able to eat much after what happened? I ate three stiff scotch and sodas, but Dorothy's appetite didn't seem puny.

I checked her eyes several times as she put away a *Tostada Grande* to see if I could detect the Hatfield gleam, but she simply looked like our friendly neighborhood banker again, having a business luncheon.

This was not your typical dizzy blond, as you probably suspect by now.

This was J. P. Morgan crossed with General George Patton.

Sex Ring in a Small Town

CHAPTER TWELVE

Oscar's face was a "study" as they say, when we walked in on Dirty Harry's body.

I tried to look surprised. It was wasted histrionics. Oscar was too busy looking horrified. "Curtains must have caught a robber in the act," I said.

"He's no robber," Oscar blurted.

"What the hell was he doing here then cleaning out my safe?" I pointed to the open safe and money on the floor.

Oscar caught himself just in time to keep from blurting out something dumb, like, "He was one of my men," and instead he said, "I don't know." Then realized that would sound dumb too, since what he'd already said indicated he'd known the man.

Finally ~ reluctantly, I judge ~ he said, "The bastard worked for me." He shot me a confused look and he wasn't putting it on. "I can't imagine what he was doing here. Actually I didn't know him all that well." I could buy that. "We'd better call the cops," I suggested.

That turned Oscar on. "I'll do it," he said quickly.

He wanted to pick his cop, I'd guess. *Fine*, I thought. *The bastard is probably thinking of the bad publicity for the company and how it will reflect on him for hiring an asshole like Dirty Harry.* Shit, who else would work at a sleazy job like company gumshoe? (Obviously, almost any hopeless case, take Oscar for example.)

I could figure out the other end of the telephone conversation. Curtains looked like he was trying to figure it out too, since he was allowing Oscar to go ahead without trying to make another trophy out of him yet. The big, black bastard reminded me of Tarzan, with one foot on the body of a cold-cocked great ape, beating his chest. (But not bellowing like Tarzan ~ Curtains wasn't the boastful type; he let his work speak for itself.)

Oscar said, "Get the Chief on ~ I've got a hot potato."

He didn't have to say who he was, so he must have called down there a lot.

When the Chief came on, he said, "I need you up here personally. Don't bring anyone you're not sure about. I'm over at my neighbor's house, right across the street from mine . . . Yeah, he's the one." (And what did the Chief ask? If it was Svengali's house?) "It looks like his big dog caught a robber in the act and killed him. There's more to it than that though."

He listened to some question, probably, "What the hell do you mean 'more to it than that?'"

"Because, he's one of my men."

More listening.

"How the hell do I know what he was doing here? I sure as hell didn't send him."

Squawking on the other end.

"No, I didn't. I don't know. The 'goddam' safe is open and some dough is scattered all over hell."

More squawking.

Maybe the Chief wasn't as securely in the company's pocket as Chiefs used to be, or as Oscar would have liked.

"We'll talk about it when you get here, but for crissakes get up here as quick as you can." Oscar put the phone down and looked as though he might be ready to puke. I was. Harry's bod had already stunk the place up like an outdoor can.

Let me summarize here, since what happened in the next couple of days was an education in small-town control by the powers that be. When big bastards are getting egg off their faces it pays to be on their side. The story made page three in the paper ~ once, with no follow-up. There was no tie-in with the shooting of Cuchillo Pete as ordinarily could have been expected, mentioning, for example, that the late unlamented killed by Curtains was one and the same with the gunman who'd tagged Pete at the VFW. Sheridan Millikan had few friends, was not married and very little was known of him ~ at least very little became public information. There was probably a lot in his company file. In fact, I'd have bet he'd once worked for Oscar as an M.P. in the Army.

I say that because Oscar suddenly got receptive to the idea of a new job somewhere else. I'd already suggested it to him in view of his (and my) domestic situation. The company probably got on his case about bringing in a rotten apple that caused them embarrassment. Yet, Oscar undoubtedly knew enough about them to merit about two year's severance pay, and not quite enough to have his body found in the desert, or in an alley behind some brothel across the border. The company was in such a philanthropical mood they even paid me a grand to have my study cleaned up. Nice eh?

Not that they would have openly bought any guilt for their bringing a crud like Dirty Harry to our "clean little town."

Oscar brought the money over personally. "A little present," as he put it. We went back together and surveyed the cleanup job. "Good as new," I said.

"Fine," Oscar said.

I invited him to stay for coffee and hit him with a copy of the Job Market section of the Retired Officer Magazine. "They want a security officer in Iraq for big bucks," I said. (Boy what a great future I was lining him up for, though neither of us knew that then.)

He looked the ad over. "That's a lot of money," he said after he'd read it. "Some guy with connections will get that one."

"You've got connections too," I told him.

He looked confused.

"Let old Dr. Pelham here get on that one. Gen. Harboldson knows everybody who knows anybody. Right now he's brown-nosing me to keep me on his payroll so he doesn't have to do some work himself."

You might think it solved all my problems when Oscar packed his bag and hauled ass, that Dorothy and I lived happily ever after. Well, I thought it would be that way. As usual, the fuckin' snake didn't waste any time coming out of hibernation and slithering around the Garden of Eden like crazy.

Enter Putt-Putt O'Dool. Everyone in town had at least heard of Putt-Putt. When his name came up there'd be a snort of laughter, or snickers, not without reason. Putt-Putt was the only public farter I've ever heard of. It was how he came by his name. Whether he farted for shock appeal, or perhaps as a one-man crusade against the hypocrisy of sneaking them off, or for other psycho reasons, he farted publicly without visible embarrassment.

If he did it as an attention-getter, he was a marvelous success.

In our town this habit first came to light when he got a job as stock boy for Safeway. In the wee hours of the morning, he and several young ladies worked in the storeroom and the store aisles, sorting, bagging and stocking goods before opening hour, and he would putt loudly. At first the girls thought their ears were deceiving them, that perhaps he had tight shoes or something. After their noses confirmed the startling news suggested by their ears, they had no alternative but to believe that here in their midst, without blushing, had appeared a public farter; the first they'd ever known. Pretty soon they hatched his nickname: Putt-Putt.

So when he appeared at my door one day, he was no stranger to me, at least by reputation. Curtains seemed to sense something different about him too, and didn't bark or growl. He simply sat like a Buddha and eyed him, one ear raised. Putt-Putt appeared unaware of the potential threat, although by then everyone in town knew Curtains had killed an intruder at my place. (Many of them were hoping for a sequel, since not much happens to brighten up life in a small town. Curtains was entertaining. But nobody tried to pet the "nice doggie" anymore when I had him out on his leash.)

"What can I do for you?" I asked Putt-Putt.

He farted. Curtains' other ear cocked up and he looked to me for a signal of what I'd like him to do, if anything. If I'd said, "kill!" it would have saved me a lot of trouble. Curtains would have taken the screen out and grabbed the bastard right there. Somehow though, I sensed he'd have done it reluctantly. Putt-Putt had the demeanor of a holy fool, maybe was one. It was in his face. His liquid-brown eyes beseeched you to love him and also said, "I mean no harm." He carried himself a trifle stooped, an assumed posture to disarm any notion he could be aggressive. The overall picture was of someone wearing a "kick me" sign that he knew God had pasted between his shoulder blades. His appearance, I would learn, was somewhat deceptive.

In response to my question regarding his presence, he said, "Sheridan Millikan was the only friend I had in town."

The poor son of a bitch. Why did my steel-trap mind leap on that and recall that Dirty Harry said if anything happened to him he'd taken precautions to see I'd regret it? I eyed Putt-Putt sharply, trying to think of something to say, but nothing bright came to mind. Moreover, it was Saturday morning and over his shoulder I could see Dorothy headed our way to perform her part in a ritual. She was wearing the same white shorts and black T-shirt she'd worn the first morning she'd trotted over with sympathy and stuff. Had that first visit been only two weeks before? When her high heels clicked onto my front patio Putt-Putt turned and, if he was more human than appearances suggested, probably got a spasm about where he lived. In any case he forgot to fart.

"Good morning," she said, taking in the scene and masking any annoyance she may have felt.

"Hi," Putt-Putt said.

I judged from the up and down of his head, that his eyes weren't missing much, especially since there was no cover charge, or maybe uncover charge in this case.

He said, "Maybe I'd better come back some other time." But he didn't mean it. He knew what the story was with me and Hot Buns or he wouldn't have been there, but she didn't know that yet.

I wasn't about to stay in suspense in any case about what he had in mind. "Now is as good a time as any to see me if we have some business," I said. "This is Dorothy McCann, my banker. You may know her."

As a matter of fact that bastard probably already had her in bed and was down to the short strokes. That's about what I'd had in mind myself for about now, and wished this turd hadn't been dumped in our punch bowl just then, but I didn't intend to let whatever he had in mind hang over our heads.

It wouldn't amount to much with Oscar safely out of town. Even if the worst came out about Harry, I thought we were in the clear. Then it occurred to me that this shit had to have a copy of Harry's recording of my purring voice suggesting to Cuchillo Pete that he should off' Sheridan Millikan for playing with his little dove, Carmen, or at least trying to. I'd destroyed the original tape, but Harry had said the machine would transmit up to a mile. After what he heard on it, the bastard would naturally keep a copy, maybe make a couple extra. That explained what Putt-Putt was doing here. He was applying for a retirement plan. I looked him over more closely.

"You may as well come in," I said. He did and I watched the way he moved. There was something pathetic in his deliberately slouching walk that I couldn't quite catalog. He farted again ~ twice. Obviously no one had ever punched him in the snoot for doing it or he'd have soon dropped that bullshit, at least around them.

Inside, Dorothy cued me how to get her out of the line of fire by saying, "If you'll set me up somewhere out of the way with the tax accounts you wanted me to look over, I'll leave you two men to your business."

A neat impromptu lie, but in view of what he knew it netted a snide, skeptical grin from Putt-Putt. I got Dorothy the hell out of there and back into my lair.

Once out of Putt-Putt's hearing she said, "Phew! What a stench. He must be rotten inside. I read that Hitler did that all the time. What does he want?"

I told her my suspicions. By then I'd leveled with her about the whole Cuchillo Pete story. She'd suspected the truth anyhow from my ingenuous remark about his omens being bad.

"What are you going to do about this one?" she asked.

"I don't know yet."

"I guess it would be a trifle obvious if Curtains did in another one."

"Probably. But, on the other hand, I'll bet I could sell tickets to it and get a medal afterward."

She laughed. "I know a cut rate printer."

"I love people who agree with me ~ sometimes. Have you got any bright ideas about how to handle it if he wants what I think he does?"

"Pay him. He looks a lot cheaper than Dirty Harry."

Putt-Putt was thumbing through Newsweek and farting when I returned. We exchanged looks."

"There's something you should know," he said. "Before I burned out I was a private eye, in fact I worked on security for . . . ; he mentioned the name of a big-time city boss. What he meant was "Don't try any cheap horse shit on me, I've played in the big leagues." Somehow he was hard to doubt. For just a flash a different person had surfaced, then dove back under cover.

"So?"

"So, I've got a copy of that tape Millikan made of you and the Mexican knife wielder."

"What makes you think it would stand up in court?"

"It wouldn't. But it would put you out of a sweet racket, if I size up the situation right."

This bastard had a lot more balls than I thought. I might have had Curtains do a number on him for all he knew. I thought of it.

I said, "So what it boils down to is haggling over your price, right?"

"Right. And it's not going to be unreasonable."

"Say it."

He laughed, probably relieved, and for once forgot to fart. He said, "My wants are simple. five hundred a week."

John Pelham

I knew a bum like him could get by on a third of that and save money down where he lived among the hairy girls and bearded goons in Hippyville. But I wasn't disposed to haggle much. It was already becoming damned apparent that my racket could be a gold mine.

"I'll give you two for starters."

"Two fifty."

That could be peanuts. Besides I thought he might be useful eventually in some aspect of a slightly crooked business. Who could say?

"O.K." I said. "How do you want me to get it to you?"

"Mail it . . . in fifties."

So I had a silent partner. I was wondering how to be sure he stayed that way. There were aspects to being a trifle crooked that hadn't really occurred to me in advance.

I thought, *How the fuck did I get into this? T*he answer wasn't complicated. I was fundamentally lazy and had the eating habit, not to mention being a horny bastard.

Sex Ring in a Small Town

CHAPTER THIRTEEN

After I got rid of Putt-Putt it would be natural enough to assume I had just one thing on my mind. Actually there were two. Female and mail. The morning mail to be exact. It might hold something that would drastically change my approach to the female angle.

Before Oscar blew, I'd arranged to meet his mistress ~ Dorothy's competition. I'd expected dynamite. What a blast in the ass meeting her turned out to be.

If she hadn't wanted to come over for a weed-kicking session, I probably could have persuaded Oscar to throw a headlock on her and drag her over. No need. Heaven was still smiling on my philanthropies.

She came eagerly, having wanted to kick the habit for a long while ~ most people have, especially if they've ever seen a lung cut out of a cadaver with lung cancer. She had; in a movie way back in High School, and had wanted to quit smoking ever since.

That really hadn't been such a long time before. She was twenty-three, knock-kneed, blond, fat, yet wearing a mini-skirt. She wore her hair frizzed in fright-wig style, God only knew why, and her makeup was all the wrong shade. Moreover, it looked like it had been applied with a shovel. In short, a gross beast. The first thought that came to mind was: *What the fuck is he doing with this in view of what he had at home?*

Then, it came to me that assholes can't stand the favors of God. Jerks like Oscar are intimidated by women they can't dominate, women they suspect are smarter than they are, women they know they don't merit. So they go dredge up one like Louisa Lockhart; a floozie, at least in appearance. She even chewed gum incessantly.

But I got what I wanted from both of them before they blew town ~ a sexual bio of their past several years. Neither had been playing around with anything since before AIDS had reared its ugly head and killed recreational sex. And just to cover my bet, I'd suggested in a manner they could hardly refuse, that they both get a general VD and AIDS test, the results to be sent to Oscar in care of yours truly, to be forwarded (after inspection). I didn't mention the latter to them. Ah, Pelham, what a scheming shit you were learning to be. Why not?

You may conjecture that I had sensational plans for Hot Buns after mail call. Unfortunately, she had plans for both of us before mail call. So I had to let her in on what I'd hoped would be a surprise. Our "all clear" signal; sort of a fucking license, you might call it. She floated into my arms and looked up at me with blue eyes suddenly turned black. She didn't have to tell me that she'd been thinking about the real thing a whole heap. This woman wanted to be loved, very badly indeed, wanted it right, and right now. We shared a record book kiss and another after coming up for breath.

Next breather, she said, "Suppose the damn report wasn't in the mail today? Suppose it got lost and was never in the mail?"

"Screw the mail!" I said. "We've been good long enough."

She laughed. "You mean you'd go for a suicide pact? To quote John Pelham, 'what a way to go (?) or words to that effect.' Should I be flattered that you'd die for me?"

"Suit yourself. It would be more becoming if you'd modestly accept the fact that you're adorable, and let it go at that." (Did I say that?) That was the last thing either of us said until I managed, "Scrootch over just a little toward the middle of the bed so we don't fall on the floor if we get too eager."

I knew right then that I'd never before been fucked. She came to meet me with everything she had. It was tight and hot and she instinctively knew how to contract the bore to grip everything where it needed it. Besides she had some kind of equipment in there like I'd never felt in a woman before. What I'm trying to say, I guess, is she coaxed out of me that extra inch, thrusting like a riveting gun, and I came so fast and hard that I groaned and blacked out with my head ground into the pillow. Finally I got focused again.

"Christ!"

She got off a real great line. "Did you come?" Then she laughed and couldn't stop.

"Did you?"

"Three times and kept on. It just stopped."

"You're putting me on."

"Uh. Uh. Three times and the last one forever."

Holy crap ~ I couldn't have stuck with her for over thirty seconds! This was some kind of sex machine.

Sex Ring in a Small Town

We lay pasted together for a long while, nibbling one another and dozing off occasionally.

The enticing smell of bacon frying and coffee brewing woke me up. I rolled out and went to the scene of the action carrying my robe.

She looked up from her work, then down at me. "Did you have something in mind."

"I can't even spit."

"I thought the smell of food might wake you up. I was about to come and get you before I put the eggs in."

"Us men are all alike."

"Not exactly," she said, groping me.

Truly spoken, if I do say it myself, the wisdom of a babe who'd just been big-dicked for the first time.

I needed those eggs. For instance, I didn't feel a thing when she groped me ~ well, not much anyhow. But I needed about a dozen eggs and vitamin shots, and another siesta.

She read the symptoms. "I've got errands to run after we eat. You should be rested up by the time I get back."

"Maybe. If you're planning to be gone till about Tuesday."

"Brave up, as the Natives used to say. I feel sure you can *rise* to the occasion. Just in case an asteroid stumbles into earth's orbit, or something, I plan to do it again before sundown."

"I'll try to last longer next time."

"It might kill an innocent young girl like me."

"Somehow, I doubt it. Pass the toast, please."

CHAPTER FOURTEEN

Dorothy, of course, was aware of my affair with the Civic Uplift League, and was remarkably tolerant of the whole thing. Complacency? Hardly. Somehow, I didn't believe there was a woman alive who could be complacent about the possibilities, with her man and Pat Sunderland alone, or even alone with Stacey Greer. I should have suspected something, knowing Dorothy. But I thought I was being clever, playing up my whole encounter with the "uplifting ladies" as comic, and any future relations as a matter of strictly commercial contacts. Of course, depending on what business a lady is in, commercial contacts can have complications too, come to think of it.

I portrayed the rich girls as just a possible leg up to get my new business started and rolling, and nothing more. Dorothy was in favor of me quitting my job and making a lot more money doing what I'd like to do. More income always makes sense to a banker.

The matter of Pat Sunderland's invite to her ranch (to ride) or my trek over to Stacey's across the hills were just as well left unmentioned, I felt. Dorothy may even have looked with tolerance on at least the invitation to the Sunderland ranch. But I didn't yet know that, or suspect her of the ulterior motives that made that true. The snake in the Garden should have been named Avarice.

That's where things stood when I got an interesting phone call. "When are we going riding?" the easily recognizable, cultivated voice inquired. The call wasn't entirely a surprise. Pat Sunderland's manner, earlier, had suggested possible plans for John Pelham.

"I've never been invited."

"You just were. What are you doing? I can pick you up."

"Where are you?"

"In front of Safeway." A point to ponder. Had the notion of riding just popped into her mind? It's been my experience that when you see a good looking young woman at a public phone, she's up to something, unless her car just broke down.

"How soon are you apt to drop by?"

"Give me a half hour ~ I've got to deplete the shelves down here a little first. Can I pick up anything for you?"

I thought, *How about condoms?* And said, "Not that I can think of. What should I wear? I only ride Western, by the way."

"Suit up like John Wayne, then. I ride Western myself out here."

I had to get used to the idea that a billionairess, at least technically, does her own shopping sometimes. Was that just a matter of projecting the image of being democratic and down-to-earth? Or was it an excuse to come to town alone every once in awhile?

Did the lady have more than girl friends? Or, perhaps, have the feeling she wanted more?

I pondered that, getting into my jeans and C-boy boots. I then flopped down in my desk chair and fired up a cigar. A '3 by 5' file on the desk reminded me I was now in business in earnest. It was hard to believe how many people wanted to quit the cigarette habit. The Surgeon General and Attorneys General had scared the crap out of everyone. Even Phillip Morris. They're now one of the world's biggest food distributors.

In my file were over sixty cards. Before long I'd need a secretary and receptionist. Carmen's sister, Angelita, popped into my head. Boy would hiring her fry my ass with Dorothy.

I phoned a few people and rescheduled my day's appointments to later in the week. Appointments were going to be educational. I'd already learned that first appointments were almost always a husband and wife, or at least a man and woman. And when one came singly later, it most often would be the woman with some other problem. A couple of the singles virtuously wanted to improve their memory or study habits ~ all the others had sexual problems, regardless of how circumspectly they were stated. The sexual problems boiled down to one thing. Their men were sorry, indifferent lovers, mostly rabbits. Whose fault was that? It was an unavoidable question after awhile. Answering it and trying to help were what was going to get my ass in deep Kim Chee. The road to hell is indeed paved with good intentions. In my case it was going to be the road out of town. Altruism sucks!

After the draining I had the day before, you might think that watching Pat Sunderland unfold from her BMW wouldn't do much for me. Not. Maybe all those dry years overloaded my storage batteries. What a totally hot body, topped by an angel face.

Pat was taller than Dorothy and voluptuous where my friendly banker was delicately formed. This was one to sink into like one of the Beverly Wilshire's custom-made soft couches.

Somehow it didn't seem as though enjoying a siesta on her main frame was going to be in order just yet though. Pity! I could almost have handled it after watching her unwind from her car and undulate toward my door.

Her attitude to date didn't exactly suggest that sex was what she had in mind just yet, if ever. I hadn't met old Croesus, her husband, Oleg Sunderland, or my reservations would have been confirmed. Although he learned to fly with the Wright brothers, he still got around like Clayton Moore (remember him? A notorious Hollywood stud, so I've been told). Later he became the straight arrow, Lone Ranger.

I met Pat at the front door and said, "Unless you want to come in, I'm ready to hit the road."

She looked me up and down slowly, taking in my togs, which included a C-boy vest in true John Wayne style.

"I don't see a Bull Durham tag a-hangin' outa thet thar vest anywhar," she finally said.

"I'm a Perfecto man." I flashed my leather cigar case. Care for one?"

"Don't mind if I do."

And damned if she didn't take one and light it before she got back behind the BMW's wheel. I was careful to be on hand to shut the door for her, and try to see as much thigh as possible. She busted me at it and grinned, then blew a cloud of cigar smoke my direction.

"Get in, Cowboy," she said, whipping the engine over and gunning it. Mine, too.

I said, "I could take my car so you don't have to bring me back."

"We've got help, more help, and limousines all over the place. You can come back in style. Get in."

I could imagine the confrontation with Dorothy if I pulled in after sundown in a Sunderland limousine, and was trying to figure out how to explain to Pat that I should be back no later than 4:30. She must have read my mind.

"I've got a dinner date with some of the girls. When do you want to get back? Maybe I can bring you."

Did she know something about my local arrangement? Little did I know yet about the Sunderland information system. I'd phoned Dorothy and told her I had to dance attendance on Gen. Harboldson and couldn't be sure when I'd be home, just in case. Life can get complicated juggling affairs like mine. I hadn't seen anything yet. "How about 4:30?"

She gave me a knowing glance.

It suggested that I should be more confiding. I said, "I've got a dinner date with my neighbor across the road."

"She's married."

"Getting divorced."

By then we were going like Mario Andretti down the road. Thank God for safety belts.

"It's none of my business, but do you have an understanding there?"

"Most men would like to, I guess. But the dinner is strictly business." Ah, Pelham, you evasive, deceitful dog.

She didn't say anything for awhile, eyes on the road, managing the cigar very nicely too.

"Dorothy is a lovely woman; clever, too."

"What the hell does that mean?" I had to ask.

Pat replied, "She's a born manager."

Was she hinting that I was in line to be managed? What woman isn't a manager where men are concerned? Hot Buns hadn't exactly scored high marks managing Oscar, though. Or had she? Hell, I had to get rid of him for her. Then a little voice asked, *Why did you get rid of him for her?*

Pat was smiling over something. I was afraid to ask what. Clairvoyant? At least damned shrewd. I had a feeling she was reading my mind again . . . down to the commas.

"I wouldn't much care to be managed," I said, lamely.

"Neither did Oscar."

Did my jaw drop? I hoped not. "Ah, small towns," I said, and had a faint glimmering of another idea that bothered me. *Big money. Super-sized money. It could just about buy anything but poverty. Certainly it could buy information.* Was I in another set of female sights? I thought, *What the hell? It beats swimming with Curtains. I guess I'll go along for the ride.* And what a ride. She passed our notoriously chicken-shit highway patrolman going 100, and waved at him. He didn't even speed up. The sonofabitch was stupid, but not that stupid. He knew one phone call would have him patrolling somewhere on an Indian reservation, where it's a long way to the nearest toilet and restaurant. I don't know if patrolmen really have a ticket quota, but I never yet saw a single one miss his quota of three meals a day on duty, and four coffee breaks, minimum.

The private drive into the Sunderland digs was asphalt the whole way ~ all twenty-three miles. It ran in a depression that looked barren from a distance, then dropped into a deep, hidden east-west canyon through their private mountain range, lushly overgrown with all sorts of shrubs and trees. At the top of it was a pass from which both sunrise and sunset were plainly visible. On the divide at the top the Sunderland buildings sprawled. The road bordered a stream as we got into the canyon, and was fringed with cottonwoods and sycamores, occasional mountain ash, and walnut trees. Blue-green Chamiso shrubs grew heavily among the gramma and love grass. Bunches of cows and calves were grazing everywhere. I wondered how many of them wore the big OS brand.

Pat anticipated my unspoken question and said, "We only run about 8,000 head. It's a hobby ranch, really. Just someplace to live."

I studied her to see if she was being droll. Her face didn't reveal it if she was. Later it would become apparent that the super rich take the damnedest things for granted. At least she slowed the BMW down enough so we weren't apt to cream some dumb, wide-eyed calf if it panicked into the road.

A long, rambling ranch house came into view across a hay meadow. Not too pretentious, actually. That was a relief. I dreaded the thought of ol' country-boy me trying to be casual rattling around in the Hearst Castle of the desert.

"That's where our Mexican gardener lives," she said as we passed that rambler.

I thought, *Holy crap! I wonder what the patron's shack looks like.* It came into view all at once as we rounded a bend. Have you ever seen a picture of the Alhambra? I couldn't resist saying, "Do you ever get cramped for space?" I was half-afraid I'd goofed and she'd tell me that was the chauffeur's house.

"Actually it's cozy inside."

We pulled up front into a long, half-circle driveway and she parked under a fifty-foot long portico and hopped out. I was still inside the BMW, gawking at a set of twenty-foot-high, carved front doors. She had to come around and wake me up. She didn't seem impatient though, or grin. Instead she said, "I still look at those doors occasionally just like you were. They were made in Mexico in the sixteenth century. It's not a lost art though. Some people can still make them like that down there."

I expected a liveried doorman to rush out to greet us, but none did. I swung out, stretched and looked around. The whole front of the house, all three hundred feet of it, was pale pink-ocher brick, pierced by high, arched windows of a size to match the door. I strangled the plebeian urge to make some real bright remark like, *Some shack!* The thing that impressed me most was the simple landscaping, a row of Italian cypresses paralleled the house, with mostly natural growth under them except for long, narrow flower beds, now bright with fall asters, mums, nasturtiums and a lot of little colorful things that I couldn't identify. Good sense had left the other side of the drive natural. There were sycamores, oaks, juniper, cottonwood and other native trees, with undergrowth running up the far slope into a forest of ocotillo; one of the densest fields of it I'd ever seen. It was interspersed with century plants, huge clumps of prickly pear and occasional junipers.

"Do you like it?" she asked, and looked genuinely expectant like a child showing off her home to a new friend.

"Of course. It's beautiful. Smells good too."

The carpet of fallen leaves lent a decayed fragrance peculiar to fall everywhere. It was so quiet I could hear the creek running over rocks at least a hundred feet away toward the hills.

"I was born here," she said.

That was a shocker. From what little I knew, I expected that old Sunderland had probably bought her at auction from Southeby's, by way of an incubator in one of the Seven Sisters. She looked and sounded like Vassar or Smith, perhaps even Wellesley or Bennington.

She said, "Daddy was Ole's partner for years."

I thought, *Ole? What a hell of a distinguished name for a billionaire.* We were interrupted by a man coming out of the house. He was wearing boots and jeans and certainly didn't look like Jeeves, or even Robert Duvall playing rancher. This flunky, in any event, was supposed to say, "May I take something in for madame?" Instead he said, "Hi, Skeezix."

She kissed his cheek, then turned and watched my expression carefully while saying, "This is my husband, Ole. John Pelham."

He shook hands firmly and looked me straight in the eyes.

"I'm glad you came out," he said. "Most people pee down their leg at the idea of hobnobbing with a fuckin' billionaire."

I laughed. Had to. Actually there wasn't much else to do. I can tell you from a little more experience that this was a man with no bullshit about him. He had it and saw no use in trying to hide what everyone knew. He was badly in need of real friends, I also discovered. I don't think that's too unusual with the very rich. Some don't want them. He did, and didn't have a single one; hadn't had one since maybe the Korean War, except for Skeezix's father, who'd been dead for twenty years.

"I hear you fly," he said, before I could think of anything to say.

"Not much anymore,"

"Me neither. Come on in."

He had to be ninety if he was a day. He looked like a well-preserved seventy and moved like an athletic sixty. The nasty thought traveled through my mind, and it was a disappointment, that this man undoubtedly was fucking Skeezix pretty often and probably doing one hell of a good job of it, even at his age. She was obviously very fond of him. Satisfied women are hard to interest in variety.

As soon as we went in, I knew what Pat meant about "Cozy inside." The entrance hall only ran back about a hundred feet and the ceiling wasn't over fifty or sixty feet high. On both sides of the hall were rustic balconies. The ceiling was sky-lighted. It was all decidedly modest. Compared to Versailles.

"What's on the agenda, Skeezix?" Ole asked.

"I thought you could take John down and show him the horses, then we can have a little lunch and go riding. I'm going to get the groceries in, then slip into some riding clothes and join you down at the stables."

I watched one of the world's classic derriere's undulate away down a hallway that departed under the right hand balcony, not giving a good damn whether Ole noticed me ogling or not. He didn't seem too.

I sighed inwardly; thinking that was probably all I'd ever see of that nice ass ~ the externals well draped. What a shot in the groin. If you live to be a million you may never guess what sort of golf cart carried us down to the stables a quarter of a mile away. A robin's egg blue, perfectly restored, right-hand-drive, 1927 Rolls Royce. Ole tooled it with the deft hand of an airplane driver.

Gnomes were busy all over down there, with little, growling garden tractors, scooping horse dooey with miniature front end loaders and carting it off somewhere out of sight. I thought maybe a thrifty billionaire had a contract to supply it to television script and ad writers.

I know horses, having owned a thoroughbred hunter at about age five and survived somehow. There wasn't a clinker in their whole bunch as far as I could see. The horses knew the Rolls Royce spelled action. Those penned came as close as they could get in order to shiny-eye us in anticipation. A herd of at least fifty thundered up from the end of an irrigated pasture and milled around, heads over the immaculate white plank fence. The dominant ones naturally ran off those lower down the pecking order, until they sorted themselves out. Ole led the way down there and went through a camel's-eye gate. They crowded around him like puppies, very careful, however, not to jostle or step on him. He talked to them like kids and tried to pat the outcasts too, but the others always ran them further away.

He looked toward me. "Pets," he said. "Spoiled. Every damn one of them."

A burro sauntered up belatedly, nipping horses out of his way, and presented himself for an ear scratching, also inspecting pockets for hidden goodies. "Baalim," Ole said. "I've had him since before Skeezix was born."

I prudently stayed on my side of the fence. I like to know my horses, and have them know me, before I get too chummy. About the time you take them for puppy dogs they'll accidentally kill you, and a rare one may do it on purpose. I had a notion the Sunderlands wouldn't have that kind.

"Take your pick," Ole said, "or would you like me to pick one for you?"

"You know 'em better'n I do."

"You done much riding? Skeezix said you're at least at the don't-fall-off."

"I used to ride a lot. I can make out with anything but an outlaw, but actually I prefer one it takes piano movers to get going."

"I can probably find you just what you want. Old Bullet will do just fine. We trot him out for old ladies and kids under two. Are you sure you want one that tame?"

"Not quite, but you get the idea."

He led the way back over to the corrals, leaving the herd at the fence, all looking disappointed. Horses liked Ole. So did I. He went into a paddock where a sleek chestnut came to meet him and dropped its chin on his shoulder. "C'mon in and meet Toper. He likes beer."

I was glad to see that Toper wasn't the monster that apple-cheeked heroines always ride in Western Romances; a 17 hand stallion, shiny, black, fiery, snorty, barely manageable. Toper was shiny enough, but ran more to love-ins than steeplechases, I'd guess. He wasn't over 16 hands. I liked his legs, especially the long pasterns that usually spell an easy trot, and the low set of his long, slender neck, coming out of high withers. The big, melting, honest eyes really did it though. You can tell a lot from horses eyes, if you know how to read them. Toper decided he liked me, or else he just liked people. We had a long talk.

Skeezix called down and said she was bringing lunch in a hamper, and showed up shortly, wearing a pair of stretch jeans and a sweater, a sure-fire bet to raise a hard-on on a saint. Mexican men, and most of their stable help, would never miss a view like that to say nothing of Americans, Kurds and Ethiopians, to mention a few others. She completely stopped work till she sat down at the folding table she'd brought to lay out lunch.

"Did you bring Toper a beer?" I asked.

"It happens I have a six pack of Corona, if you'd care to do the honors. He drinks from the bottle."

And sure enough, he did. That undoubtedly set me up as aces in his estimation. After lunch we saddled our own horses. It's a good way to sort out the phonies who've done their equestrian trick at some LA or New York City riding club where stooges do all the work. I suspect both Ole and Skeezix had their eye on me. I passed the final course when I asked, first of all, for a hoof pick and cleaned Toper's feet thoroughly. He had nice, trim black hoofs, the kind that are hard and healthy, cupped high, and freshly shod. At least I wasn't apt to go ice skating with him.

I'd wondered if Ole actually planned to ride, or even could get on a horse, till I saw him leap on one like a jumping jack coming out of its box. He was riding a horse Custer would have loved, one that was either going to run or try to get rid of any rider so tame he didn't want to. They took a half-mile circuit at a dead run, taking the edge off him and came back in a cloud of clods. I recalled that someone had seen Custer thundering toward the battle of Gettysburg a few days after they made him a general, with his staff strung out a mile behind trying to keep up, and their comment that he rode like a "circus rider gone mad." Ole's goddam horse obviously took arms like a weight lifter's to haul him in during the first ten miles or so.

Skeezix and I went at a walk, trot, lope. Ole was seldom in sight, moving in and out at a run. If he knew that horses sometimes went ass over hula-hoop, he didn't show it.

"How old is he?" I asked her.

"Well, he was a fighter ace in World War One. The youngest one, but nonetheless he has to be ninety at least."

"Does he do everything like that?"

"None of your derned business." But she laughed.

I hadn't even thought of that. But if she thought I was being clever, that was O.K. with me.

We had a great day and she deposited me in my driveway at 4:30 sharp, after another Daytona 500 cruise during which we passed our chicken-shit highway patrolman going the other way. She waved again. She was one "fo' dollah" pistol, for sure. So was Ole.

The last thing he said to me was, "Come out any damn time. I mean that. Next time I want to take you down to my airstrip. Got some dandy little planes." He did too. Seventeen of them.

Sex Ring in a Small Town

CHAPTER FIFTEEN

After Skeezix dropped me off, I collected my mail from the box, then went in and staved off an affectionate attempt at homicide by Curtains, long enough to get him out in the back yard. He rushed through a piss and charged again. Suffering his affection was like training to be a gladiator. Curtains loved to romp and thought he was still a loveable little armful of wiggling puppy. To escape total maiming, I would sooner or later flop on my face and play dead. He always tried to root me up with a big wet snoot, loving every minute of it, especially when I growled at him.

After surviving that, I escaped to the patio and mixed a scotch and soda, got a cigar going and scanned the mail.

Sex Ring in a Small Town

The return address on one letter demanded attention first: Dulaney Studios in LA. In the Army, Captain Diamond Dan Dulaney managed to cause me more trouble than anyone I'd ever met. His formula was simple ~ he tried to be my best friend twenty-four hours a day. In his case it was a sure-fire recipe for disaster most of the time. On the other hand it was Diamond Dan who finally plucked my ass out of the jungle, under a heavy fire, one jump ahead of Charlie, after I got shot down.

Diamond Dan and Dulaney Studios take a little explaining. When I first met him he'd just been recalled to active duty as a chopper pilot, more or less due to patriotic inspiration: inspiration anyhow. As he explained the circumstances: "I got my fuckin' discharge and like everyone else I said, *Thank God, they'll never get me back in the mother-fuckin' Army!* Obviously I was dead wrong. Anyhow, back then I found a bunch of grifters going around California selling home repairs to dumb old folks at about three times what they cost. We formed squads of threes. As junior grifter in my squad, I was first contact man, going door to door, pointing out obvious defects that could be easily repaired, and discovering if the people owned or rented. We were only interested in owners with good credit ratings. A follow-up man came by in a few days and explained that all the stuff could be done for a few bucks down and a small monthly payment, with us arranging all the financing and work. He foretold the coming of Mr. Wonderful, head grifter, who would be by in a few more days and show them how to get something for almost nothing. In the rackets, Mr. Wonderful is called the "closer." He carried the contracts, some before and after photos of our earlier miracles, and had a gift for the shit a mile long. We weren't exactly stealing either ~ only gouging. We'd get a good contractor to actually do the work at a fair price, discount the note to the local bank with no trouble since we only operated with owners with good credit, and pocket more than we paid the contractor. Mr. Wonderful got the lion's share. I told myself, *shit, I can do that!* I made up my own team and went through Northern California and Oregon and came back driving a Mark VI free and clear, with a hundred grand in my pocket, all in six months, and looked around for something else to do. That's when Dick Stone entered the picture, the greedy son of a bitch.

To make a long story short, Dan explained how Dulaney and Stone Productions started a con even better than home repair. They rented studio offices, sound stages and all the appurtenances of TV production and sucked in people who'd always wanted to be in movies. They included some remarkable extremes. They asked for a $100.00 contribution from the sucker, actually taking only fifty, since, as Dan said, "If it went a cent over fifty clams and a court decided we were not legit, it was a felony."

He told some other interesting details, such as, "Did you ever hear of the Hollywood stretch couch? It was used for auditioning. Iowa schoolteachers on summer vacation were the most cooperative. They'd do anything. You should have seen some of the pictures they'd show you to prove they'd do anything, even before you auditioned them. Then, that bastard Stone got greedy and conned a char woman from UCLA. Later we conned a big wig from there and did he ever burn when he found out he'd been taken for fifty bucks for a few lousy feet of footage with him in it. He didn't want to look like the asshole he was, but when he happened to hear the char woman's story he saw his chance and sicced the bunco cops and fearless, investigative press on us. I walked into the studio coffee shop one morning and hadn't even put my hat in the rack when the wisdom of 'big tipping' became crystal clear to me. A waitress said, 'Blow Dan! The joint's full of cops and reporters looking for you guys!' I blew, got into my Mark VI and stopped only for gas before I whipped over the Nevada line. Whoever heard of extradition for a debatable con? Then I arranged a patriotic recall to my duty as a chopper pilot in the service of my country, and here I am."

By the time I got his latest letter, he'd been a civilian again for at least ten years. He was into the movie thing big. Dulaney Studios was the biggest mail order porno-flick outfit in the country under Adair Productions labels. The bastard was rolling in money, had his own Grumman Gulfstream, and for the past two years had insisted on taking me, and my late unlamented, to Copenhagen with him at Christmas. Fortunately, I seldom saw the *late* after we checked into our hotel, or I'd have had a terrible time.

"Copenhagen?" you may say. "What ever happened to Paree?" Yeah, Copenhagen! You can have Paris, and Rome too. If you want to know what the hell the big pull is in Copenhagen, go find out. As a clue, the Danes, unlike Americans, are not hypocrites about sex. Jimmy Swaggart couldn't make page three in Denmark. Diamond Dan's letter, like all of them, was brief. It read: "My new fuckin' unlisted number is . . . What the hell is yours? They wouldn't give it to me, even though I swore I was your brother and our mother was dying. Give me a ring. Christmas is on again if you're game."

I decided to call him right then. He answered personally on the first ring.

"Dulaney."

"What's an important executive doing answering his own phone?"

"I delegated everything but delegation." He knew whose voice it was. Everyone recognizes my voice. Makes it tough to do obscene phone calls.

"Are you busy?"

"Not too. What the hell's new?"

"Did I tell you I'm a widower?"

"No. What happened?"

I told him. He got off the subject. He'd probably screwed her a time or two, but Diamond Dan used women for one thing ~ to get it off and forget it.

No sentiment there. Maybe not so strangely, it made him irresistible to most women. They sensed him as the greatest challenge of their life. Someone to nurse, to introduce to the tender trap and make whole. He never bit. In every such case that I'd observed, his final comment always was, "The dumb fuck!" Followed by a loud guffaw. However, there wasn't a mean bone in his bod. He asked, "What're you doing this week end?"

I should have known what was coming and said I'd be busy as hell. Instead, I said, as I usually did, "Nothing special." He often dropped in for a day or two and kept out of contact with the business as much as possible. I could have told him I expected to be getting dehydrated with a sensational blond, but I planned to keep Hot Buns out of his sights, in fact out of his ken, knowing him. But it was too late to make that easy to do.

He said, "Good. I'll fly in on Friday night. Meet me sevenish."

"Is the Mafia looking for you?"

"Fuck no. The bastards pay me protection. I just need a rest so don't lay on the dancing girls."

"I don't know any." A monumental lie. I could probably have got the Civic Uplift crowd, Dorothy, and every prospective whore in town if I'd advertised his arrival and what he did.

I didn't intend to have my private stock infected just after I got a pure food ticket. Anyone who stuck it in after an optimist like Diamond Dan, was asking for real trouble. If he didn't have AIDS, it ranked among the major miracles, along with the Immaculate Conception and the fact that Ronny Reagan got a second term, or even a first.

It was a sure bet Diamond Dan hadn't reformed. He figured a week when he didn't get a piece of strange was a total loss. Regarding the suggestion that he reform, he once said, "Me? I'd rather die." The odds on that were rising right smart, in my opinion.

Sex Ring in a Small Town

Normally Diamond Dan's visits were something to look forward to. I had mixed feelings about this one. It was food for a lot of thought and I was deep into some of it when Dorothy let herself in and came out to the patio to join me.

Curtains went to meet her, and since I didn't hear a commotion, I knew who it had to be. I heard her talking and skirmishing with him all the way back. She said, "Get down you big idiot, you're mussing my skirt. Stop. No. Get away. All right, one kiss. Now, behave." And other words to that effect. He shot through the door grinning and so did she.

I met her with a kiss. "I was planning to muss your skirt too, if you didn't get it off quick enough."

"How about a drink first?"

"It's a civilized joint. That sounds reasonable. We can even postpone protocol from your lusty host till after dinner, if you feel like eating."

"I feel fine now. I'll whomp up some rations after a sun downer."

"The sun's already down."

"Don't quibble."

"O.K." I said. "You mix and tune mine up and I'll build a fire. It's getting chilly enough."

"Good thinking, *mi corazon*."

So I started my first fire of the fall. My fireplace was flanked by two picture windows and had a long, soft couch facing them. There was still an afterglow in the sky when I got the fire going, highlighting the partially bare pomegranate branches outside, a perfect frame for a cozy fire.

We sat on the couch, shoulders touching, with the lights out, and let good Scotch warm us inside. I can't recall being any happier up till that night. It's probably the way Adam felt just before he had to go out to apply for his first job.

I decided to come clean on my earlier activities that day, in case I was found out, and got a happier reply than expected.

"Do you realize what you've done?" she asked.

"Not really."

"I don't know a soul in town that's had an invitation out there. Few people have ever seen Ole Sunderland socially. He drops in to see me when he has to, at the bank, but that's about it for visits to town. He's even taken me to lunch a time or two. What did you think of him?"

"I think he's a great old guy."

"That's what I think. How did you get along with him?"

"Fabulous. I got an invite out to see his airplanes."

"For God's sake, go."

"Do I sense a scheming banker's mind somewhere here?"

"Damn right! If you like money, a darn good motto is, 'court billionaires.' How can you go wrong?"

"Easy."

"How?"

"By having them suspect you're trying to use them."

"They're used to it. I've been trying to steer him your way."

Probably true, yet I had no intention of using Ole for anything.

She went on. "He's probably got a few aches and pains you could banish with hypnotism."

A light went on. I sketched in the rest of the scenario, "And then we tap into his secrets of success, right?"

I felt her tense slightly, since the tone of my voice didn't suggest wholehearted support of that tactic." Why not?" she asked, sounding defensive.

"Because it's not right."

"How about having a half-nuts knife-wielder go after old Sheridan Millikan?"

"Dirty Harry asked for it."

"You need moral justification? How about this: money corrupts, so you're being a philanthropist by trying to reduce Ole's vulnerability."

"How about increasing my vulnerability in the bargain?" I had to laugh. "You bankers sure like dough."

"That's not it," she said, sharply. "I just never want to be poor again. Did you ever live in a little, crummy mountain cabin that the winter wind whistled through at night, nursing flu under a blanket about as thin as a threadbare tablecloth? Did you ever stumble through snow barefoot to go to school? I did. And I'm never coming close to that shape again . . . no matter what!" She almost shrieked the last few words.

I was shocked and couldn't think of a thing to say. Then I realized that her voice had cracked on the final words and she was sobbing. I set our glasses on the coffee table and took her into my arms. A flood of tears was on her face when I gave her a gentle, salty kiss.

"I'm sorry," I said, and meant it.

She managed to shudder out, "It's just that . . . every once in awhile I remember it just like I'm back there, coming home from school in the dark ~ to nothing. Absolutely nothing! Not even anything to eat pretty often. My parents hated each other, hated us, hated the world they lived in. Can you blame them?"

"Who could?" I said, realizing exactly where she was coming from. But I still couldn't see myself telling a hypnotized Ole, "You'll remember absolutely nothing when I wake you up," after figuratively rifling his pockets by going through his stock positions with him about once a week.

There had to be a better way to make Dorothy feel safe at last, and I intended to find it, even if it meant going back to work for old Norbert. Five grand a month isn't too bad coupled with a colonel's "overly generous" retirement pay, earned in exchange for his sense of humor.

A little later she whispered, "Forget what I said. I'm just scared out of my wits sometimes, even yet. Afraid they'll take it all away again."

Of course, I couldn't forget it. I could sense her terror as a very real thing, hearing her explain it. What a hell of a way to grow up.

She stayed the night with me, curled up in my arms with my hard-on throbbing against her every time I woke up. She was dead beat, so I wasn't about to wake her. I thought about getting up and using the good old Jergens, but decided to store up for later instead. Was I reforming? Giving up the habits of a lifetime? Actually, I was dog-tired too.

Sex Ring in a Small Town

John Pelham

CHAPTER SIXTEEN

In the morning Dorothy told me, "I forgot to tell you in the midst of all my nonsense last night ~ I've got to go to the big city for a seminar. I hate like hell to leave you, oh love, but it's important if I want to get ahead.

I thought, *Hot damn! Maybe that'll get her out of town while Diamond Dan is around.*

"I'll be back for the week end," she said, leering at me.

So much for eluding Diamond Dan. Well, I'd have a couple of days alone. I'd almost got used to it before she came on the scene. But now the prospect didn't please me. We had a touching little goodbye ceremony that threatened to put us both in intensive care.

Happily she didn't have to leave till late, so we lolled around and dozed awhile.

I wondered what I'd kill time with alone, racking my brain for what I did before. Of course I could always invite Carmen and her sister over. Not. Either one could have been suicide, so far as I yet knew. I had them safely in the bank with Brother John. I haven't introduced Brother John to you yet, but never mind, he's a sort of super-chaperon; I'll explain later. Don't ask me what I was saving them for. I've tried to hide the obvious from myself. But it looked like I was in for a lot of TV or reading. Books had the edge. They usually do unless something is on PBS, usually a program produced in England where either committees must be smarter, or else genius is allowed free rein.

Come the dark of night, Pelham with a book, a scotch, a cigar, Curtains faithfully by my side: about 9 P.M. he alerted me that he wanted to investigate something out front. I got out the old GI .45 just in case and let him through the door, with the house dark behind me. I peeked out cautiously. He was on the porch but not growling or barking. I turned on the porch light. He was actually wagging his tail. We had a visitor the other side of the screen. Beano, who'd bit the bishop.

"Hello, Beano-who-bit-the-bishop," I greeted her, opening the door.

She popped in like she lived there. Inside it took her about ten seconds to make it to the refrigerator. She plopped down in front of it, looking hopeful. What can you do? I fixed her up with scraps otherwise destined for Curtains. He didn't even complain, watching her 'scarf' them down. The big jerk probably had designs on her wiggly little bod. Recalling her owner's trim little 'thang' undulating down my hall a few days previously in tight shorts, I thought, *Well, it just runs in the family, I guess.* Stacey Greer's number wasn't in the phone book; unlisted, no doubt.

Who could blame a girl who lived mostly alone for that? While I fiddled with the phone business, Beano slowly put away her food, a delicate eater, or else Curtains made her nervous sniffing her jewel. Every time he did she sat down and he looked at me with an "oh shit" look.

I had three options with Beano: leave her in all night, keep her in my yard, or put her on a leash and walk her home. The latter somehow appealed to me, since a crystal clear recollection of something or other up at Beano's house recurred to me, not that I was planning to be unfaithful to my new love ~ maybe just test my faithfulness. You guys will know how it is. Besides there was always the nasty prospect of AIDS out there all over to reinforce virtue. I didn't yet know that was small risk in Stacey's case, like none; nor why that was so.

My .45 was in the pocket of my canvas windbreaker as I set out for Beano's house. I left Curtains inside, disapprovingly guarding against "bug" planters and the like. He barked just once after I closed the front door. It was his "boss-you're-a-real-bastard-sometimes" bark. I was probably scheduled for the "shoulder" when I got home. That's when your good old dog or kitty faces three quarters away from you at all times and won't look at you. It can last for hours, days or even weeks, depending on the gravity of your offense.

It took awhile for my eyes to adjust so starlight showed up the road. The night was one of those nice, crisp, high-desert fall beauties, crystal clear, that seemed warmer than it was since no wind was blowing. Our breath condensed into clouds.

A car was parked in Stacey's drive, but the house was dark. Closer, I recognized the car as a familiar BMW. I thought, *The ladies are gone in Stacey's car, uplifting valiantly somewhere*. I rang the bell anyhow, in case there was a basement game room or something that showed no light outside.

Sex Ring in a Small Town

You never know what kind of digs the rich may build for security, or just because they're different, eccentric ~ even screwy.

No response. Well, at least I knew how to put Beano into her own run. The path ran along the big garage. She really didn't want to go in, whining a little. I told her, "Look, fathead, you're house is warmer than my yard would be, and I don't know if you're housebroken or I'd have let you stay with us."

You may conjecture that I talk to dogs. Its' not hard to get the habit if you've had a wife to whom you have nothing to say. I stuck a finger through the chain link fence to 'skritch' Beano goodbye, and got a grateful lick. No hard feelings. Basically, dogs beat hell out of people when it comes to dispositions.

Across the extensive back yard I noticed a flickering light, apparently a TV reflecting on a drawn Venetian blind in a window along the long rear "L" of the house. I assumed a gardener or maid might live there and figured it might be a good idea to tell them I'd brought Beano home.

I'm not a natural-born window peeper anymore than anyone else, meaning, I'm a confirmed voyeur; so I sneaked a look through the only-partially-drawn blinds to see, if possible, who I would be telling about Beano. Close up, it was easy to see into the room. Who the hell is careful about drawing blinds with fifty miles of empty desert outside? In this case someone should have been. There was a skin flick playing on one of those giant TV screens. I, somehow, couldn't restrain myself from watching the action for awhile. It wasn't one of those phony Playboy things. You know the kind I mean, with a lot of thrusting of invisible parts, with nary the sight of a single erection in a month of movies. This was the real McCoy, but it made no difference with respect to erections, since this one was about Lesbians.

The flick had two good-looking, big-boobed babes having at each other.

When I got my first look they were fondling one another's tits with some kind of oil on their hands and it didn't look as though their enraptured faces wore the phony contortions of professionals. This was someone's honest, homemade movie, and well done for its kind. The proof that the two actresses were actually aroused was their hugely erect nipples. Take a look-see over the Playboy imitations, by contrast . . . pure hoak. Here were two people who knew all about female arousal for the obvious reason that they were females. Asshole rabbit husbands should be required to watch this sort of thing, upon a signed complaint by their wives, somewhat like a drunk drivers' clinic.

I could feel my wand rising to the occasion. I'd always had a yen to join a couple of lesbians in an act like that one, whether they were queer or not, especially two that beautiful. I almost forgot to look and see who was watching this show. It probably won't take a gigantic, intuitive mind to figure that out. Pat Sunderland and Stacey Greer were on a huge bed, piled high with pillows on which they were semi-reclining, their eyes glued to the action. Guess what they were wearing. Not much. As far as I could tell, nothing but wedding rings. My palpitating desire of the day before to see Pat's delectable ass disrobed was about to be granted by a beneficent God. I decided to send a substantial check to some worthy charity. They had prepared themselves to ape the action on the screen. I watched them get up on their knees and pour some oil into their hands, then start gently massaging each other's breasts. They used their full palms to massage, fondling gently, but with their eyes glued on the TV show. And there, in all of its lovely reality, was Pat's abundant ass, facing directly toward me. But she wasn't what awed me. I couldn't keep my eyes off her smaller, dark-haired partner. My, what clothes can conceal, even shorts. Naked, Stacey was a perfect Greek statue, in warm flesh tones as the originals had been painted.

Her hirsute triangle, a woman's most alluring, jealously guarded treasure was artistically perfect, abundant, symmetrical, enticing. Looking at her gave me a perfectly awesome, throbbing hard-on. I had an almost overpowering urge to whip the bad boy out and run off a charge on the spot. More overpowering was my curiosity to discover where the tableau inside was leading. Plenty of time to go home, put on some of my own flicks from the Diamond Dan private collection and get out the good, old Jergens, if need be.

Obviously the two inside intended to mimic the screen, probably had done this before. Pat put the video on "pause" then pushed Stacey down on the bed as the two on the screen had done by then. She poured a generous portion of oil on Stacey's body and smoothed it around evenly. Then she coated herself, raptly fondling her own breasts as Stacey watched. Stacey started involuntarily thrusting her pelvis toward an invisible lover, devoured by uncontrollable passion. This was obviously what turned her on best. She continued to thrust her hips, then ran her hands slowly between her legs and back up her tummy.

Then Pat suddenly attacked her, throwing herself on top of her and kissing her savagely, all the time caressing her oiled body. They were entwined, rubbing together precisely right to massage one another in their most sensitive spots.

I thought, *What's queer about that? Why not get it off however you can if it floats your boat?* I was a trifle shocked, since I'd assumed that Ole was probably still able to do it the way a young woman liked it. Obviously not. As for Stacey, it was common knowledge her husband came and went, no pun intended. I was going to learn more about that before long. In any case here were two women doing what lots of women were learning to do, rather than secretly hide gin bottles in their undies and nip at them to get through the day, or hang themselves in carriage houses, which practically used to be a national pastime.

An equivalent orgy with another man wouldn't be my cup of tea, but there are men and men. With some it's genetic, I suppose. But a lot of women go Lezbo due to the "quarterback syndrome" as much as anything. And what's that? Fast and impulsive may be fine in football, but it doesn't get it done in bed. Dumb "rabbit" men, in my opinion, create some lesbians. What is a rabbit? someone may ask. The saying about their m.o. is: "wham, bam, thank you ma'am."

Rabbits suck! Ask any woman who was stuck with one, married or not, and later found out the difference. They're fingering each other across the land; read Dear Abbey if you don't believe it.

I still had a hell of a rail on by the way, and was thinking of fisting off on the spot. Inside they were getting to the short, spasmodic humping and got off a simultaneous orgasm, I'd guess. Afterward they kissed gently for awhile. Pity more men don't learn to be as tender, or tender at all. Pity that women like these seldom learn there are men who can be.

It didn't come to me as a surprise that women have a hell of a lot more sexual staying power than men. These two were not ready to go to the showers yet. They turned the action back on and we all watched the two on film do just what they'd been doing on the bed. Pat and Stacey must have learned that this turned them back on. I wondered how often they did this sort of thing. Mandrake the Magician could have learned, but my strange set of ethics ruled it out.

A sub-title announced the name of the next game. The film had probably been done in Europe, because there was sound, but it was barely audible to me. The subtitle was: "I'll bet I can keep from coming longer than you." The two on the screen lay, propped up on pillows, legs spread and oiled their hands, then started massaging themselves, first with deep pressure, then with deft fingers to their clitoris. This wasn't acting either. Anyone could tell from their rapt expressions that they were transported with passion.

This segment, too, would have been splendid sex education, especially to show where the clitoris can be found and what it can do. A movie like that might cause a sexual revolution all by itself.

Stacey and Pat were starting the same thing on the bed. It wasn't long before they started thrusting their hips and breathing rapidly. These four were truly well sexed women.

The subtitle now read: "I'll get you so hot you can't stand it." The larger actress rolled over and started to gently suck and tongue the other's breasts. Pat did the same to Stacey ~ with the same outcome. Both of the women so ministered to started to thrust wildly, one on the bed, one on the screen, raising their buttocks and arching their backs.

The subtitle now read: "Oh sweet heavenly Christ, I'm coming!" and the big bitch switched to kissing the other hard on her lips. Stacey got the same treatment and shortly, collapsed, legs crossed, gasping for breath.

After that Pat and her screen counterpart acted out the subtitle: "I'm not waiting for anything!" They obviously needed their turn badly by then.

What a hell of a time I was having, any way you look at it. Pat had a body that defies description. And something I particularly like in women, abundant pubic hair, in her case honey-blond. Her busy finger was buried in it, working expertly, as she lay back, lips parted, breathing heavily. Stacey was watching, spellbound, aroused again, caressing her breasts with one hand and working her clitoris again with the other. Pat couldn't have lasted a minute before she started thrusting spasmodically, then, like Stacey had, back arched, came like an avalanche. I could hear her ecstatic moan even outside. Stacey obviously got it off again with her, aroused by watching Pat's passion.

Was that going to be the end of the show? Hardly. It was time for a new flick. I was surprised to see something as tame as Butch Cassidy and the Sundance Kid. They started at the part where Sundance pretends to be a rapist and attacks his girlfriend.

Pat disappeared somewhere about then. Stacey intently watched the screen antics and held a final frame on pause. She looked around as though she wondered where Pat had gone, just as I did. She knew. I didn't. A figure dressed like Sundance's came through the door by which Pat had left. It wore a mustache and slouch hat just like Sundance. This had to be Pat made up. Stacey feigned fear, even giving a phony scream. The menacing rapist slowly approached the bed, while Stacey remained frozen, a helpless rabbit hypnotized by its stalker.

Then Pat launched her attack, fully clothed. They wrestled, Pat forcing kiss after kiss on her victim, who gradually submitted and responded. Then came the real shocker for me. Pat rolled partially off Stacey, unbuttoned her pants and slid out the dildo she had strapped on. She oiled the end of it and gently rubbed it up and down on Stacey's entrance, the latter now coming to meet her eagerly. Pat gently put just the tip in, sliding it easily up and down to assure that Stacey was well lubricated. Stacey grabbed the rapist's buttocks and thrust him into her, coming to meet the attack. This was more than I could stand. I unzipped and decided to play a little lets-see-who-comes-first right there. I wouldn't have known, or cared, if it was ten below and snowing.

Pat obviously knew exactly what her partner wanted. Past experience had assured that. There would be no lack of communication between a pair like this, such as ruins marriages. Pat had been told exactly what to do, how and when, so it suited her partner. There was no unruly ego involved to screw it up for them.

Pat started with long, slow strokes, then she increased the tempo, finally getting down to short quick strokes, fully inserted, Stacey, head thrown back, eyes tightly closed, moaning and gasping.

Sex Ring in a Small Town

I felt like that too, except that I knew it was best to be quiet under the circumstances, and I wasn't about to close my eyes. I wasn't missing a thing.Stacey and I had a mutual orgasm, as I arched off a load on her porch. Maybe I should have made a loud noise as I did it, like her, and got caught. No telling where that might have led. (Sadly, jail was one possibility.) Inside they shut down for the night with a little, tender after play. Pat was not the type that wanted a dildo, I suppose. It gave me a clue about Stacey; she was probably capable of being at least a switch hitter, where Pat was a true dyke by choice. A word about their paraphernalia for you studs ~ they could have had any size they pleased, yet what pleased Stacey was just average, the standard six. I made a note to get some of that sort of paraphernalia for the use of my customers, if need be.

I suppose they slept together, since they were still in bed together when they turned off the lights. I wondered what Ole would say if he knew. Or Stacey's husband. For my part I said, "More power to them." Also, "Thanks, ladies."

I drove by in the morning and Pat's car was till in the driveway. I thought, "How sweet. Lovers." And a damned sight more satisfying lovers than the national average. I don't give a damn what anyone does in private. It's nobody's business.

CHAPTER SEVENTEEN

Dirty Harry had been trouble enough, but for real trouble I was going to learn that philanthropy laid it all over him. My first expedition into hard core philanthropy was due to the minster's wife, Liz Leonard. I still can't recall what he was minister of: "ya seen one ya seen 'em all." Liz came to me first for the usual reason ~ to help her quit smoking. She not only thought it was a dirty, dangerous habit she couldn't kick alone, but she couldn't afford outrageous cigarette prices.

I fixed up the smoking thing in the usual manner in short order. When she was about to leave she mentioned she had one of her terrible tension headaches. Unlucky me. It was 2:30 P.M. and she was my last appointment of the day.

So I said, "We can probably fix that too if you've got time."

She had time. Her headache went away easily and she felt great when I woke her up.

She bubbled, "That's wonderful. I've been having them so often lately. I wonder why."

My motor mouth ran on, "Maybe we can find that out too if you want to try." She wanted to try, or at least try something.

I must tell you of my best therapeutic device, "the great impersonal voice, such as I'd used on Carmen." The patient is convinced they are talking only to a disembodied father figure that is their best friend, an entity whose functions are to listen politely, deftly suggest, never judge or criticize, a voice that could well be inside them, or might even be God. With the *voice* one has very private conversations with an absolutely trustworthy confidant.

With patients fully into this mode I have witnessed some most revealing insights into the human condition. Here is an example with Liz Leonard: "Do you have any idea what might be causing your tension headaches? You may talk freely. I am your friend; only a voice that will never be able to reveal anything you say."

Long pause here, as though Liz is deep in thought, or actually traveling to some other place. Then considerable frowning and several deep sighs. The voice that finally talks is not quite hers.

"I hate him."

"Who?"

"My husband."

"Do you really?"

"Yes."

"Why?"

Long delay, as though dredging up information, gasping and uncomfortable twisting in the deep, overstuffed chair.

"I don't know."

"Did you ever love him?"

"I don't know what love is."

"What makes you say that?"

In a higher pitched voice, "I just don't." Hands clench into fists and thereafter alternate between relaxed and tensed, whitening her knuckles when she clenches them.

A couple of weeks earlier, I'd have become alarmed at that point. Instead I smoothly put in a distracting question.

"You never loved any man?"

"I love the man who runs the second hand furniture store."

"When did you know him?"

"Now. His name is George."

"What does George do that your husband doesn't?"

"Nothing. He delivered a chair. I gave him a cup of coffee. He's just nice. Considerate. He listened to me and seemed interested."

"And your husband doesn't?"

"No. He talks all the time himself. Never shuts up."

"About what?"

"Religion."

"Religion?"

"Yes. God. The bible. Scripture. I wish the son of a bitch would shut up just once. He doesn't know a thing about real religion . . . being good and having faith."

"Have you thought of getting a divorce?"

"I can't."

"Why not?"

"I couldn't support myself and Audrey. I don't know how to do anything."

"Audrey is your daughter?"

"Yes. She's only seventeen."

"This is a no-fault state. You can get a divorce and he has to support you both."

"On his salary?" She laughed.

I noticed for the first time her Salvation Army Thrift Store clothes. No wonder she was having tension headaches. I couldn't think of anything to say. She could.

"I could stand it if I didn't have to sleep with him. He's just like an animal, puffing and snorting and jabbing the big thing in me and he goes on forever. When it's all over I'm so nervous I can't go to sleep for hours. I'd like to kill him."

A light went on. "Do you have orgasms?"

"I've read about them. I don't think so. No. I'm sure I've never had one."

"Not even masturbating after he leaves you dissatisfied?"

"I couldn't do that!"

"Why not?"

"It's a sin."

We were at a dead end. I knew from what she said that he certainly never got her off playing with her clitoris. The bastard and his type don't know what a clitoris is, or if they do they think playing with one is kinky. That's when I got a sensational idea. I said, "Did you know that people can change their personalities and become a more comfortable person, just like an actress changes roles?"

"I sometimes daydream that I'm someone else."

"Who?"

"Well, lately, Maud."

"Tell me about Maud."

"She's a character in a Romance I just finished."

"What sort of person is she?"

"A woman of the world. Self-assured. Attractive. With plenty of money. She's an executive and independent."

"A feminist?"

"Yes. She has this wonderful apartment and good clothes, eats in good restaurants."

"Would you like to be Maud?"

"Yes. Very much."

"All right. You're going to relax for three minutes and think about becoming Maud. At the end of that time you will hear this voice again and start having adventures as Maud, your other self."

"Oh, that will be wonderful."

She looked so happy I got scared that it might not work. I had no idea if it would or not, or what she was going to do as Maud, but I had three minutes to think it over. I was breathing fast, a trifle awed by my own imagination and audacity, and what society would have to say about what was forming in my mind. This woman's problem, like most, was at its root, sexual. I intended to try to give her a fighting chance at satisfaction, and happiness. I was watching the second hand on my watch. In exactly three minutes I said, "How are you, Maud?"

A different, more cultivated and confident voice answered me, "I'm just fine."

"Where are you?"

"In my apartment."

"Where is your apartment?"

"In a tall building in Seattle. I can see the Sound and the ships out there."

"Would you like to describe your apartment?"

"It's big."

"What else?"

"Light and airy. Furnished in Danish Modern."

"Are you happy?"

"Oh, yes."

"Do you recall our talk about relieving tension?"

"Yes."

This was astounding. She apparently knew she was both Liz and

Maud. " Good. As Maud you are independent of men because you are sophisticated and won't let just any man use you. You pick and choose. You know how to relieve your sexual tensions till the right man comes along. You don't have tension headaches anymore, because you know how to do that."

"Yes."

"Now, you will be absolutely alone so you can relieve your tensions privately."

Silence and a frown. I thought she might wake up and spoil her chances, or worse yet, remember what I was trying to do to her. Boy would a small town see that as sexual harassment. I quickly reinforced her state, then said, "Just go in on the bed and relax. The door is to your right."

By then I'd done a number one furnishing job on the bedrooms, having observed how useful a private room had been in Carmen's case. Nothing like a good bump of anticipation. I'd also hooked up Dirty Harry's purloined equipment for making sophisticated movies on the sly. Do you suppose some of Diamond Dan had rubbed off on me?

I prompted Liz-Maud to undress and relax on the big bed. I had to tell her what to do, just as I had Carmen, and even guide her hand at first. Let me tell you this: sin, or no sin, masturbation comes naturally. I feel sure Doctor Ruth will confirm this. Maud fumbled a trifle for exactly the right place, but found it every time. She was soon breathing harder and thrusting like an experienced hand at it. She got her first orgasm right there.

You may wonder if that got me charged up after my experiences of the night before and my taking care of the situation. What the hell do you think? This was a good-looking woman in her late thirties. I'm all too human. If I didn't suspect that ministers were all Billy Goats, pumping hell out of half their congregations, I'd have been tempted to teach Liz-Maud the rest of the drill. Pity we can't shove

AIDS back up the monkeys.

I then got Maud back into her clothes and back into Liz, totally without conscious recollection on her part. However, I was sure that Liz was going to be a confirmed masturbator from then on. She now thought it was sophisticated, which it is. Moreover, she was aware of what she'd been missing. She looked ten years younger. I wondered if her dunce husband would notice.

Why did I get all this on video tape? Why did I rerun it to see how it came out? She grew prettier as the episode progressed. Don't ask me how. Maybe it was "a miracle, brother." It took my mind off Diamond Dan's impending visit. Just then the phone rang.

"John?"

It was a voice only faintly familiar, since it was unexpected. "Who is this?" I asked, cautiously.

"Ole. Ole Sunderland."

Did he suppose I wouldn't know which Ole? I decided to take the plunge. "What the hell is a billionaire doing making his own phone calls?" It was the right tack.

He guffawed and said, "I'm too cheap to hire a secretary. That's how I made my money. How about coming out flying?"

"When?"

"Can you make it tomorrow morning? Maybe come out for breakfast and then we'll defy gravity afterward."

"I'll cancel a few appointments. It sounds good to me."

"I heard about your business. It ought to make a million. How's it doing?"

Thinking of what had just happened, I said, "You wouldn't believe it."

"I suspect I would. In fact I want to talk about it with you. There may be something you can do for me . . . for a fee, of course," he quickly added.

The poor, rich bastard. He wasn't used to getting favors. Didn't expect any. As I said, he needed a friend.

If I hadn't before, right then and there I decided to be his friend if I could.

CHAPTER EIGHTEEN

You may wonder if Carmen and her sister, Angelita, had slipped my mind. They never slipped the mind of any man who'd ever seen them. Besides, like Ole, the poor kids needed a friend. More philanthropy, right? And leading me to the same place maybe. Poor Cuchillo Pete couldn't make bail, so he was still in slam awaiting trial. If I was any judge, he was on his way up for some real hard time. What a tragedy. The girls' protector taken out of circulation. With Pete's knife out of the picture, every self-styled great lover in town would be out to minister to these little, lonesome doves. It was a thought that bothered me so much I had arranged to see them the morning Ole wanted me to come out flying. I was torn between two desires.

Sex Ring in a Small Town

I solved the conflict by calling and, rather than rescheduling their appointments, having them come over that very evening.

I observed as soon as they arrived that away from their keeper they were two different ladies. Each vied with the other to keep my eyes only on them. And each kept her eyes only on mine. What a mental fucking I was getting. They were making out pretty well too, come to think of it. I barely managed to escort them (from behind, of course) down to my lair. Both wore tight, short skirts, spike heels, black nylons and skin-tight sweaters. Their glossy black hair trailed almost to their waists. What legs! What butts! What a hard-on! "Again?" you may ask. All it takes is the right inspiration. Recall that the wise old heads recruited virgins to warm Solomon.

Since this isn't intended as porn, I'll give only a brief summary, no clinical details, kids, of what I did for the two girls.

1) Reinforced the no-smoking business.

2) Introduced the truest friend a girl ever had ~ the disembodied voice.

3) Created Brother John a phantom lover who very realistically would keep down their tensions. I recalled that psychic piece of ass I'd arranged years before in the Army. If it worked for a man, why not a woman? Thenceforth Brother John would be their sole male sex partner.

Why do I emphasize male sex partner? Well, variety is the spice of life. I also gave them a second, special personality each and had them learn to do, with a phantom lover, a repeat of what Pat and Stacey had done the night before. Strictly for therapy, of course. In their secondary personalities as sexpots, neither had the slightest hesitation about that. In fact, I suspect their primary personalities would have been just as willing; something I would one day discover, or die in the attempt. My time was too limited that night to find out.

Of course, I had to forego the dildo bit, since I didn't have one yet.

4) In the girls' secondary personalities I could do no less than give them an opportunity to learn to give an expert hand job with Jergens. To keep down my tensions, which they'd really done wonders in raising. It didn't take long under the circumstances. Alas, suppose Dorothy came home and I couldn't even get aroused? I'd think about that, tomorrow, like Scarlet O'Hara.

I really got a good, relaxed sleep that night. I don't think Ole was primarily interested in me as a fellow aviator, not even at first. He'd learned enough about me from various sources, including Skeezix (Pat), to have plans for me. Ole had a sex problem, and it wasn't that his lovely, young wife was a lesbian. Old as he was, here was a man who wanted to enjoy life to the fullest. But, of course, I didn't know that when we went down to his airplane hangars in his Rolls Royce taxi. He had six hangars and needed that many to house all his birds.

"Did you ever fly a SPAD?" he asked on our way down.

The SPAD was a WWI antique, mainstay of Allied aviation in fact. Famous American ace, Eddie Rickenbacker, had scored his many victories flying one. All the American aces flew French and British planes, since America, where airplanes were pioneered, had not followed through and built an aircraft industry.

To Ole's question about my ever having flown a SPAD, I told him, "Nope. And I'm not sure I want to."

"How about a Sopwith Camel or SE-5?"

"Ditto."

He laughed. "I flew 'em all in the last, great, gentleman's war."

"I didn't know there was such a thing."

"There isn't, but recall that WWI was the war to end all war."

"And make the world safe for democracy."

"Right. Anyway, fighter pilots were the last knights."

Ole had the SPAD equipped with oxygen, something unheard of in WWI, even though they climbed up to where you needed it. They must have had bright lights swimming in front of their eyes up there. I took it up to 18,000 feet, just to see if it would go that high. Ole had told me, "The higher the better. The way to attack was high and out of the sun. That's how we got to be aces. Fuck that Lufberry Circle shit and dogfighting. I made one balls to the wall pass, hit and ran. Even then I knew I'd rather be rich and live a long while to drink and screw a lot than be a dead hero."

Well, that made sense. I got to 18,000 easily and had a notion it might go to twenty. I descended and gingerly tried some elementary aerobatics, which aren't part of the Army flying curriculum, but we all had to try them. Then I made a controlled crash back on Ole's strip, after about an hour in the air. I fervently prayed that Ole subscribed to the old aviation saw: "Any landing you can walk away from is a good one." I shut it down, unstrapped and crawled out. He met me, grinning.

"You got talent," he said.

"How's that?"

"One take off . . . three landings."

"I walked away from all three."

"I noticed. I could have done it myself. Want to try the Sopwith?"

"Not on a bet. I need a drink."

"Why not? I've got something else that may interest you more; a little business proposition."

Damn near anything but snakebite would have interested me more than getting into another one of those antique instruments of the devil.

He took us back to the house, if you can call Hearst Castle Southwest a house.

"Let's go up to my study."

We took an elevator from the ten car basement garage up to the third floor tower. The room we came out in was at least forty feet square. When Ole had a tower built he did it right. The carpet was like a golf green. He noticed me testing it.

"Executive perks," he said. "Would you believe that in some companies they have rules about how deep a carpet pile each executive position is entitled to? Same for the kind of fixtures in the executive cans. Speaking of cans, if you need one, that's it," he pointed to a carved door next to the elevator.

What impressed me most was the view on all sides. You could see the stables and the airfield, of course, but also the valleys on both ends of their canyon, yellow rivers of shimmering fall-cured grass, with hazy, purple mountains piled, range on range, to a pale horizon where they became one with sky.

Ole's voice called me back from drowning in the view.

"Breathtaking, isn't it?"

It wasn't what I expected to hear from a ninety-year-old billionaire, especially in a voice more like a thrilled little kid's. "Money has its compensations," he continued.

I wondered if he was being funny; also if he expected me to say something. If I had, it might have been to observe that money hadn't built that view and it didn't take money to look at it. I had a feeling that would have got no argument from him.

"How about that drink now?" he said.

"Sounds good to me."

He pointed to the bar and said, "Mix your own. It's all there. I'm a piss poor bartender."

I'd have bet he missed piss poor by a country mile at anything he tried to do. I fixed myself a good, stiff scotch and soda and he took a Glenfiddich straight. Then he offered me a cigar from a mahogany humidor, took one himself and we both lit up. It was the best cigar I ever tasted. Probably smuggled.

He flopped into a king-size, high-backed executive chair behind

Sex Ring in a Small Town

a desk about the size of a ping pong table, hoisted his feet up on it and motioned me to a chair equally plush. It was beside him, rather than in front of the desk where he knew I might feel like a job applicant.

He speared me with a set of very keen, blue eyes. "I know a lot about what you're doing," he said.

That wasn't hard to believe. I thought of how chintzy Dirty Harry's salary had probably been. God knows what real money can buy.

A thought occurred to me, *Holy shit!* I wonder if he had some gumshoe watching Skeezix, who took in our act the other night and reported the whole thing. It really didn't seem like Ole's style.

What he said reassured me. "I know you're doing a lot of good already, helping people quit smoking. You're not charging some of the poor ones a damn thing, I've heard."

Now how the hell would he know that?

He continued, "You've got a good heart. It will probably get you into a hell of a lot of trouble before you're through."

What a prophet he was! For example, there was Diamond Dan due to blow in pretty soon. He always managed to whip a few new paving blocks into the road to hell.

"I've read a lot about hypnotism," he said. "I've tried self hypnotism and can't get it to work. My mind keeps thrashing around too much. So I want you to hypnotize me."

"Why?" I was a trifle dumfounded.

"To improve my memory, among other things."

I was too surprised to pick up on "among other things" just then. But here was a mighty man who couldn't be sure what he proposed wasn't placing him in the clutches of a schemer. This was exactly what Dorothy had been shooting for me to do, and now it had dropped into my lap. This could be a ticket to billions. And I still couldn't see it. I simply wasn't built right.

He had obviously thought of that and said, "Naturally I've taken a few precautions about what you may do to me. We'll be on hidden camera." He laughed. "You'll also be one of the best paid 'private screen' actors in the business if you shoot square with me."

I looked him right straight into those chilly eyes and said, "I'd shoot square with you, or anyone else, whether you paid me or not."

"I already figured that. It's why you're sitting there."

He wasn't easy to hypnotize, as he'd said, his fertile mind grabbing and analyzing everything. If he hadn't been hyper-willing and stuck with me patiently, he'd have been one of those people that supposedly can't be hypnotized. It took at least an hour. When I was sure of him at last, I gave him the usual reinforcement so it would be easier the next time.

I couldn't think of a thing to do on the memory angle. I simply took a scattergun approach and told him his memory would improve every day. It was pure optimism, assuming his mind knew more about it than I did. If it didn't I sure as hell had no idea what to tell him, or anyone, that they should do as a memory improving exercise.

Driving home that evening I was sure of one thing. I liked the old man and intended to be his true friend. Equally as well, I liked the check in my billfold. It would take care of paying Putt Putt for a long while. I suspected that Ole liked me, too. I didn't know the half of it. Or what he really wanted from me.

Sex Ring in a Small Town

John Pelham

CHAPTER NINETEEN

I read in a national newsmagazine on the subject of "safe sex," that Carmen, a High School Girl, was sure she wasn't going to get AIDS from her boyfriend because he loves her and wouldn't do anything to hurt her. Shades of the B.C. comic strip in which one of the characters laments that all of the dragons have been slain, leaving no real challenges, and B.C. retorts: "How about stupidity?" And here's another darb from the same magazine: "a prostitute thinks she can't transmit AIDs to her true lover because she's had a hysterectomy."

So, looking back, I conclude I'd inadvertently entered the lists to joust with the dragon of stupidity. But only indirectly. God helps those who help themselves.

Sex Ring in a Small Town

I was merely trying to arm them for their own salvation. Come to think of it, that's supposed to be the church's preserve. Maybe that's why the church is always the first to frown on efforts like mine. Competition. Besides my solution worked, the problem went away, the "victim, er, whoops, client" didn't need to toss money on the collection plate for a lifetime.

Which brings up dirty old money, the reason I fell into the witch doctoring trade. I merely thought I was earning it before the High School football coach showed up.

"I'm Coach Lawson," he said, shoving out his hand and giving me the Hollywood ivories grin.

So what? I thought and would have liked to have said, "No shit? He was the kind that thought he had an anthropoid grip and used it to impress people shaking hands. Also to maim those he could. My old man made us all milk cows back in Wisconsin and my jock strap program ever since has included grippers or hard rubber balls squeezed a few hundred times daily. I gave the sonofabitch a little of his own medicine and he tried to let go, but I hung on and he got a hand to nurse with liniment. All the while I was giving him back the Hollywood ivory business.

"Glad to know you, coach. I've heard a lot about you." In fact I'd heard he was a candy-assed little puke. Little described him. About five seven. One of those who went out for every sport in school and never earned a letter in anything. You see them on the end of the bench at every football game, never getting up, except to ass pat some jock who's just come off the field after making a big play. Maybe the coach gets so desperate in some game he says to a Lawson-clone, "Get up," and they think it's their big chance until he concludes, "I'm sending in the bench." It's surprising how many of them end up as High School athletic directors; either that or big game hunters. A .458 Winchester gives them exactly the odds they need to feel Macho.

Lawson showed up the week Diamond Dan was still hanging over my head. I'd given Ole's memory and Liz Leonard's tension their treatment, Carmen and Angelita now had Brother John, I'd done a little window peeping and, although I haven't mentioned it yet, done my first anesthesia job for a local dentist. A patient was allergic to painkillers.

Coach Lawson said, "I've been reading about hypnotism."

I thought, *So he can read ~ cool!* By then I'd let him in as far as the living room. Curtains sat next to him after he sunk into one of my big chairs, eyeing him to chalk out the spot where he planned to drill him a new asshole if I gave him the word.

"Does he bite?" Lawson asked. I wondered if the son of a bitch read newspapers.

"He killed a robber in here not long ago."

"Oh? Yeah. I heard about that. He doesn't look dangerous."

Here was one who'd play with Sidewinders because they were little. "You'd better look again."

He did, and sensing what I expected Curtains drew back his lips from inch and a half long incisors and let out a low growl.

Lawson looked like a tourist who just recognizes that he's put down a bare foot too close to a rattlesnake. He tried to grin and got off a great line. "Nice doggie." He actually put out his hand to pat Curtains and got the damnedest growl I'd ever heard from my faithful friend. The hand retracted like magic. The bastard at least had physical reflexes.

"Why don't you just forget the nice doggie, and he'll leave you alone."

"Wouldn't it be better if you put him outside?"

"As long as I'm here he won't do anything I don't want him to . . . or at least he never has up till now . . . what can I do for you, by the way?"

He gave me a sickly grin. "Well," eyeing my faithful companion all the while, "like I said, I've been reading about hypnotism and our dentist told me you're really good at it."

"And?"

"I thought maybe you could inspire my football team."

I got a picture of that and couldn't help laughing. The famous local Lions hadn't won a game in seven years. I'm not kidding. And just then I recalled that I'd heard Coach Lawson had been on board exactly seven years. Now he was after psychic steroids as a last, desperate measure of self-preservation, no doubt.

A great idea grabbed me, or at least it seemed like a great idea because it could be good for a laugh.

"Why not? I'll start with you and you can judge for yourself what I can do for the team."

The stupid asshole said, "Start with me? What for?"

"To inspire you." You should have seen the look on his face, as though it was inconceivable that anyone failed to recognize that he had been on the mountain talking to God, that he, by gum, was inspired to the max already.

He said, "I don't think I need it."

To cut a long story down, I agreed to come down the next day before pre-game warm up and do a group number on the local eleven, even the subs, just as I'd done for the Civic Uplift League. The next day was Friday. I was looking forward to the return of Dorothy. I was not looking forward to the Return of Diamond Dan, Episode I.

I really didn't need to be reminded what gymnasiums smell like. Almost everyone knows. Better than battlefields, but nothing like flower gardens. Recalling my dismal years in schools, even their hallway odor makes me feel like puking.

And I had to thread my way through several hallways to reach the gym since Coach Lawson had the mother wit to get the principal behind his last ditch campaign to win. He was street-smart enough to know that otherwise he might be suspected of attempting witchcraft by his fat-faced leader, Principal George Reedy. So we picked up Reedy on our way to the gym.

About fifteen minutes later I had a gym full of morons out in the mental daisy patch browsing on inspiration-weed. Coach Lawson and Reedy led the way, would you believe? What an opportunity to send them all down to a recruiting office and improve the town overnight. Even at that, it probably would have raised the average I.Q. of the Army or Marines. Instead I hyped them, especially with the notion that they'd all be back in dreamland if, like Mandrake the Magician, I gestured hypnotically at them. I always wondered how the fuck Mandrake gestured hypnotically; still do. Actually, I told the bastards if I looked at them and counted three they'd be out with the birdies and could hear only my voice caroling signals at them. And, of course, I told them if they didn't go out and rah, rah, rah for old Hudson High, the commies would despoil their mothers and girlfriends.

I escaped into fresh air and sunlight through a fire exit, booked for several reinforcement engagements. Let me get ahead of my story here and say that the team started winning as of that night, and never lost another game as long as I worked on them. It was a fact that may have saved me from leaving town in the manner of the Shah of Iran. Small towns can be dangerous, especially in the face of two unforgivable offenses: obvious intelligence, and success. Come to think of it, so can large towns. In any event, the deadly Lions marched on to victory that very night, their first win in seven years. The suspense of wondering whether it would happen again may have been too much for Coach Lawson.

The next week he was to come to me and say, "Reverend Leonard's wife told me you cured her tension headaches. Maybe you can help me too."

I'd thought, the week before, that hypnotizing him would be funny, and I hadn't changed my mind. I wanted to discover just what made a little puke like him tick.

John Pelham

CHAPTER TWENTY

Dorothy got home about the time I was ready to head for the airport and meet Diamond Dan. I had played out several scenarios in my mind about how to prevent the natural consequences of the inevitable meeting of Diamond and Hot Buns. I came up with a blank. Only prayer was left. Maybe she'd be the first woman I'd ever seen who didn't, at least figuratively, throw herself into his lap, panting. Maybe he'd miraculously got religion; better yet, morals. Maybe a Deus ex Machina would descend through the roof and snatch me to Glory, to forget it all and have a flaming centuries-long affair with Venus, or at least Helen. Maybe the assessor would lower my tax rate. The phone next to my chair rang. I jumped, then picked it up.

"Hey, Pel," a familiar voice said, "I'm at the fuckin' Savoy in London, so you don't have to pick me up." I thought, *Thank God, a reprieve,* and said, "What the hell are you doing there?"

"Some assholes want to corner the skin-flick business in the common market."

"That's about as common as markets get, isn't it?"

"Don't knock it. I'm getting a five million consulting fee. Already got half of it up front. How does that grab you, buddy?"

"Peanuts."

"Haw. Haw. Haw." There's no laugh like Diamond Dan's. I used to think of selling tickets to it in Nam.

"Are you coming through here on your way back?"

"Can't say yet. I'm picking up a new executive chopper at the factory and may ferry it back myself. Maybe I'll stop by and show it off. Let's count on Christmas for sure."

That, of course, meant Copenhagen. Christ the times we had there. "Maybe," I said. "Depends on if I can get away from old Harboldson." He'd worked for him too in Nam. I didn't think it was a good time to bring up my thriving new business with Diamond. A good time to do that would be never plus thirty days.

"Screw Harboldson! Ciao!" and the connection clicked off.

I literally let out a hell of a sigh of relief. Then I fetched a big hooker of Scotch, lit up a stogy, and was feeling gangbusters when Dorothy rang me up on the phone.

"It is I. Home from the wars." A little reunion was in order.

As I said before, philanthropy really sucks, or did I say that before? Before I really figured that out, I hired Liz Leonard as a part-time secretary. I checked it out first with Dorothy to make damn sure she wouldn't be suspicious. She thought it was a nice idea, " . . . because Liz can really use the money . . . and that husband of hers . . ." She threw a hand to her forehead like an undone virgin in a melodrama. Need I say more? Pure philanthropy all the way around. I really wasn't thinking of watching Liz relieve her tensions if it got boring around my office.

What got to me about her case was honorable poverty. She could only afford crummy, cheap cotton underwear and thrift store clothes. She deserved a heap better. She had honest, direct eyes, nice even teeth, shiny, clean, neat hair and she always reminded me of a soap commercial. She smelled good without using perfume. What I'm trying to say is, she was just a hell of a nice person, making the best of a tough row to hoe.

I can't imagine why her "suck-hole" husband wasn't suspicious of me. Maybe it was my overwhelming aura of virtue, helping people quit the filthy weed. Besides the bastard was a football fan and Coach Lawson told him about the team's new secret of success. Then too, our local dentist, Dr. Muscovy, was praising me as heaven-sent to help treat patients he couldn't touch before except like they did in the Dark Ages.

I had a sweet deal going all the way around. Pity the most humane aspects of it were something society deems illegitimate and/or sinful, if not actually illegal. I tried hard as hell to avoid hubris in my role as God's surrogate, but had indifferent success. And what do I mean by that? Well, you've probably heard the adjuration, "Vengeance is mine, saith the Lord." I couldn't resist helping him out occasionally when it looked like he was a trifle too busy to notice an aggravated case.

For example, take Coach Lawson's tension headaches. Naturally, I had to get to the root of them in the manner I did with Liz Leonard, didn't I?

Once I got him out of his usual trance and into a hypnotic one, I asked, "Is there some person whom you strongly admire and would like to be?" He seemed to be reflecting quite awhile. I waited. Obviously it had been the "would like to be" that was puzzling him.

Finally he said, "I not only would like to be, I am Napoleon."
"Napoleon?"
"Yes."
"Bonaparte?"
"Yes."
"And you're also Coach Lawson?"
"Yes. They're very fortunate to have me."
"That's true," I said. "Sometimes common people are ungrateful, though."
"Very. But I can overlook that."

I almost asked him how he felt about Wellington and Blucher, but was after bigger game. I had to be sure he knew the voice addressing him now was disembodied, really something enchanted inside him, an entity that would never, could never, betray him. And would never ridicule him. When I felt he was assured of that, I asked him what he thought was at the root of his tension headaches. If you live to be a million, you'll probably never guess.

He said, "I'm in love with my tight end." (Who isn't?)
"Explain that."
"Joe Reedy. The Principal's son. He plays tight end on the football team."
"And you're in love with him? You mean . . ."
"Yes. I'm a switch hitter. AC, DC"

So what? I recall a quote from one of Caesar's contemporaries: "Caesar is a husband to every woman and a wife to every man." And let's not forget Ganymede, beloved of the God's on Mt. Olympus. And I certainly couldn't forget the other side of the coin, lovely Pat and Stacey, having at it in the manner that turned them on. Judge not. But then there's AIDS.

I made a note to check out Joe Reedy and see what his druthers were. Then I might ~ just might ~ relieve Coach Lawson's tensions to his heart's desire.

I knew that Napoleon was also aware he was Coach Lawson, so I said, "Have Joe Reedy come over and we'll reinforce his inspiration to make all-state tight end."

The day Joe Reedy had his appointment, Liz Leonard's daughter Audrey was in my office waiting to drive her mother home. If drive sounds affluent, get this: their only car was a 1969 Datsun, dented and scratched. It only ran thanks to my handyman Alfredo, who tinkered with it whenever needed.

Audrey was a young edition of her mother. Very pretty and clean, with honest eyes, long brown hair down to the middle of her back. This, as the saying goes, "Was eatin' stuff." The same kind of clothes her mother could afford didn't camouflage a sensational body. I'm an "ass man" and she really turned me on whenever I looked at hers, which was as often as I could manage. I wondered if she had some tensions I ought to work on.

If she did it was pretty obvious what could be causing them when Joe Reedy walked in, looked at her, mumbled, "Hi Audrey," and blushed.

I got him off the hook by quickly escorting him down the hall to the bedroom I'd fitted out to do double duty as a second office. I noticed that Audrey blushed a trifle herself. I thought, *Maybe Diamond Dan would like to cast these two in a sex education movie . . . Why Diamond Dan?* For the moment I had another matter to consider regarding tight ends. Joe Reedy was already prepped by my group sessions with the football team to take a quick trip into dreamland. You don't need details of my conversation as God's surrogate in this case. In a nutshell I discovered the kid was a virgin.

He did have a normal set of hots for Audrey, though. Every straight male in the High School probably did. In Joe's case, he said, "I'm in love with Audrey Leonard, but I don't think she likes me."

Christ, how dumb young men are, compared to young women. She'd almost raped him with her eyes, was probably out there now, pretending to look at a magazine and thinking about laying him, with her thang twitching. I made a note to do something about their sex education if the opportunity presented itself, whether I got it on film or not.

That left Coach Lawson's designs on Joe Reedy to be coped with. A couple of sessions more with his eminence, Napoleon, enabled me to redirect his libido. Hypnotism is a potent thing. After the second reinforcement session, I was sure Coach Lawson/Napoleon Bonaparte, was convinced that Putt-Putt O'Dool was: the most attractive potential sex partner in town. I wished I could watch the courtship that was bound to ensue.

CHAPTER TWENTY-ONE

Somewhat to my surprise, Ole called and made an appointment to come to my place. I was in for a second surprise when Curtains met him. Maybe the pooch sensed his great age and had an innate respect for that. More likely, however, it was the instant bonding of two fighters, both fearless. Curtains allowed his ears to be scratched without blinking an eye, then smiled. He heeled behind Ole and flopped next to him when he took the same big chair Napoleon had a few days before.

"I'm pooped," Ole said, closing his eyes and massaging them with his fingers.

"Headache?"

"A little. Just tension."

I wondered what was able to make him tense. It wasn't long in coming out. Why he chose to trust me was puzzling then; still is, as a matter of fact. Maybe he was trying to acquire a son informally.

He said, "Some people play chess for mental exercise. I play Wall Street. It takes as much out of you as a tennis match sometimes."

I recalled some sport or other who found out what Wall Street was really up to, and concluded, "It's a crap shoot."

"How about a drink?" I asked.

"You've got a customer. About a double, double, double of Scotch." He pulled out his carved leather cigar case and offered me one. While I was pouring he said, "What I really need is a good piece of strange."

This little shocker put my mind to work. Knowing what I did about his young wife, I wondered if that strange implied, after all, that Pat really was fucking the old boy and he wanted some variety.

I took the plunge. "With your dough, I'd think you could have a harem." I handed him a half water glass of Glenlivit and an ice water backer.

He sipped a bit, then took a bigger swig. "Ah," he breathed, "The nectar of the Gods."

I thought he might be planning to slip the punch on my "harem" ploy, but he didn't.

"Buying a harem never was easy and it's out of the question today."

"AIDS?"

"That's one stumbling block. A dependable pimp is the main one. Eunuchs are scarce outside the Arab world. If you found a clean concubine you'd have to have her watched day and night to keep her that way. A piece of ass isn't that important to me anymore; never was, come to think of it." He puffed on his cigar and began to look more relaxed. One of his problems was he didn't have anyone to talk to. He went on, "I'm pushin' ninety-one. Makes you wonder if you'll drop dead any second. But life is still sweet. I don't think a damn bit different or feel much different about things than I did when I was twenty, not that I'd care to go back and live it over again, especially getting shot all to hell."

I said, "I'll buy that."

"Did you get shot up too?"

"Only near misses. Just enough to shit my pants a couple of times."

"I've done that," he said, and laughed.

It was hard to believe, looking at those eyes. "Forgot to gird my loins," he explained. "No time." He laughed again. "What happened to you?"

I told him how me and my Uzi survived Charlie when I was shot down in Nam.

"War is a nasty business," he pronounced. "You wouldn't believe where I got shot all to hell."

"Try me."

"I had a twenty millimeter explode almost in my lap. I was leading a B-17 raid. Should have been in an asylum instead. I was almost fifty years old, a B.G.; could have been sitting on my ass in headquarters, or fucking a nurse." He was silent a long while. Finally he said, "The fuckin' thing blew my cock off. Imagine that? You've probably heard of a few cases like that. Bound to happen." He snorted. "It wasn't as funny then. And it hurt like hell. My co-pilot got us home. Pity it didn't take my balls off with it. I have to sit down and piss like a woman and wipe off my balls afterward. I still get it off though, occasionally ~ in wet dreams. Imagine that!" He snorted again.

Well, that answered the question about Skeezix. If she'd been straight he could have used a dildo on her, but she obviously didn't need anything a man could offer, except a stroke or two for her ego from damn fools who hadn't yet caught onto her. It was Stacey who needed a man and perhaps didn't realize it.

"I'm going to level with you. You probably wonder what I'm doing with a young wife."

I started to protest that it was none of my business and he held up a hand to cut me off.

"I know what I want to say. Don't interrupt. Looking at Skeezix probably turns you on. If it doesn't, I pity you. But a man can forget any aspirations there."

I opened my mouth and left it open when he quickly said, "She's queer as a three dollar bill." He was watching me closely. I'm sure I looked stunned enough he didn't suspect I already knew that. "I knew that when I married her. I did it to protect the kid. I loved her like a daughter. One day when she was about nineteen I ran across her and a girl she had up visiting from college. Oh, they didn't see me, but I caught them having at each other across the creek from the house; going at it like crazy and having a hell of a lot of fun, I observed. They got it off with tongue jobs and even necked like a man and woman. I was too dumfounded to get the hell out of there; besides I had a natural curiosity to know what two women did. I never even hinted to her that I knew. One day, though, years later, when she was out of college, I asked her why she had so little to do with men and if she thought she'd ever get married. She leveled with me then, and I suggested we get married so men would leave her alone. And that's how May and December got hitched in our case. Does it sound cold-blooded?"

"Just the opposite. Almost too civilized to believe, but not cold blooded by a jug full."

"We ought to learn to be more civilized."

"I'm all for it." That was the whole point of my philanthropy, aside from my own healthy curiosity and Billy Goat Balls. Let's not kid ourselves about Brother John's purpose, for example. I was saving Carmen and Angelita as private stock, just in case, until they were ripe for testing.

In response to my reply, Ole went on, "Good. That's why I came here."

After getting this far with my story, I can't say "you won't believe this" because you undoubtedly will. He wanted me to fix him up, just like the guy in boot camp, so he could have fantasy fucking, whenever he wanted a little.

"You think you can do it?" he asked.

"Hell yes. That's how I got into this business." I told him about that old affair.

"That's fabulous, I may be old, but I'm not dead by a long shot."

So I built into him a harem of his very own. I had no doubt that it would take some reinforcing sessions before he could do it alone, but right then and there I took him back to one of the king size beds and left him to have a mental orgy. When he came out an hour later he looked a lot happier and more relaxed than he had when he'd complained he was pooped.

"Did it work?"

"Like a charm. To be more precise, like a fuckin' charm."

"Good."

"What's the tab?"

"Not a damn thing. We're even for flying your SPAD. Who the hell ever gets to fly a SPAD these days?" I really didn't want a damn thing from him, then or ever.

"Bullshit!. You'll need something someday. How about a case of Glenlivitt for now?"

"Deal."

He left looking mighty happy. Curtains and I saw him out and both of us were smiling. He was a great old son of a bitch. Tough. Honest. Rich. Horny. The last was what really impressed me. An inspiration to live as long as I can.

He wasn't driving the '27 Rolls. He had a Bugatti of unknown vintage. It sounded like an old threshing machine, but I later learned it could go about a hundred and fifty miles an hour. He always held it down to a conservative hundred due to the condition of our local highways.

As he drove off and waved, I thought, *What a helluva friend he could be. Or enemy.* I loved the old bastard.

John Pelham

CHAPTER TWENTY-TWO

Dorothy had attracted the attention of the top men of her bank chain. No surprise if some of them had seen her at that seminar. They must have found out she was getting a divorce, too. Once upon a time that might have been a reflection on the bank. Today it's an invitation to the dance.

I have no doubt that she was fully qualified for almost any banking job, but also felt sure that she was about to be blessed by the civilian equivalent of that military female promotion system I mentioned before: "fucking up." In any case she was in line for the district manager's job. It required her to take several more seminars on the finer points of banking. Such as, no doubt, how to screw lifelong customers without arousing their suspicions till it's too late.

Sex Ring in a Small Town

"Don't get eye strain studying by the midnight oil," I cautioned her, seeing her off to the first of these seminars. It netted me an arch look. Curtains had his paws on her window sill and licked her hand goodbye, while she patted his round noggin. She eased her Olds 98 out of my circle drive and I waved goodbye, feeling a sinking sensation. I had a lot of emotional investment there, and so did Curtains. We both liked this lady a lot. I was sure wedding bells were in our future.

I thought, *If those bastards running the bank have their way, she's more apt to get back strain than eye strain.* In my opinion there was little chance of that. She had the love bug worse than I did. There's no truer heart than that beating in the breast of a woman who's been loved right for the first time.

I watched her car out of sight, wondering how I'd spend evenings alone for another week. Industrious toe-nail scraping on the asphalt behind me got my attention, especially since it was accompanied by a series of eager little whines. Beano-who-bit-the-bishop was straining at her leash, happy to see John-who-has-the-refrigerator. I discovered Stacey on the other end of the leash.

"Hi," she said, looking deliciously hippy and chesty in black sweater and slacks.

It didn't occur to me just then that she knew Dorothy had left town for awhile. "Coffee?" I asked, feeling my spirits pick up right smart.

"I thought you'd never ask."

"Lead the way and I shall precede."

She did. What a lovely ass. Did the fact that I knew about her and Pat turn me off? Or the added fact that Ole had called Pat "queer as a three dollar bill?" Fuck no! I didn't think this one was beyond recall for a major (or a colonel) modification.

I followed Stacey down the hall, recharging the batteries Dorothy had discharged a trifle earlier. Beano, now off her leash, was already seated before the refrigerator, looking hopeful.

"She's a quick study," I said. "She visited the other day and got Curtain's scraps."

"Did you bring her back?"

"I started but she slipped off Curtain's leash. His snap was too big for her collar ring, I guess." A nifty, quick fib, eh? What if I'd said, "Yeah, I did and boy did I get an eyeful through the window of that back bedroom." She'd probably have had a seizure, or at least invented a new lipstick shade blushing.

"You know where stuff is. You fix while I get the fireplace going."

"Oh, great! I love fireplaces on chilly days."

Before I left on that chore, I tolled Beano and Curtains out the back door with a porkchop bone apiece.

Did I then miraculously whip Stacey into the hot tub inside ten minutes, like Mike Hammer? Sadly, no. We sat facing the fire, balancing coffee cups, at opposite ends of my big couch.

She surprised me with a question, "Are you and Dorothy planning to get married when her divorce is final?"

Actually at least, I was, but said, "I'm not sure either of us wants to risk it again after what we were through. Would you do it again if you were single?"

She looked like I'd waltzed her off the floor she'd expected us to dance on, across the portico and into the bushes, and I quickly said, "It's none of my business."

"It's all right." Then, after a long silence, as though she'd been debating whether to tell me more, she said, "I really haven't had a bad marriage. More like none at all."

"Oh?"

Having gone that far she plunged ahead. "We only made love once . . . on our honeymoon." She laughed, a short staccato snort more wistful than amused, then added, "And I got pregnant." What she'd said was unexpected. A stunner, in fact.

I couldn't help but be my loveable self and exploded, "Jesus Christ! What the hell's the matter with him? Do you live together?"

She didn't seem offended or taken aback. It was probably about what she wondered herself. "He's in Samoa right now. With our son."

"What the hell are they doing there?"

"Proselytizing for the church. He's really very religious."

I got a picture of them in somber business suits, going from door to door, startling the barefoot locals who would be wearing lava lavas and sarongs, and probably jogging their memories about an old custom where missionaries were baptized by total immersion in big stew pots.

"Did you know this about him before you were married?"

"I really didn't know much about him at all, except that he was a star quarterback here in High School, and later in college; we both went to State."

Shades of tight ends ~ Madison Avenue will cook in hell for brain washing generations of American girls about football heroes. She continued her sad story, "One day he noticed me for the first time, proposed and we got married in a few days."

She looked and sounded far away. "I suppose I was lonesome. I never knew my mother, and my father had just died."

A light went on. She'd suddenly got very rich.

"Does the church finance his proselytizing?"

"Not entirely."

"So?"

She laughed. "I'm not as naive as I used to be. In fact I'm getting cynical."

It was an advance explanation of what she knew she was going to say next. "I have the impractical idiot on an allowance. Four thousand dollars a month."

"Jesus!" I said, "If he gets et by the 'ny-tives' somewhere, can I apply for the opening?"

"Why not?" she said, and gave me a no-doubt-deliberately-undecipherable look.

Regardless, it grabbed me right where I lived. Remember Stacey was the one who needed the dildo.

I thought, *Slow down, boy. You're an almost married man, in love. I also thought, "You know that's horseshit, Pelham. You've been the route. You don't really give a shit about any of that true-blue crap anymore, if you ever did.* Beware the man with his balls recently restored. And the other kind, too. The Coolidge Effect survives everything but rigor mortise, and perhaps castration.

"How about I fix breakfast?" I suggested, to give her a chance to get off what might be a touchy subject. "I'm aces with stuff that comes frozen, like hash browns ~ can even slice ham and seldom bust sunny-side-up eggs."

"I'm not a breakfast person. Coffee is fine. If you want to eat, Beano and I can hit the road."

I almost leaped up, grabbed her and blurted, "Jesus Christ, no! Don't rush off in the heat of the day." I did say the latter.

She said, "Do you really have all that stuff in the refrigerator?"

"Derned right."

"You'll make Dorothy a wonderful wife." She laughed. "Or did she stock your refrigerator?"

"Scout's honor. I kept a well-stocked refrigerator even before we started holding hands."

It was easy to read her "holding-hands-my-ass" look, but she only grinned. "I'm a nibbler during the day," she said, returning to the breakfast subject. "Maybe a salad at lunch. Then by dinner I'm starving and fix a regular meal."

"Even when you're alone?"

She nodded. "I've got so I almost like to be alone . . . most of the time."

It brought to mind my window peeping episode and I suddenly recalled her warm white bod, lovely and aroused; but not alone. "Why don't you come down for dinner then?" I suggested. "Sevenish."

"Why don't you come up for dinner, sevenish? I'm expecting a couple of business phone calls and have to stay home tonight."

All of this, of course, told me what I should have suspected.

I hadn't told her Dorothy would be out of town, but she knew. I didn't hesitate. Besides I wanted to see the inside of her place, especially the TV room in that back wing.

My heart wasn't in my work all that day. Liz Leonard showed up a little early and I had more coffee with her and smoked a cigar in the kitchen. Sometimes little old ladies in tennis shoes, of either sex, come to see the doctor by the front entrance, even though I'd put up a sign pointing the way to my professional lair. They could all smell stale cigar smoke, even the slightest whiff of it, and would wrinkle their noses like they had discovered dog shit under their fingernails.

I sifted the 3X5 cards for the day's appointments. They were fairly typical. Three new cigarette-quitting hopefuls, one from a small town at least a hundred miles away. Word was getting around. Two others were clients that had backslid, sneaked off a weed, and needed reinforcement. The local librarian was coming in for a concentration treatment, to improve her Dewey Decimals, or something.

We were also experimenting to see if we could speed up her reading and retention rates, and how much. I was getting really interested in that sort of thing.

It was going to be a light day, actually. There were a couple of women who wanted to learn to relax. I knew how to read that in the long run; it was spelled t-r-o-u-b-l-e.

Nonetheless, I couldn't turn them down, not even the homely ones. Whenever I thought I ought to, I'd look at how happy Liz looked compared to the first day she'd come to me.

She was turning out to be a first-rate girl Friday. I really liked her. I could talk to her without reservation. And, for you nasty minds, I had no aspirations there. Well, not just then anyhow. She was the kind I could have married and tried my damnedest to stay true-blue to until death did us part. She was pretty. And still stacked every bit as well as her daughter, Audrey. The latter prompted me to think of starting a defloration service. I'd have bet a bunch that Audrey was still a virgin, and lost.

My rough estimate was that I had at least a one thousand dollar day ahead of me, if we collected all that it would bring due. That's twenty thousand a month of five-day weeks, gang. I could make it on half of that, even paying off regularly to Putt Putt. I was waiting my chance to pay him off permanently. Something was bound to turn up.

Incidentally, Napoleon and Putt Putt had become a local item. Could it be Putt-Putt was gay? What else accounted for seeing them together several times, usually head to head, deep in conversation at the local coffee shop, totally unaware of my presence?

And Napoleon hadn't been back to see me about tensions. I still reinforced his team's fight though; once a week. So far no one had suggested paying me. Maybe they thought it was my civic duty. In time the team would get a booster club, due to me, but too late to pass the hat.

That day was a perfectly legal one, for the most part. Nonetheless, it could have earned me a lynching. Three ladies with tension problems, for instance. They all replicated Liz Leonard's case, including the treatment I gave them. Not one of them had ever had an orgasm with a man. Most of them had accidentally discovered how; by reading Jackie Collins. Two shame-facedly admitted they masturbated when the tension got to be too much for them, generally after they'd been raped by their rabbit.

I, quite simply, provided private surroundings for them to relax. I started what amounted to a hypno-whorehouse for them, all in their minds. Did they have a movie star that turned them on? You'd be surprised how many did, and who they were. What the hell ~ no double standard here; Ole had his harem, why not the ladies?

As time passed, I even started clubs among them. Lord knows what happened when they took it from there. I can imagine. Like Pat and Stacey. Read Dr. Ruth or Ann Landers where letters from this kind glory in their revenge.

These clubs, of course, were not pure philanthropy, though they netted me nothing but good will. I simply had too much other business to fit them all into my rooms. If I'd lasted, maybe I'd have had an architect build me a seraglio. I had all the paying customers I could accommodate. And they weren't all women by a long shot. At any given time I was apt to have a couple of men and a woman in adjoining rooms, relaxing at $100.00 a rap. Running full blast, the three surplus rooms were good for $300.00 an hour, helping frustrated souls get it off like Ole.

That was a hell of a lot better than I could have rented it for doctors or lawyers. Or as a health spa, though it might have qualified as that in a sense of the word. It was a hectic living though.

Despite all that diverting stuff, I was looking forward to dinner with Stacey Greer and got there at seven on the dot.

I regretted not being able to take Curtains up there for a social call on Beano, but there was always the chance that some of Dirty Harry had smudged off on Putt Putt. I sure as hell didn't need my current business on video tape ~ that is, someone else's videotape.

John Pelham

I had a lot of it on my own tape and that could be dangerous enough; Lord knows what I thought I could do with it. It could backfire like Nixon's White House tapes, a thought that had occurred to me. A time bomb ticking?

Sex Ring in a Small Town

CHAPTER TWENTY-THREE

Stacey undoubtedly had been looking forward to a *tete-a-tete* as much as I was, and had obviously been peeking out the window occasionally, because the door opened before I could ring the bell. "Enter," she said. "Do I see the perfect guest with a bottle of vintage wine in a grungy sack in his hand?"

"You see a guest with tulip bulbs in a grungy sack in his hand. Two dozen to be exact. I noticed you like plants. These are rare."

"You angel! I love tulips. They always look so brave and cheerful waving their heads around on a windy spring day." She kissed my cheek. Her lips were soft and warm, lingering longer than necessary. Holy shit what that did for me!

"What's your poison?" she asked."

"Scotch and soda," I told her, wrestling off my coat and being careful not to bump my .45 into anything. Of course, being a native born and bred she'd have understood the wisdom of carrying one, especially out there at night. She probably carried a .38 automatic in her purse wherever she went.

"Hang it in the hall closet," she said over her shoulder, "then follow my footprints down to the kitchen and watch me be domestic."

The house was lit up for a party. I wondered if anyone else was coming. I passed a large front living room and formal library opposite each other across the hall. Further along, divided by the hallway, were the dining room and family room. The former was set for just two, with all the formal dining doo-dads including a silver candelabrum. A fire was crackling invitingly in a fieldstone fireplace in the family room. How totally cool. The hall passed between a pantry and bathroom into the kitchen, a real country kitchen for sure, with another fireplace at the far end of it and a breakfast nook beside it. The whole house was tastefully decorated in a blend of contemporary and antique, accented by Mexican and Indian pieces; eclectic, but with emphasis on comfort, and nothing clashed.

She handed me a scotch that passed the sight test, obviously heavy on the booze. I thought, *I hope she's plying me with liquor."*

I looked around for evidence she was plying herself with liquor and didn't see any. "What're you drinking?" I asked.

"I'm a vodka martini freak before dinner, but I'm going to whip up a salad before I have one. Then we can sit in front of the fire."

I raised my glass in a solo toast. "To Beano and Curtains, our best friends. By the way, where is Beano?"

"Out back. Sulking. She's such a beggar at the table. I'll let her in when we're through eating."

Stacey was obviously no novice in a kitchen. I'd expected she might have a cook to handle guests. But cooks destroy intimacy, come to think of it. That didn't occur to me at the time. I've been a slow study with women. But I do learn.

She finished the salad, poured herself a martini from a prepared pitcher of them in the refrigerator and tuned up my scotch. Still working on our Mrs. Malaprop gag, she said, "I'll precede this time," and pointed the way.

Two monster overstuffed chairs with hassocks were angled toward the fire on each side, with an end table each, furnished with Moorish lamps, ashtrays and silver cloisonne coasters.

She invited, "Light up an evil weed if you want to. It won't bother me. I tried to give up cigarettes all my life, but was never able to until you helped me, so I don't really miss them. Besides they cut my wind skiing."

My expression must have telegraphed my surprise. "I do lots of weird stuff to keep me out of trouble." I'd buy that, almost; but I could have said something about orgies. Of course, they're my kind of trouble.

She raised her glass and saluted me. "Trouble," she said. "May it keep its nose out of our affairs." She knew more about where our affairs might be headed than I did. However, it was an appropriate toast under any circumstances.

I returned the salute. "Amen. A nice sentiment. Improbable, but a nice hope."

"Are you a pessimist," she asked, frowning a trifle.

"Far from it. I still believe in Santa and the Tooth Fairy."

She giggled, then her mood suddenly changed. "Have you had a lot of trouble?" she asked.

I thought of the beauties of Nam, then wondered how much she knew, or surmised about my late, disastrous marriage and how it may have twisted me.

That question caused me to ask myself, however, *Has my life really been the pits?* It really hadn't.

"If I fall over dead here in your chair, I'd have to say that life's been pretty good. No complaints. How about you, aside from a religious freak husband?"

That didn't ruffle her in the least. She thought awhile. "Outside of Dullsville sometimes, I guess most women would like to trade places with me."

At least she hadn't had her clod husband around long enough to discover that he was a lousy lover, like some had. A question popped into my mind and I asked her, "Who would you like to trade places with, if anyone?"

"The Red Baron. I always wanted to be a fighter pilot."

I laughed and so did she. What a nice laugh she had, open and friendly, a joyous sound like laughs should be.

"Are you a pilot?"

"Uh. Uh. Ole Sunderland tried to teach me to fly, but he said my coordination in the air is terrible." That caused her to laugh again at some thought. "What?" I asked.

"Ole told me if I solo'ed I'd probably 'bust my lovely ass,' as he put it. But I'm a pretty good rider. He told me to stick to horses. I was born on a ranch and lived there till I left for college."

"Do you have a horse?"

"Three. Ole keeps 'em for me. He's an old sweetie. You should meet him."

"I have."

"What did you think of him?"

"He's a four dollar pistol alright."

She giggled. "I never quite thought of him that way, but it's true." After awhile she added, "That's probably the way he sees himself ~ he still thinks he's twenty."

Twenty? Had Ole patted this sensational ass, or tried to do more, or done more? After all, he'd told me, holding up one finger, "I could do more for a woman with this finger than most men could with everything in their arsenal." I wondered what she'd say if I told her about Ole's harem?

We hit the bottom of our drinks and she asked, pretending to be drunkenly slurring her words, "nuther one?"

"Why not?" I watched her "lovely" ass to the door. She was wearing a dark green, clinging jump suit. By the time she undulated out of sight I knew I wanted to lay her something fierce, knew I would be looking for an opening to head that direction and my other "true love" could be damned. Boy was Mrs. Pelham's little boy John changing.

The chance wasn't long in presenting itself. She came back, set her drink down, then mine, then leaned over me with one hand on each arm of my chair, perched there and simply looked into my eyes. Then she lowered herself a little and put those warm lips on mine, her eyes wide open and dark, naked invitation plain in them.

Again I was amazed at how soft and warm her lips were, like a little girl just out of her bath. I took her shoulders in my hands and lifted her a trifle, looking down her jump suit in the bargain, then lowered her on top of me. She snuggled down and then rolled into the big chair beside me. Our lips came together naturally and clung probing each other a long while. I was conscious of everything she had, pressing eagerly against me. And I had a classic hard-on throbbing directly against where a woman really lives.

This wasn't leading to supper. We'd have been in bed in another five minutes if the goddam doorbell hadn't clanged.

"Shit!" Stacey muttered. My sentiments exactly. "We can't ignore it with the place lit up like the Big Apple. I'll get rid of whoever it is and be right back. Don't go away."

I wasn't going anywhere. I took a substantial gulp of my drink, feeling like Gangbusters, my hard-on lying in wait to greet her return, when Pat Sunderland's voice in the hall folded it up like a dishrag in no time. What a helluva time for her to drop in. Here, one can see my real genius as a lover ~ Don Juan got caught by a jealous husband, anyone can manage that, but consider what I got caught by. Few ever have.

Obviously Stacey couldn't push Pat out the door. Obviously Pat was going to butt in and find out who was there or die in the attempt. She certainly hadn't been told by her little patty-cake-friend that she was having a *do* that evening. I heard Stacey say, "I'm entertaining a neighbor you know. Come on in and join us for a drink. Have you eaten?" What the hell else was she going to say?

I couldn't hear what Pat said, but Stacey said, "I can throw on another steak with no trouble at all." Her voice sounded a trifle rushed and guilty to me, but I knew what we'd been doing, and what we were about to do, so maybe I just imagined that. Pat came in first and I could get up since she'd folded my hard-on into a limp biscuit. She couldn't wipe the startled look off her face quick enough.

"Hi," she said, and I knew she was making a mighty effort to make it casual. Nonetheless she'd had the look for just that first instant, of a jealous lover, or outraged husband. Undoubtedly a lot of factors caused that look: she knew that Dorothy had left town just that morning, that we were practically engaged, and therefore my presence here suggested I was an untrustworthy philanderer. Ergo. Her own turtle-dove was far from safe in my company. All the more so, since Pat probably drew the same conclusion I did about Stacey's weakness for Sundance, and need for a dildo. Stacey may have been just-like-that for girls, but she liked boys too. I was on the hot seat.

I probably didn't help a damn bit by saying, "Us widowers will do just about anything to con a free meal we don't have to fix ourselves."

The way the dining room table was set didn't exactly imply a Salvation Army soup kitchen, even to my unperceptive-clod, male mind. Stacey sidestepped an embarrassing situation by disappearing to get Pat a drink. She took her time about it, damn her, but I couldn't blame her for that.

Would you believe that Pat graciously bowed to the inevitable, had her drink and left as quickly as possible, even saying, "Three's a crowd?" Better not. If she had I'd have suspected she had another girl friend on the string.

The fact was she stayed for a steak and hung around afterward like a vampire. What had started out to look like it might be one of my better evenings had turned into a real bummer. Pat was still there when I thanked Stacey for the meal and headed home in the cold night air. I needed it. It was a real relief from the charged atmosphere inside.

On the other hand, if I hadn't been an accomplished window peeper, I wouldn't have noticed a thing. I should have circled around to see if Pat had come by because she wanted to play games. I didn't want to know. Or think that maybe I'd heated Stacey up so she needed Pat to get it on with. The situation reminded me of all the times I'd been shot out of the saddle by the bastard with the convertible in the days of my youth, when my *shit* old man hadn't let any of us have a car till we were eighteen.

CHAPTER TWENTY-FOUR

The next morning I called Stacey late enough to be pretty sure Skeezix was gone if she'd stayed overnight.
"Hello."
"Hi. Have the tulips come up?"
Long Pause. Then, "Click," a dead line.
I thought, *What sort of adolescent horseshit is this?* The answer was pretty obvious after I thought it over. An ultimatum had been delivered by a jealous lover. There had probably been a big spat, followed by hot wet kisses and love-making. After all they had been friends almost from the cradle, in addition to being lovers. What the hell right did I have to horn in there? In any case I didn't think it was a good idea to call right back, or to storm up there indignantly and

demand an explanation. She probably wouldn't have answered the door anyway.

So when Dorothy rolled back in Friday night I was still a virgin, so to speak. I was out back getting wood for the fireplace when the phone rang. I picked it up on the patio extension.

"Hello, my love, I'm back. Are you glad?"

"I was just thinking about you, trying to figure out how to slip you into my crowded schedule."

"I'll be over and slip you into something while you're thinking about it. But first I can use a shot, and a hot soak."

"You twisted my arm, you sweet talking devil."

"I'm on my way."

The next couple of hours were enough, almost, to return me to the path of virtue and rectitude. In the middle of the night I very groggily picked up the jangling telephone and heard a little, uncertain voice say, "Why don't you come up and we'll take up where we left off."

I had to say, "You must have the wrong number." If Dorothy woke up she must have heard me say "wrong number," since she didn't ask who it was, then or later, and women always want to know that sort of thing. Besides I might be reforming. Who am I kidding? I had a clear recollection of Stacey's petite, hard-body, eagerly pressing against me, asking for something she probably only suspected was out there somewhere waiting for her, and those startlingly warm lips. It was all too much for my billy goat nature.

Dorothy's seminar had certainly deepened her appreciation of money. Saturday morning she was full of such remarks as: "They're the smartest people in the world. And, you have no idea how sweet Banking is on the inside."

I'd have bought "shittiest" and "crooked" in place of smartest and sweet, with a lot fewer reservations than I did her starry-eyed appraisal. Screw them. Their kind ruined the deregulated Savings and Loan business, as I recall. Ivan Boesky and Mike Millken were just about to be found out. The great deregulator, Reagan, will be found out sooner or later. History will rank him for presidential impact on the well-being of America, in last place, just below Hoover and Jefferson Davis.

However, my motto is, "never let a little ideological difference spoil your relations with a sensational piece." That afternoon we were just waking up from a post-lovemaking nap when a horrendous roaring engine overhead shook the whole house.

"What's that?" she asked, sitting up startled.

I knew. It could only be the nonpareil, Diamond Dan.

"Relax," I said. "It's the end of the world. Nothing to worry about. As a matter of fact it's a helicopter, and unless I'm wrong an old friend has checked out of the Savoy in London and is about to check in the Pelham Arms."

The idiot obviously intended to put on an air show, because I could hear the whirly bird circling for a return pass. We quickly threw on some clothes and rushed out into the back yard. The yard wasn't unobstructed enough to land in or he'd probably have done it, and Curtains might have got his head chopped off trying to kill whatever was attacking us.

He came back, hovered and yelled down through a P/A system, "Meet me at the airport, Pel. Who's the blond?" With that he swooped off into the wild blue and putted out of sight over the ridge.

Dorothy looked at me for a further explanation. "He's an old friend," I said. And not being able to think of a way to get out of it, added, "You wanna come to the airport with me to pick him up?"

"Do you have many old friends like him?"

"Not a one."

"What kind of accent is that he talks with?"

"Bronx. Strictly a city mouth. And the worst I ever heard, come to think of it . . . are you coming or staying?"

"What do you think? What does he do?"

"He piddles around the film industry." Boy, if she only knew.

Diamond was in the airport waiting room scoping a magazine. He glanced up and noticed Dorothy first. It took him quite awhile to discover I was with her. She got a real mental molestation on the spot. It's a wonder she didn't feel him slipping it in.

Get this picture of God's Gift to Women. Five-ten and health-club lean. Six-two in his John Wayne uplifter boots. The boots had engraved silver toe plates inlaid with turquoise. He wore his trademark pants, stone washed jeans with specially tailored belt loops to accommodate a four inch carved belt with a saucer-sized solid gold buckle; the buckle was decorated with turquoise, coral and diamonds. He had a matching watchband. A golf shirt, of course, to show his delts and biceps which he kept bulgy by lifting weights. What sort of a face went with this? Lean. High cheek bones, John Barrymore's nose, deep-set light blue eyes, straight brows. A Hollywood Civil War mustache and sideburns, topped off with an Elvis' 50's hairdo, duck-tailed in back and heavily sprayed so not a hair was out of place. With his teeth in he also had a wonderful smile. His complexion was baby pink, which complemented his wavy, distinguished graying hair.

In short, an irresistible hunk to almost all women and, if I do say so myself, looking like a prosperous Border-town pimp. Eventually he noticed me. He popped up and walked over briskly, hand extended, shook, turned his eyes back to Dorothy, and said, "I don't have to ask you what you've been up to, Pel?"

"Dorothy, this is an old friend, Dan Dulaney. Dan, meet Dorothy, my banker. You caught us in the middle of a business discussion, so I brought her along."

He laughed, but didn't say anything. His expression said it for him,

Business, my ass. On Saturday? A telling point.

Dorothy was apparently going to be one of the majority of women captivated by him. They tried to blind one another with ivories and I almost said, *Hold it for the cameras.*

She said, "Pleased to meet you."

And get this; he bowed over her hand, kissed it and said, "Charmed, my dear."

Holy moley. Nobody else I know can carry off that syrupy shit without netting a laugh. She looked like she was going to trip him and beat him to the ground. I thought, *Wait'll she finds out the bastard is rich.* Well, I've had my time beaten before. With dismal regularity, come to think of it. I'd rather have it be Diamond Dan than Coach Lawson or the Rev. Leonard, to name just a couple. Besides there was Stacey lurking out there.

On the subject of beating my time, who should walk in just about then, but the world's second greatest lover, Xavier Fernandez? He, Dan and I had had some good and bad adventures together in Nam and elsewhere in the Army, usually drunk at the time. Hev, as he was generally known to his friends, was also known as the poor man's Harry Bellafonte, though I can't imagine why. He was better looking than Bellafonte, for one thing. He hailed from somewhere in the Caribbean. "What the hell are you doing here, as if I didn't know?" We hugged like a couple of lunatics. We'd gone to the Army's Mohawk airplane driver school together way back when and followed each other around, borrowing money from one another, for ten years before he burned out on the Army's chicken-shit and slow promotions and took a job flying for Diamond Dan.

"I'm flying asshole's Gulfstream, to keep him from killing himself." Then, pretending to notice Dorothy for the first time, which was a bunch of shit too ~ he'd probably already screwed her mentally like Diamond had, maybe twice. "Whoops! Pardon my language, ma'am. I didn't notice you there."

This smooth article knew how that would fly with a sensational-looking blond whose ego was everything you'd expect.

"What did you say?" she asked. "I'm so used to John's language it must have sounded normal."

Boy, did she ever blow my casual business acquaintance story there. Diamond put a hand over Hev's mouth. "Ne'mine. He's just an ignorant field hand, ma'am."

Do you imagine that ruffled the field hand? Sorry to disappoint some of you. He got unmuzzled and said, "Yassah, Massa. I'ze sorry I demeaned us in front of the quality."

He was grinning like an evil genie. Deep in his heart he was already planning revenge. He'd probably piss in a bottle of Diamond's choice scotch, or something equally outrageous sooner or later, then tell him after he drank it.

"Unless you've laid something on we've got to get to right away," Dan said, "I want to give you guys the tour of my new Gulfstream before we head into town."

What a machine. He must have put two million bucks worth of extras into it. It had beds, a movie theater, computers, galley and dining room, all compact but luxurious, and the normal seat compartment handled only six. Diamond didn't believe in dragging a retinue around with him. He thought "yes-men" sucked; one reason he wasn't about to go broke. I recall hearing him say several times, "Look at the world through rose-colored glasses and you'll soon be looking at the want ads for a new job." True. I wonder how bastards like Harboldson survived. They all love "yes-men."

I was ready to make the supreme sacrifice and not only bartend all evening at my place, but cook steaks. Dorothy rescued me and took us all to the country club. Country clubs are worse than officers' clubs in my opinion, which is to say a half-mile from the peons but a million miles from real society. However, the town banker gets you the best in one, something like a commanding general. It was,

"Oh, good evening, ma'am. Nice to see you again." And we didn't get seated in the draft from the front door or in front of the can, or the kitchen.

Diamond and Hev were what a woman like Dorothy needed. They listened politely to everything she said, and asked questions as though an interest in her opinions was the uppermost tenet of their most sacred beliefs. Flattery will get you a lot with most women, though they all profess to be impervious to it.

All I'm sure of from the shank of the evening on, is that I woke up the next morning with a darb of a headache. Everyone obviously had plenty to drink. I'd like to have slept about two days, but the phone woke me up around eleven A.M.

"Aren't you men ever going to wake up?"

"Oog!"

"That bad, eh?"

"Worse."

"I got some super little pills from the banking industry for surviving business dinners. I was in the same shape a few minutes ago. They really work."

"Bring some over." I collapsed into a recliner. I could vaguely recall that Dorothy had insisted us old Army types would want to reminisce and that she needed to go home to bed after a hard week.

Her pills really worked. I almost came to life. We were having a dynamite Bloody Mary together in the living room when an apparition appeared at the hall door.

It wore only baby blue nylon briefs, and was barely recognizable as Diamond Dan without his hair spray or false teeth. Pretty familiar togs for short acquaintance with a lady; I still wasn't cynical enough to wonder whom old Diamond might have been visiting after I passed out.

"How do you feel?" I asked him.

"Great. Why?"

I also didn't suspect he might have brought back a little supply of the same kind of pills that had revived me.

A phone call dragged Diamond away and he was gone about a half-hour. By the time he got back, more or less dressed and polished, I'd recovered enough to be thinking about eating, so we all had breakfast, Hev, having shown up, fully clothed, in the meantime.

"I'd like to stay around a few days," Dan said, "but a hot deal just broke with a lot of dough hanging on it."

I could believe both remarks. He was still sticking it into Dorothy mentally, running neck and neck with Hev. What a duo. They were almost as horny as me, the dirty bastards.

Diamond Dan flew back to Hollywood in his Gulfstream, having a ferry crew to fly the new chopper. That night I got a call from him. His first words were the corny old Hollywood dialogue from movies like Hells Angels. "Well, I cheated death again."

"I can believe that, if you were doing the flying."

"No way. I co-pilot only. No time to stay proficient. That's why I keep Hev around. Well, not entirely. He pimps for me too."

"Speaking of cheating death, you should have tried out the SPAD I flew the other day."

"SPAD?"

"Yeah. SPAD. S-P-A-D. Like Eddie Rickenbacker."

"No kidding?"

"Nope." I told him about Ole's stable of antiques.

"I'd like to meet the old guy. He must have a shit-pot full of money to keep a bunch like that flying."

"Enough, I guess. He was an ace in WWI."

"How old is he?"

"Ninety, pushing ninety-one."

"I'd like to meet the old bastard before he dies."

"He says he's not planning to die."

"Good. Now, down to what I called you about. Are you fucking your neighbor across the street?"

"How you *do* go on. She's not my type. I told you we had a business relationship."

"If you aren't laying her you ought to have your head examined."

"I didn't exactly say I wasn't fucking her; I said she wasn't my type. Hell, I take on a charity job every once in awhile."

"That sounds more like it. That's mighty big of you. Hey, she's every man's type. I was thinking of getting you sessions with a good shrink for Christmas."

"You're nothing but a fuckin' jewel, buddy. All heart."

"Again, that brings me to what I called about. Do you think that blond charity job would like to be in pictures?"

"Skin flicks?"

"Why not?"

"I doubt it."

"Money talks."

"How much money?"

"Lots. A quarter of a million for starters."

"Peanuts. She's got her eye on a multi-billionaire."

"Who?"

"The old guy with all the airplanes."

"Jesus Christ!"

"No, Ole Sunderland."

"I want to meet him for sure."

"Why? To con him?"

"Nobody puts the grift on that kind. I've got a legit business deal he might go for."

"Such as?"

"Buying up one of the major studios. I'm getting tired of looking at rushes of pubic hair."

"I'll bet."

"How do I get to meet this guy? You think you could swing an introduction?"

"Maybe. I'll think about it."

"You do that. Meanwhile, back to your banker."

"Call her up. Put the proposition to her. You can never tell. She might figure a bird in hand is worth two in the bush. Lovely bush, . . . and a quarter mil' isn't peanuts." I was confident she'd tell him to shove it, of course.

He said, "Actually, I'm thinking of doing a quality soft porn thing. She wouldn't have to do anything but sit around in restaurants with some handsome stud and do some courtship stuff, all on the up and up. We haven't appealed to the really big audience that wants to see some romance before they get to the hair and sweat. So *I* might just call her up."

"No screwing?"

"No screwing. If we do any of that, we'll get a double."

Why was I believing this bullshit? Well, for one thing he was right. Women, especially, want some romance in even skin flicks. I never met a nice one yet that wasn't turned off by the straight thing, wham, bam. It's the hard-drinking ones too far down the line that buy the stuff called "Stroking Studs," and that sort of horseshit and stroke themselves off with the boys.

He said, "Meanwhile, work on the billion bucks. If you bring this off I'll give you a piece of the action."

"Like what? The last million dollar deal I put you onto you gave me an electric toothbrush."

"Hell. That was a practical joke. You said you didn't want a cent."

"Pure rhetoric. Send me a 'finder's fee' contract on this one and I might go for it."

"How much?"

"Ten percent of the gross I get for you."

Diamond Dan seldom gets serious about anything. You can tell when he does because he gets quiet. He was quiet for a long while.

I thought maybe the connection had broken, when he finally said, "You're on. Ten percent may be a little high if we get up into the real big numbers, but I'm serious about going legit. I just don't want to have to fuck with bankers anymore."

"All bankers?"

He laughed. "Investment bankers."

I'm going to shorten this business to say that I interested Ole in the fabulous, traditional Christmas junket to Copenhagen.

He said, "I'd like to romp around a big bed with a half dozen bosomy Scandahoovian whores. Hell, I'm a Swede myself."

CHAPTER TWENTY-FIVE

My faithful-girl-Friday, Liz Leonard, showed up that Monday morning very late. Her face was a dead giveaway that something was gravely wrong. Since she said nothing, I finally asked, "You're looking a trifle peaked, Liz. Are you under the weather, maybe coming down with flu or something?"

She tried to smile. "I'm not feeling up to par, that's a fact."

"Why don't you take the day off and go home?"

"No! I don't want to go home!"

Later, after my last morning appointment, I looked across at her and she was crying quietly. I crossed to her desk and put my hand on her shoulder. "Tell Papa."

Then the dam broke. She started crying like a kid.

Tell me," I said, again. "It always helps."

"I can't," she wailed, and tried to look at me.

"C'mon back here in my other office. If someone comes in they'll think I beat you."

She tried to follow me and ran into the corner of her desk, blinded by tears. I had to lead her. I knew that sanctimonious son of a bitch of a husband of hers had to be somewhere at the root of this much grief. Once in my inner office she fell into my arms like a heartbroken kid wanting to be comforted. I knew it would be best to let her cry it out awhile. I just held her gently. Finally her sobs let up a little and she drew away and looked around for a Kleenex.

I gave her my handkerchief. "Sit down," I invited her. "You can tell me all. I'll never tell or make any judgements, you know that."

She looked at me, absolutely torn between her whole life's social conditioning to face adversity with a stiff upper lip, and the dire need for a friend.

Finally she said, "I can't talk about it. Not to anyone."

But I knew she had to ~ otherwise, as bad off as she was, she might kill herself. So I put her to sleep without asking her by-your-leave. What the hell. I'd never done it before, but this wasn't like taking advantage of a woman.

Here is the blow-by-blow of what had devastated her, in her own words.

"I started to work and remembered I'd left behind the Christmas cards I had to mail; so I drove back. I let myself in as quiet as a mouse, since the Reverend had been working late on his sermon and I knew he'd want to sleep till noon, at least. I was about to slip out again when I heard a noise in the back of the house somewhere. It was a funny noise, like a hurt animal.

I thought maybe Audrey had accidentally left her dog in her bedroom when she left for school, so I slipped back and very quietly opened her bedroom door so I wouldn't wake up my husband. My first thought when I looked in was: *Someone has Audrey on the bed and is raping her.* Before I could scream for the Reverend to come help or move to pick up something and try to hit whoever it was, I heard Audrey moan and say, 'Oh, Daddy, Daddy, do it to me hard!' She and her father were doing it like two barnyard animals, him thrusting away like a pig, the way I hate it. He wasn't forcing her. She loved it. I wanted to just slip away and go somewhere and never come back. But Audrey opened her eyes and caught me. She said, 'Oh, my God, it's Mama!' He jumped off and stood there with his nasty big thing still standing up and it was even throbbing and said, 'Oh, Liz!' It would have been funny if it wasn't so disgusting. I said, 'You horrible, horrible man!' He said, 'She seduced me the first time!'"

How long has this been going on?' I asked them. He was too scared to lie. He said, 'Since she was fourteen.' Imagine that, three years. By then his dirty, big dong was almost shriveled up. Audrey hadn't said anything. She'd got covered up under the bedspread. I asked her, Did your father force you? She said, 'Oh, no, I love him. I really love him.' Then she said, 'It isn't like the dark ages when inadequate women like you were raised dumb. He needs me for God's work! You can't help him release his tensions so he can really do God's work.' I couldn't believe my ears. I screamed, 'You little slut! You're a monster! And he's a monster! Neither of you know what God means.' He started to cry then, like a big, fat baby. Would you believe it? Big tears rolling down his cheeks. Then he shouted in his preaching voice: 'Forgive me Liz! Forgive me, God!' I said, 'God may forgive you, but I never will!' And I ran out of the house. I wanted to kill myself. Knowing him, I know he had to finish up to relieve his tensions. They were probably back at it before I was a block away. I felt like throwing-up."

That was the end of Liz's story. I changed her into her other personality as Maud and left her sleeping peacefully.

It wasn't hard to figure out what had to be done. I had to find some place for her to stay ~ a refuge away from the memories that might drive her to suicide. And I had to wipe those memories out of her consciousness permanently. Where to put her? I couldn't keep her with me or people would jump to the wrong conclusion. Where else? Ole Sunderland had told me to call him if I needed a favor. I sure as hell needed one in this case.

He answered his phone on the first ring. "Sunderland here."

"Ole," he insisted I call him that although I wasn't exactly comfortable doing it. "It's John Pelham. I need a little help on something damned delicate. I hate to bother . . ."

"Bother, my ass. What the hell do you need?"

I told him Liz's sad story.

"Jesus Christ! That rotten bastard! Bring her out here. We'll put her up and see that no one bothers her."

So I drove Liz out there. Ole met us at the front door.

He said, "I told Skeezix about her. She'll be right down and take it from here."

Liz acted like she was still in a daze and went with Skeezix like a dog on a leash. "Don't worry about a thing, John," Skeezix said. "I can handle this. I can give her a job, too. There's no need for her to go there again." She didn't say home. Liz had started to cry again.

Ole said to me, "You look like you could use a drink."

"About a double, double double."

"Follow me." He led me to another study on the first floor, a lot smaller than the tower room and showed me the bar. "Help yourself." He flopped into a king size leather executive chair and propped his feet on his desk.

I tossed off a quick, straight shot, "Ahhhh!"

"Christ, you really did need a belt. I used to feel like that after flying a mission in a SPAD. No parachutes. You knew if you got shot down in flames you couldn't walk on air. Sooner or later it got to you and you got tight as a fiddle string. We all drank like fish, ... you're getting tight as a fiddle string running that show down there. Do you think the people you're helping give a shit for you? Sooner or later someone is going to blow the whistle. I wouldn't be surprised if that woman's husband goes after you when she doesn't come home. I'm going to offer you a parachute."

I waited to hear what he had in mind.

"I've got a job for you."

"What?"

"How the hell do I know yet? I'll think of something. You're dead honest. I need someone like that. They don't grow on trees. How about administrative assistant, whatever the fuck one of those is?"

We both laughed. I said, "I've seen some of those. I should pay you if what you have in mind is apt to be like the usual Admin. Assistant's job."

He laughed. "Don't worry about the details ~ we'll figure them out as we go along. I guess I can afford a pretty fair salary in the meantime."

I thought about it all the way home, and after I got there. The more I thought it over the more it sounded like charity. Curtains met me at the door and we had our usual wrestling match. "I'm glad you're not after my balls," I told the big, black ape, and got a grin. He knew exactly what I said.

The next morning I put in a call to a retired friend, a fellow madman who'd taken his psychology degree with me in the Army. Only he went ahead and got his doctorate and worked at it. I knew something about him the rest of the world didn't, except for a few hundred ladies? And assorted close friends like me. He had a worse set of billy goat balls than I did, and as soft a heart.

I didn't mince words with him, after the usual, "Hey, pal, what the hell is going on, and what have you been doing, etc."

I said, "How would you like to take over a cushy racket?" I knew the bastard would. He's widowed like me and would draw to an inside straight ~ playing bridge! So I took my first step in turning over my business to someone cut out for it better than I. I simply couldn't cut and run on a lot of people that needed me.

The next morning I got a call from the Rev Leonard. I had expected one the night before. Maybe he was used to driving Liz out for a night. He, of course, wanted to know if I knew where Liz was.

"I haven't the foggiest," trying to sound genuinely alarmed.

"Have you called the police?"

"I don't think that would be wise just yet."

"Why not?"

"She's getting to be at that difficult age."

I could barely strangle the urge to say, *Most women are at a difficult age when they surprise their husband fucking their daughter.* I said, "I hadn't noticed. She looked O.K. to me when she left here at noon yesterday. She said she was going to do a little Christmas shopping."

"If she comes in, let me know."

"I sure will."

"I'm worried."

"Are you sure you shouldn't call the police?"

"No, she's done this before."

I thought, *I'll bet, you gold-plated prick!*

A few months have passed since then, and I'd bet he still doesn't know what happened to her, unless he or the police checked with the passport people.

On the Gulfstream, headed for the Christmas escapade in Copenhagen, were Hev and Diamond up front in the cockpit, herding the bird, and back in the passenger compartment were, yours truly, Dorothy, Ole, Skeezix, and the latter's new social secretary, Liz.

I thought Liz was making a remarkable recovery from the whole thing. In fact she looked like a kid going to a Christmas party. Did she ever look good in a form-fitting jump suit with proper makeup and hairdo, maybe for the first time ever. Skeezix was transforming her into a real beauty. I wondered what else she was planning to transform her into, if she hadn't already.

Sex Ring in a Small Town

John Pelham

CHAPTER TWENTY-SIX

This was the third time I'd been looking out an airplane window on the approach to Kastrup Airport, and I had yet to see the ground till we'd busted about five hundred feet on G.C.A. final. Quite disgustingly, Hev greased the Gulfstream onto the ground, rather than making one of those controlled crashes the airlines specialize in; one's fellow pilots always hope you'll stub your toe and bounce, at the very least. He'd pulled a grease job coming into Kennedy and did it again, damn him.

When we deplaned it was the usual Copenhagen thirty degrees; typical December. We were met by Diamond's exec. producer of his second unit that he had shooting some kind of porno-extravaganza downtown.

Sex Ring in a Small Town

We whipped through customs and got our baggage into a Dulaney Productions Lincoln limo and headed for town right smart.

Let me fill you in on Diamond's relationship to the Danish capital; it undoubtedly stems from a state policy put remarkably well in a literary classic known as Sexiary Tourist Guide for the Sex-Life of Copenhagen, which I quote verbatim: ". . . Today a new fairy-tale is being written, one which will make little Denmark even more famous than Hans Andersen was able to. The fairy-tale is about a country whose government have been planning so much ahead that they have given people the right to a free and uninhibited sex-life."

It was a natural environment for an American boy who'd graduated from selling overpriced roofing jobs to the elderly and dumb in Northern California.

We might have stayed in stately splendor in a grand hotel such as the Hotel d' Angleterre, a Danish institution, or the ultra-modern Sheraton Copenhagen, but Diamond's needs and connections took us to another first-class hostelry; never mind the name. I don't want Copenhageners to get wry necks staring at the windows of the top two floors in passing, wondering if Dulaney has a unit in town working up there. Actually he has one up there most of the time; it's safer from a bust than in La La Land, loose as that is most of the time.

We entered from the rear alley into a garage that most people probably don't know exists, and went up in private elevators that serve only the top two floors. They don't even connect to the kitchen and bar, since Diamond has his own, which employ ultra-discreet personnel.

The Sunderland's and Liz had a suite, Dorothy and I another, and Dan and Hev each had their own for convenience in entertaining sundry strumpets, all in a row down the hall. I'll drop a clue here; ours had a nice view of the center of town.

When we were settled in with our luggage, Dorothy looked out the window and said, "I want to go see the Mermaid."

Everyone wants to go see Copenhagen's famous mermaid, the Little Mermaid of Andersen's fairy tale, sculpted by Edward Eriksen. She sits on a rock on the *Langelinie* promenade with a view of the harbor.

"Seen one mermaid ya seen 'em all."

"I intend to take full advantage of a chance to be a tourist and see the sights."

"Me too. I notice there's a hot tub in here almost like mine. Would you like a conducted tour?"

She gave me an arch look. "Maybe. What's in it for me?"

"Cripes, you've only been around old Diamond twice and you're beginning to sound like him."

"I always thought like him."

"I guess we all do."

"Not Honest John Pelham."

I looked at her for a clue to what she was driving at. I didn't get one and had to ask. "What does that reflection on my healthy avarice imply?"

"I've been chatting with Ole Sunderland."

"And?"

"He says your talents have done wonders for his memory."

I thought, *Oh, oh. The balloon goes up. I knew what she had in mind for him if I ever got him in my Svengalian clutches.*

"You don't know the half of what I've done for his memory, sweetheart."

"So?"

"I'll draw you a specific diagram. He's one of the shrewdest takeover artists in the business. And he's more dangerous than a Carl Icahn, since he never gets publicity when he does it."

She looked at me for reaction and I only looked expectantly at her for the rest of the diagram.

Finally she said, "You - we - pick his brain. Anything he takes over appreciates in price anywhere from half again to double in a matter of days. He buys, we buy. We all get rich."

Just to argue, I said, "He's already rich."

And she, quite predictably, said, "And we ain't."

I thought I might as well take the bull by the horns. "I can't see it."

She flared at once. "Why not?"

"It ain't honest."

"How about sicking a mad knife wielder on Dirty Harry? Was that honest?"

"He asked for it. I did that as much for you as for myself."

"And you'll be doing this for me, and indirectly yourself, whether you think so or not. It's Christmas. That's the Christmas present you can give me."

"I'll think it over."

"Start now or you may have a very dry vacation in Copenhagen."

I don't take "cut-your-water-off-if-you-don't" threats from women. It's the cheapest thing to do with sex. Using it as a weapon is the best way to kick love straight out the window, I put it as succinctly as the case demanded. "Fuck you, sweetheart."

She replied, overly sweet, "Are we seeing another John Pelham here for the first time?"

She was indeed. And I thought it was a good time to tell her about it. "Damn right. I don't take cheap threats. Furthermore, it's almost impossible to spend a dry vacation in Copenhagen. Ass comes up out of the ground."

"How about AIDS?"

"As you found out, a man doesn't have to take a dip in the deep, quiet, inner recesses to get it off."

She thought that over. Finally, she must have cooled down a little and said, "I'm sorry." It's possible she was. I was willing to buy that just to get off the subject. But it chilled whatever I had in mind for the immediate future. I headed out the door instead of for the hot tub.

"Where are you going?" she asked.

"Down to see Diamond Dan. I just thought of something. I'll be back." I didn't say when. I got back about two hours later, after a trifle of what is sometimes known as libating. Ole Sunderland came over and joined us. Diamond ran some of the most salacious skin flicks for us that it's ever been my questionable pleasure to look at. He was having trouble occasionally, during the showing, with his wide screen electronics. "You're a communications and electronics genius," he said to me, "or at least you've horse-shitted old Harboldson into thinking so. How about fixing this fucker?"

I did. In the process I found a big closet full of electronic shit related to his video setup. Some of what I saw aroused my curiosity, but I didn't ask him about it. The thought went through my mind, however, that it would bear looking into later if I got a chance alone.

What Diamond said about a communications and electronics genius gave Ole the idea he needed to give me that job he'd mentioned earlier. "You really are a communications specialist?" he asked me. "I mean not just a hobbyist?"

Diamond said, "The sonofabitch was the brains of the Army's ELINT (electronic intelligence) before he retired, and I might add, pissed them off big time by retiring."

"I told the bastards they could always promote me to B.G. and I might think about staying."

"I thought you were strictly a pilot?"

"I was scared of falling out. The last ten years or so I flew Harboldson around, but I also flew a desk in the electronic spook business."

Ole didn't pursue the subject further, but it would bear some mighty interesting fruit. After awhile he and Diamond started talking big deals and I tuned out, thinking of my difficulties with Dorothy. I'd really thought we might have wedding bells in our immediate future. I wondered if she'd been doing parallel thinking, or was primarily interested in me for other reasons. I was beginning to lean to the latter. She'd set me up in the Svengali business, in a sense of the term. I was dreading the thought of going back to the room and facing her. However, I knew I had to go sooner or later and the sooner the better. I unlocked the door and walked in cautiously. She wasn't there.

John Pelham

CHAPTER TWENTY-SEVEN

This was beginning to shape up enough like my not-so-great, late marriage that I felt like puking. I staved that off long enough to look around for another drink. I found the bar and looked for Scotch, but obviously some local had stocked the bar and it had a small refrigerator full of Tuborg beer and a shelf on which was a lone bottle of Aalborg Akavit. Normally I'd as soon drink kerosene as Akvavit, despite all the bullshit about its quality, etc. It's the Dane's favorite for *skolling*. I thought, *What the hell.* I poured a hooker, and opened a Tuborg, knowing I'd need a quick chaser, and did the classic *Skol*, looking myself in the eyes in the mirror above the bar, lowered my head, tossing it off and looking at myself again - and what a face I looked at. I tossed down some Tuborg to put out the fire.

However, don't knock local dynamite. After it sat awhile, it felt like another one, and another one. If Dorothy came in during the night, she found me passed out on the divan. Danish modern, of course. Someone came in and lovingly (maybe) covered me with a blanket, because I was under one when I woke up and headed for a glass of water, or several. What a fuckin' hangover I had. I went back and collapsed on the divan for another couple of hours. When I woke up I found some of Dorothy's' little hangover tablets and a note that read: *Gone to a business meeting with Ole and Diamond ~ honest.*

I staggered into the bathroom for more water and scarffed down a couple of the little black pills, then back to the divan again. It was almost noon when Dorothy woke me up.

"Sorry to bother you, but I thought you might have died."

"So did I. Thanks for the pills."

We looked at one another warily.

Anticipating a question I might have asked, she said, "I went out to find something to eat last night when you didn't come back. I was starved. Did you find the dining room?"

"Uh, uh. Where is it?"

"Down the hall to the right and around the corner. Bar right next to it."

Somehow, I didn't think I'd need a bar for about a week. "What sort of business meeting did you go to?" I asked. I had visions of a meeting with Hev or Diamond on a king-size bed. Women have been known to do that sort of thing when piqued sufficiently.

"I met our genial host at dinner last night, and Ole with him. They were looking for someone to put together a deal for them. They were talking about investment bankers to thrash out the details of the sort of thing my girls out at the installment loan desk do every day of the week. I got the notion they figured it would all be over the pretty head of a small town banker. Are big business men really that thick?"

"I've never talked business with one, so I don't know. I've read the Harvard Business Review and my guess is the Japanese would never have sunk us economically without American business schools to fuck up our board chairmen and CEO's. The likes of Henry Ford, or Walter Chrysler, or Edison would have tied them in knots, but none of those guys ever went to school beyond the fourth grade, as I recall. Schools didn't have time to brainwash them."

We were avoiding discussion of our little falling out, but not kidding one another about what was really bothering us. I decided to have it out. Maybe it was the Akavit's after-effect. I felt horny.

"How would you like to get married in Copenhagen?"

She looked genuinely startled, even pained. I didn't know that she'd reached a decision about us based on her little business meetings.

She bit her lip. "I don't think so," all the while not looking at me. "I don't think I'm ready to get married again."

"Why not?"

"Isn't this a little sudden? Do we have to decide this instant? I might have said yes a month ago."

"And what's happened since to change your mind?"

"Business, for one thing."

"Our argument for another?"

"That too. You were being a little immature."

There's nothing that pleases me half so much as to have some snot-nosed bitch tell me I'm being immature.

I snorted. "When the hell have principles become immature?"

There was something in the look that netted me from her that put me on guard. I'd seen that look before. My ex was good at it, particularly when she was making such stunning remarks as, "The pill has liberated millions of women," or "Why can't a person do what they want to?" The look was what is called *possessed*. A devil lurks behind such eyes, not the person one thought they knew so well.

"You can't eat principles," she said.

"Neither of us is starving," This wasn't leading anywhere that would improve the situation.

She blurted. "Starving is relative. As a matter of fact, I'm going to be a lot further from it than I was yesterday morning. I was just hired as Comptroller of Dulaney Productions."

"I'm not surprised. Did you read your contract? Watch out for the final clause in it that he's bound to have picked up from the Army that reads: 'Such other duties as required'."

That must have stung her female pride.

"You think that's all he wants? When Dan hired me, Ole said, 'I wish I'd hired her first'."

(Ah, now it was Dan. How cozy.) I got in deeper by observing "Why didn't he top Diamond's offer then? He could."

She was obviously thinking that over. The connotation took a little of the pleasure from her triumph in letting me know she could now buy and sell me.

"Am I permitted to ask how much he's going to pay you?"

"A quarter million a year." That was a sum to rave over. So I did.

"Congratulations. This makes you a real catch. You could support me in the manner I'd like to get accustomed to. Will groveling help?"

"Don't be immature again. As a matter of fact I'm moving into another suite."

"Hev's or Diamond's?" I inquired.

She slapped me hard, instead of laughing it off. Another goddam prom-queen tactic in my book.

I returned the compliment hard enough to knock her on her ass.

I half-expected her to get up screaming, biting and clawing. Instead she gave me her Devil Anse Hatfield look as she got up. Her face was red, but she wouldn't have a black eye.

"If I had a gun I'd kill you," she said.

"I believe you. And being scared of getting shot isn't the reason I'm apologizing for doing that. I lost my temper."

She only looked at me, not softening the "I'll kill you" look a single bit. Then she headed for the door. "I'll send someone back for my things."

She stormed out and almost ran over Diamond coming in. He looked startled. "What the hell was that all about?"

"What they call a lovers' spat,"

"It looked more to me like the smoke settling after the Gunfire at the OK Corral."

"Actually it was. The honeymoon is over. The whole affair is over."

"Tough shit." There's always another one coming down the road."

Then he dropped the subject. "I came to give you a key to my suite. I'd like you to check out my electronic setup. You saw what it was doing last night. It acts like it's got Saint Vitus Dance. No hurry."

"I might as well hurry. I won't be doing anything else, I suspect."

"The place is yours all afternoon. Ole and I are going to be across town with some other people; the ones I met at the Savoy that want to tie up porno-flicks in the Common Market. We might not be back till midnight. I'm taking your bitch along; whatever else you say about her, she's one hell of a banker."

"She's not my bitch any longer. You're welcome to her. You should have seen the look she gave me."

"I can imagine. I probably saw the same look when my five wives tried to shoot me after we split up."

"Five?"

"Okay, Actually seven, but I'm still married to two of them, technically."

I thought, *Holy Shit! This guy is serious.* But not too serious.

He laughed his booming, "Haw! Haw! Haw!"

I wished I could take it all as lightly as he seemed to. I felt raw inside, as though I needed mama to console me after stubbing my big toe. A little tact on my part and the blow-up wouldn't have taken place. And I'd have been stuck with the equivalent of the Hatfields versus the McCoys without knowing it. *You lucked out, boy,* I told myself. *In a few days you'll forget all about it.* The question is, nevertheless, what to do right then, not in a few days. I was horny; maybe there's something to be said for Satan after all. I decided to get something to eat, then tackle Diamond's electronic instrument of the devil to take my mind off things. I hoped I wouldn't meet Dorothy anywhere. After all, I had meant it when I asked her to marry me. I was probably in love with her. Therefore, I was already asking myself why I should hang around for Christmas with a pall hanging in the air. Looking at her and being reminded it was all over would be painful. Why not grab a SAS flight to New York and a domestic flight home? I might even be able to get a direct flight over the pole.

CHAPTER TWENTY-EIGHT

Diamond had everything I needed to do a thorough trouble-shooting job. I looked over that back closet where the central control unit was and wondered what the hell kind of stuff he had hooked up that required a control console that complicated. It didn't take long to figure out. He had the whole complex covered with hidden cameras and mikes, in every one of the suites. Of course, in his business, the utility of that was obvious. On the other hand I made a note not to be starred on candid camera loping my mule in the can or watching a sexy video. What a laugh old Diamond and Hev would get out of some footage like that of me.

I experimented with the console and discovered that each apartment could be photographed from several cameras; there wasn't a nook or cranny outside the closets that couldn't be shot by some one of the cameras. After a little messing around I discovered that the five-foot square screen could be viewed in its entirety or electronically separated into four segments, showing different angles of the same scene. When I got to Ole's suite with the scanner, I was just mortally forced to stop and do a thorough inspection of a plumb fascinating scene. Skeezix was standing by the phone in her birthday suit. I got a pleasant pang looking over that classy ass, just as I had the last time. In fact old junior was rising rapidly again. She dialed some number and I noticed a light flash on one of a bank of phones in my control booth. That bastard Diamond also was able to monitor all the phone calls in the place. I threw a switch on the phone and, as I expected, overheard Skeezix phone line ringing a number on a master speakerphone in my booth. A second phone light flashed on the control panel. She was obviously calling another suite, but whomever she was calling didn't answer right away, then I heard another woman's voice come on. Skeezix said, "I guess we're going to be alone all day. Everyone but John went out on some kind of business. Why don't you come over? Maybe you can massage the kink out of my back."

I thought, *What is this, John boy?* She didn't waste any time breaking in a substitute for Stacey. *I wonder if she and Stacey had a falling out, or if this is only a substitute for the road.* I recognized the other voice; my ex-secretary and girl Friday, Liz Leonard. She said, "I'll be over in a minute."

I wasn't about to go back to trouble-shooting under the circumstances. Moreover, if whatever was on the agenda forced me to relieve a little of my tensions watching, I was certain I wouldn't be on candid camera when I got my rocks off. I threw the bolt on the inside of my booth, just in case someone popped in. I had no idea who else might have access to the inner sanctum.

With the reception fine-tuned, I leaned back in the console chair, a nice-overstuffed executive job that reclined as well as rotated. I'd bet a fig that old Diamond spent a lot of time there; no telling what he did, but quality time anyhow.

Shortly, Liz came through a private door from an adjoining suite. From the surprised expression on her face when she saw Skeezix nude, I guessed maybe this wasn't an old routine. I adjusted the sound monitor. It came across crystal clear.

Skeezix said matter-of-factly, "I suppose the hotel has a masseuse, but anyone can do it. I'll tell you how." She lay on her stomach on the king-size bed. All you have to do is straddle me and work your fingers into my back. I'll tell you where. I have some oil on the nightstand that's soothing. Put it on your hands first, then work it in."

Liz did as she was told, having to hike her skirt up to straddle Skeezix. She worked tentatively, starting at the shoulders, seeming to be embarrassed.

"Down a little further, and work with your thumbs, just a gentle pressure."

Liz did as she was told.

"Right there. That's the spot. Ahhhhh . . . , that's wonderful." She lay passively, enjoying the massage, "You don't look comfortable. Why don't you slip off your skirt so you don't have to strain to straddle me?"

Liz blushed.

Skeezix laughed. "It's just us girls. No one is coming in. I locked the dead bolt on the door."

"I don't know if I should," Liz said.

I wondered if she had some inkling of where this might be leading, and I wished I'd had time to put her into sophisticated-Maud-mode before this started. Her bashfulness might ruin a great scene before it got started.

"Go ahead. It's part of what I expect from my traveling secretaries.

If you don't think I'm paying you enough, I can give you a raise right now."

"Oh, no. It's not that. You're more than generous. I guess I've just been sheltered."

"Then it's time to start getting over it. I won't even look if you don't want me to."

Liz slipped off her skirt and slip and I noticed she'd probably had access to a good conditioning center since she'd gone to work with the Sunderland's. She was trimmer than she'd been, with the housewife's tummy gone. I recalled her daughter's classy ass and had to admit it had nothing on her mother's now. I watched her again straddle Skeezix and resume her massaging. This went on for several minutes.

Skeezix purred, "There's nothing like a massage to relax a girl and make her feel like a million. I studied massage in college. It's a conditioner, just like exercise. Let me give you one." She got up and in a take-charge voice said, "Take your blouse off and get on the bed."

Liz did as she was told, not certain she should, I suspect. She wasn't yet sure of what was going on.

Skeezix straddled her and started to skillfully massage her back. "You can't really do this with a brassiere on." She unsnapped it and tossed the ends aside and continued to massage. She worked her way gradually down to the lower back, artfully getting a lot of body contact with her legs all the while. "Doesn't that feel good?" she asked.

Liz sighed. "Wonderful." I'd have bet a wad she was beginning to warm up, just as Skeezix knew she would.

After another few minutes, during which the massage included the sides of Liz's breasts which protruded beneath her from lying on them, and her hips, which Skeezix lifted and let fall several times, each time wrapping her arms farther around in front, she said, "Why not take your clothes off, Liz? They're just in the way of a good massage." She started to pull Liz's panties down and the other dutifully raised her body to let them slide off. "Now I can get your legs. That's the ticket, and your feet too." She worked down them, working the muscles gently and oiling as she went. Then she worked back up and cautiously moved her hands closer and closer to where I could see pubic hair peeping from between Liz's partially spread legs. Her fingers finally touched there, as though by accident, then moved away and back again. Liz let out a little pleasured sigh and started to work her hips involuntarily.

"Turn over now," Skeezix ordered.

Liz did as she was commanded, avoiding Skeezix's eyes, and blushing, but not resisting. The latter continued her massaging of the legs, working back up to the critical spot and this time gently stroking the moist lips of Liz's vagina. She got no resistance or protest. Liz's eyes were tightly closed and she had begun to breathe heavily. An experienced finger sought what it was looking for and went to work on a clitoris that I suspected had been erect early in the performance, before Liz had even turned over. Boy was I learning something about seduction. Skeezix lowered herself gently beside Liz, continuing to massage her clitoris, then leaned across her and kissed her breasts, tonguing them and sucking gently, then moving downward, kissing gently all the way until she reached the spot where her finger was massaging Liz. She rearranged her position slightly, then spread the outer lips of Liz's vagina and moved a soft, warm, slippery tongue there in place of her finger, flicking it up and down. I could hear Liz's ecstatic little moan over the sensitive sound system, and watched fascinated as her hips rose to meet the tantalizing instrument of her pleasure. Skeezix was skillful at this, knowing right where and how to work and with what rhythm.

I wondered how many others she'd done this to, since that day long ago when Ole had observed her and a school mate at it. The game was over pretty quick. Liz rose in one final ecstatic thrust and cried, "Oh, my God!" then thrust several times more and subsided, gasping for breath.

Skeezix shifted her position and covered Liz, kissing her lips gently, then more roughly. Liz was completely in her power now, responding to whatever she desired. I had a monumental hard-on, of course, but wasn't sure what I was going to do with it, or when. I thought, *It'll keep. This is too rare a thing to miss any part of.*

Skeezix said, "Do you think you could do that to me? I'll tell you how if you don't do it right." Liz blushed deeply, but said,

"I can try." I knew that she had jumped a huge hurdle and in her own person gained admission to the world she'd read about in Judith Krantz and Jackie Collins, the world she fantasized about as Maud, and now she was reveling in every second of it.

Skeezix rolled onto her back and spread her legs. What a delectable cunt she revealed, as I said before, amply endowed with a luxuriant growth of honey-blond hair. I could imagine what it would be like to shove what was throbbing in my pants through that lovely, warm hair and thrust it in deeply. I fantasized doing just that while I watched and could feel the beginning of an orgasm. I wondered if I was going to cream in my pants.

Liz looked like a quick learner. She didn't hesitate after she started, and being a woman could feel exactly where she should be stroking with her warm tongue. Skeezix was thrusting to meet her from the first and never had to tell her a thing, soon breathing rapidly and moaning.

They all seem to; men are more inclined to gasp or groan, or at least all the ones I've heard ~ I know I do. I'm a noisy lover, as many woman have observed; and a "strong man" as a Japanese hotsy bath girl observed when I arched a series of loads several feet in the air after she stroked me off with lotion.

I don't think it took more than a minute for Skeezix to get it off. She was more wildly unrestrained than Liz in the final seconds, perhaps through experience or being more highly sexed.

I thought, *What a magnificent stroke of luck to stumble onto this set up just at this time. Thank you God! Also Diamond Dan.*

Skeezix recovered, "Maybe you'd better get dressed, just in case someone does come. I imagine after that you could use a nap. I know I could."

Now that it was over, Liz avoided looking directly at her, and was probably very embarrassed. She'd get over that, I guessed. Stacey hadn't looked embarrassed. There had to have been a scene somewhat like this when Skeezix and Stacey went at each other the first time. I figured Skeezix had been the aggressor then, too. Stacey came fleetingly to mind. Had she just been replaced? She'd avoided me for a long while before we'd left to come to Copenhagen. If she'd done it being true blue to her girl friend, she'd miscued.

Liz quickly dressed, but didn't resist when Skeezix kissed her goodbye; in fact, she returned the kiss with interest, then left by the door she'd entered through, looking back once bashfully and blowing Skeezix a kiss.

Skeezix bolted the door behind her. I soon discovered why. From her bedside table she took what looked like a night kit. Only it was a lot more than that. From it she extracted a life-like vibrator and a tube of lubricant. She tested the batteries and found them working, put a dollop of grease on its end and lay back to tantalize herself. She probably had figured that it was too soon to expect Liz to do the male impersonator role with a dildo strapped on her, without undue embarrassment. That was most likely true. Obviously I'd been wrong about Skeezix not wanting to be penetrated. She also confirmed what I'd heard. The more some women play with themselves, the more they also want to copulate, or at least do the equivalent in this case. I wondered why Stacey hadn't returned the compliment the night Skeezix had played the part of the Sundance Kid.

This was more than I could stand. Much as I deplored the absence of a little lotion in my sanctum, I whipped the boy out and decided to play *burnout* with Skeezix. It wasn't going to be easy. This was a magnificent, beautiful, voluptuous woman, with everything that turned me on, in spades. Her face was heavy with passion, lips opened and drooping slightly, as she started to breathe hard, head thrown back. I could feel myself coming as soon as I started to stroke. Meanwhile, she was getting deep penetration and vibration at the same time. Then suddenly she stopped, as though she'd heard someone. The sensitive sound system didn't pick up any unusual noise.

Her seeming apprehension stopped me for a minute. She withdrew her equipment and reached for the phone, dialing a number. I wondered whom she was calling. Maybe she'd changed her mind and was going to take the leap with Liz. I turned the light-rheostat up a little to see if I could make out what suite number was flashing on the master phone system, in case she was calling in-house again. When the light flashed, it was for my suite. I was only nonplussed for a minute, then I picked it up where I was and said, "Pelham here."

"John, this is Pat," she said, husky voiced from passion, and I watched her fondling her cunt as she talked, "I guess we've been deserted by the busy little bees. Are you hungry?"

I'd have said I was if I'd just eaten a whole cow. "I guess. What do you have in mind?"

"Come on over. I've got a hamper of stuff in the fridge that I had the kitchen bring in. Even a bottle of divine champagne. Do you drink champagne?'

"Beats Akavit. When should I make an appearance?"

"Anytime. I'm just lounging around. Give me a couple of minutes."

"I'll be there." I watched as she went into the bathroom and switched the screen to there, picking the right switch the first time, and watched her get ready for my arrival, by washing her hands and getting the oil off them. If she'd sat on the john I would have tuned out ~ watching gals on the can ain't one of my kinks.

I knew she'd be wearing nothing but a robe, perhaps perfume, when I got there, unless she did one hell of a quick change.

She opened the door as though she'd been standing by it waiting, probably had. I tried for eye contact with her at once, wondering what I might detect. She didn't avoid my stare. Her pupils were huge and dark. This lady had plans for me.

Just for the hell of it I said, "Did I come over too soon? Would you like me to split to give you a chance to put something on?"

She laughed. "You mean the robe? You won't lose your head and attack me if it slips open, will you?"

She sounded emphatic. Looking at me all the while, she locked the dead bolt and let the robe slip open, facing me. She smiled, but said nothing. No instructions are necessary on a package of that kind. I grabbed her and devoured her lips. I tried to get my tongue down to her tonsils, and she followed it right back and gave me the same every time I withdrew it.

"Come into my den, darlin' " she said, when we broke for breath. She led me into the bedroom where she and Liz had just put on their act for me.

"Are you wondering what will happen if Ole should come home?" she asked. "Don't. He never comes into my bedroom. We have what you've heard called a marriage of convenience. Did you suspect that?"

"Yes." And I thought, *If you only knew what I know, you'd probably have the vapors.*

"In fact," she went on, "he's often said if I find a man I really love, he'll give me a divorce and a dowry, though I don't know why he should; daddy left me almost as much money as Ole has."

I wondered why she was telling me this. Had the fatal Pelham charm finally penetrated? I doubted it. "Are you trying to buy me?" I teased.

"If need be. Somehow, I have the feeling that won't be necessary."

"I have the feeling you're right." I had been peeling my clothes while this was going on. She was already in the middle of the bed, her eyes speculatively on mine, then on my body. I wondered if she'd ever had a man before, and, if so, how many. Somehow, I didn't think so. At least not in a long time. Wishful thinking. Was I willing to risk AIDS for her where I hadn't been for Hot Buns? Yes! I'd never been so horny in my life. Something about her and the situation was irresistible. There are times when every human is vulnerable; when the most faithful husband, wife or soul mate in the world can be taken by some one temptation at a certain enchanted moment.

"I haven't had time to take a shower today," I said. "Let's start there."

She got up quickly and led the way. It was one of those wonderful showers with a head that gave any kind of stream you wanted. They're better for women than men, but we didn't need one. I soaped us up and we slid together in a long, slippery embrace, during which we groped each other repeatedly. My dong was standing up like a flagpole, and stayed up all the while I dried and got back to the bed.

Further preliminaries were pretty short. I slid it into her while devouring her voluptuous, greedy lips in a long kiss and gently moved it fully in, feeling her muscles contract around it.

Like many of the inexperienced kind, she had probably read and watched everything from the Perfumed Garden and Kama Sutra through, the Kinsey Report, Masters and Johnson, The Joys of Sex and more. This woman knew, instinctively or not, how to pleasure a man. I fought a tremendous battle to keep from erupting in a couple of minutes and lost. It was wasted philanthropy. At the same time I could feel her coming and coming, and hear her. She pulled her mouth away and gasped, cried out, moaned and muttered, "I love you's" and "Oh, God!" for minutes, even after I came and was simply holding her.

When it was all over she was crying in my arms. She said, "Don't mind me. Sometimes I do that. God, that was so wonderful."

She didn't break down and confess that it was the first time for her with a man. Not yet. I was in love again. I sat across the table from her in the breakfast nook and let her feed me from her hamper. Suddenly she laughed. "How will I ever face my dear, old husband, having sinned twice?"

"Twice?"

"Yes," she said. "We're going to do it again, aren't we?" Then she giggled, and after a moment added, "Only this time somewhere else. Some of them may come back early.

"My crib will do." I told her about me and Hot Buns.

"Good" she said. "I never thought she was your type."

We sneaked over to my room and I tossed Hot Buns' bags in the hall. Suddenly I was very weary.

"How about a nap before we sin again? After-all, I am *supposed* to be taking a nap." She would have dropped dead if she knew, why I knew . . . exactly what she meant.

EPILOGUE
MUCH ADIEU ABOUT SOMETHING

What Ole had in mind for me got me out of Copenhagen before I had to spend much time being glared at by Hot Buns. What is it about women who split off an affair, allegedly getting what they want, that they have to stay bitchy about it, as though they didn't really want the split? Do they want to own you forever, anyhow? I think, yes. Perhaps I looked too complacent about the whole thing.

Ole and Diamond found a community of interest. Diamond wanted a safe place to make any kind of movie he pleased, and Ole wanted a number of things, such as a secure communications snooping system to monitor the world's financial community. He'd already determined he needed a large seagoing vessel to house such a snooping arrangement and had optioned one.

A set up like that would provide him immunity from control by any nation on earth. The ship he got also had enough room for a floating movie studio and accommodations for all sorts of people. It was a surplus troop transport and barracks ship, eight hundred feet long and wide enough that it would just go through the Panama Canal.

You can guess who was hired to put in the snooping system; Mr. ELINT (Electronic Intelligence) himself, yours truly. I was on a plane, headed for the U.S. in short order. I wanted to go back to Uncle Sugar to pick up Curtains anyhow, and terminate my affairs back home, then join the ship before it left port in New York.

Such being the case, why am I sitting on a patio at Ole Sunderland's villa high over the picturesque little harbor of Portofino, sipping his scotch and smoking his Havanas? Well, what the hell, Portofino is a small town.

Getting here started when I put out the "For Sale" sign on my place in my former, fabled "small town." I heard familiar toenails scraping the blacktop as I stood out admiring the sign and turned to find, you-know-who: Beano-who-bit-the-bishop dragging her mom.

Ergo, dinner again (at 6:30 this time) at Stacey's. Big chair in front of the fireplace, necking a bit again, with Pelham raising a hard-on a cat couldn't scratch, just like the last time with little, wiggly Stacey. This time I got the tour of the Video bedroom, but not the salacious movies. We made our own. Was it sensational? Well, let's put it this way: I was horny again, as usual, and she was lovely, warm, willing, tight, enthusiastic as only a tyro can be and I had no scruples about double crossing my new love in Copenhagen." What the hell, for all I knew Skeezix might be in bed at that very time with Diamond, Hev, (more likely, Liz) or her teddy bear. A hard-on has no conscience. I'm damn glad I layed Stacey, even though philanthropy usually sucks.

Sex Ring in a Small Town

"Much later," as the subtitles frequently tell us, Stacey said, "Where do you intend to go?"

"Down to my place, if you don't think I should stick around for the night."

"I mean when you leave town."

I didn't come close to leveling with her, in view of her connection to Skeezix. I did tell her about a job in my specialty as an electronics engineer.

"Where?"

"Genoa."

"Italy?"

"Not Illinois."

"We've owned a villa in Portofino for ages," she said.

"The name sounds familiar. Where is it?"

"About twenty miles east of Genoa."

What a come-on. I rather liked the idea, though. How did I know the Sunderlands owned a villa there too?

So, let me tell you about the current situation six months later. I had to forsake my well-known scruples and create a secondary personality, like Maud, for Skeezix and Stacey. The four of us have had some wonderful times in bed together. I always wanted a gang-bang in reverse. Am I married to Skeezix? No. She didn'tthink it would be the right thing to do to Ole. She said, "Maybe if he dies." I hope he never does.

All this has presented no complications. It is a little tricky at times, juggling the four with the Countess Graciela Rosetti who decided she wanted to quit smoking. In my opinion, she'll never quit smoking, though she's given up cigarettes with my help. She also induced me to make her husband, the Count, who is an internationally famous mathematician, stop embarrassing her by carrying a security blanket like Linus. He does have his uses. He owns seventeen castles up and down Italy. I've screwed her in all but three so far.

The other girls get pretty tied up with one another sometimes. Some lecher with a good memory may wonder what happened to the two fabulous sisters, Carmen and Angelita. Briefly, they now think Diamond Dan is Brother John and he is making them the queens of porno flicks. Regarding his aspirations to acquire a legit studio, Ole convinced him he should have his head examined if he went that route. And speaking of Ole, he and I are sitting here drinking his booze and watching the sunset through cigar smoke.

I am saying, "What do you think of these, Ole?" and handing him two letters to be read in order.

The first was postmarked in LA, where a well-known, up-and-coming female financier is making her mark as comptroller of Dulaney Productions. It reads: "I miss you." The second, written by me, says: "But the point is, if you'd had a .38 that day in Copenhagen, *you wouldn't have missed me.*"

Diamond sent me another electric toothbrush in a padded envelope. I am sitting here with the envelope in my hand, and can see his, and Ole's floating studio and spy ship, the SS Raptor from where we're sitting. It's anchored out in International waters.

PS: I almost threw out the envelope after I saw the toothbrush, before I noticed a smaller manila envelope in it, which I carefully drew out, expecting a snide card ~ inside was a certified check for $500,000.00.

Let's see ~ added to $400,000.00 for my house ~ hell, I'm almost a millionaire.

This was one of those occasional exceptions to the rule of philanthropy . . . it doesn't always suck.

* * *

Sex Ring in a Small Town

John Pelham

Sex Ring in a Small Town

John Pelham